The Dark Sword series

"Grant creates a vivid picture of Britain centuries after the Celts and Druids tried to expel the Romans, deftly merging magic and history. The result is a wonderfully dark, delightfully well-written [series]. Readers will eagerly await the next Dark Sword book."

—RT Book Reviews

"Another fantastic series that melds the paranormal with the historical life of the Scottish highlander in this arousing and exciting adventure."

—Bitten By Books

"These are some of the hottest brothers around in paranormal fiction." *—Nocturne Romance Reads*

"Will keep readers spellbound."

—Romance Reviews Today

DONNA GRANT

St. Martin's Paperbacks

This is a work of fiction. All of the characters, organizations, and events portrayed in this novel are either products of the author's imagination or are used fictitiously.

HEAT

Copyright © 2018 by Donna Grant.

All rights reserved.

For information address St. Martin's Press, 175 Fifth Avenue, New York, NY 10010.

ISBN: 978-1-250-10957-6

Printed in the United States of America

Our books may be purchased in bulk for promotional, educational, or business use. Please contact your local bookseller or the Macmillan Corporate and Premium Sales Department at 1-800-221-7945, ext. 5442, or by e-mail at MacmillanSpecialMarkets@macmillan.com.

St. Martin's Paperbacks edition / February 2018

St. Martin's Paperbacks are published by St. Martin's Press, 175 Fifth Avenue, New York, NY 10010.

10 9 8 7 6 5 4 3 2 1

To lovers of dragons and Dragon Kings—
There is nothing more magical, enchanting,
or thrilling as dragons!
Thank you for letting my Dragon Kings
into your hearts.

ACKNOWLEDGMENTS

A special shout-out to everyone at SMP for getting this book ready, including the amazing art department for such a gorgeous cover. Much thanks and appreciation goes to my extraordinary editor, Monique Patterson, who I can't ever praise enough.

To my fantastic agent, Natanya Wheeler, who fell in love with dragons!

Hats off to my incredible readers and those in the DG Groupies FB group for keeping the love of the Dragon Kings alive. Words can't say how much I adore y'all.

A special thanks to my children, Gillian and Connor, as well as my family for the never-ending support.

PROLOGUE

Long, long ago . . .

The smell of death permeated the air, sinking into everything. Nikolai stood next to his deceased mother. He nudged her as he attempted to flap his small wings. His stomach rumbled with hunger as fear took root. He looked around and saw the body of his father not far off, but he didn't go to him.

It was the horror of it all that sent Nikolai burrowing beneath his mother's wing. He didn't know where to go or what to do. The last thing his parents told him was to remain close.

He had no idea how long he stayed, starving, scared, and alone before something large blocked the sun. He peeked around his mother's wing and saw the giant shadow that flew over him. It passed thrice more before he felt the ground shudder when the dragon landed.

Had they returned to kill him?

Suddenly, his mother's wing was lifted, and he found himself staring into the obsidian eyes of a silver dragon. Nikolai warily watched the large dragon. He felt the push against his mind and hesitantly opened the link.

"*Hello, lad,*" the dragon said.

Nikolai lifted his head and released a growl of warning, hoping it would send the Silver away. Nikolai was the son of a great dragon. He wouldn't cower, no matter how frightened he was.

The Silver glanced behind him before he returned his solemn gaze to Nikolai. The black orbs were filled with sadness. So was his voice when he asked, *"What happened?"*

Once more, Nikolai growled.

The Silver stared at him, admiration flickering in his dark depths. *"I'm no' here to hurt you. I've come to help. Now, tell me what happened."*

Nikolai paused, unsure what to do. He wanted to trust the Silver, but fear held him in check. He rubbed up against his mother for comfort—and guidance—but her scales were now cold.

He was alone. Save for this one dragon, who claimed to want to help. There really wasn't a choice for him. Nikolai had to take a chance. He drew in a breath, his chest puffing out as wisps of smoke drifted from his nostrils. *"Ivories came and fought my da. Then they killed mum while she hid me."*

"They would've likely killed you, as well." The Silver released a long sigh. *"Do you have anyone I can take you to?"*

Nikolai shook his head. If he had other family, he didn't know of them.

"Then I'll care for you."

At this, hope filled Nikolai. *"You'll help me?"*

"I willna allow you to starve, lad, or leave you to the dragons who did this. Because they will return. I must talk to your King, however. He needs to know what happened."

"Who are you?"

The Silver smiled. *"Ulrik. King of Silvers."*

King? Nikolai was shocked to find he was speaking to a Dragon King.

"*And you are?*" Ulrik asked.

"*Nikolai.*"

"*Well, Nikolai, can you fly yet?*"

He shook his head as he walked from beneath his mother's wing. "*Mum and Da have been helping me.*"

"*Then we need to get you in the air.*"

Nikolai stretched out his wings and flapped them quickly as he jumped into the air, but he promptly fell to the ground, awkwardly tripping so that he landed on his face. He shook his head and got back up, repeating the process again and again while Ulrik gave words of encouragement and praise, as well as pointers.

Growing tired, Nikolai tried once more. He set his jaw and jumped as high as he could, his wings beating frantically. The wind glided over him a heartbeat before his wings caught a current.

And this time, he didn't fall.

With each beat of his wings, he flew higher.

A large shape came beneath him. Ulrik smiled up at him. "*Your parents would be proud.*"

At the mention of his family, Nikolai dipped a wing and made a wobbly turn to fly over their bodies. Ulrik remained with him the entire time.

After several passes, Nikolai said, "*I doona want to leave them.*"

"*I know, lad, but you can no' stay either. We'll return with some of my Silvers to give them a proper burial.*"

Nikolai's stomach rumbled then, reminding him that it had been hours since he'd eaten. "*I'll hold you to your word.*"

Ulrik's response was a nod of approval. They didn't speak again as they approached the land of the Silvers. It bordered the Ivories', and though the two clans weren't enemies, they weren't exactly allies either. That was something Nikolai's parents had felt relevant enough to teach him as soon as he hatched.

Nikolai's wings grew tired, but he refused to say anything to Ulrik. He still wasn't sure what to make of the fact that the King of the Silvers was taking him in.

No sooner had Ulrik begun to descend from the sky than he suddenly swung around. The King's wing nudged him, and Nikolai obeyed the silent command. It wasn't long until he saw the reason—Avgust, the King of the Ivories, was flying toward them.

The three landed. The fact that Nikolai didn't trip over his feet made him puff out his chest as he stood next to Ulrik—even if his wings did tremble from the exertion. The two Kings shifted to their human forms. Word quickly spread, and soon, both silver and ivory dragons gathered around them.

"What are you doing with one of my dragons?" Avgust demanded.

Ulrik glanced at Nikolai. "Helping him."

"He should've come to me."

"He just learned to fly," Ulrik stated. "He was orphaned and alone, his parents killed by other Ivories."

Avgust's gaze swung to Nikolai. "Is that true, lad? Did Ivories kill your parents?"

Nikolai nodded, his gaze locked on Avgust.

Avgust turned to his dragons. "I want those responsible brought to me by day's end tomorrow." Then he faced Nikolai. "I'll see justice done."

Nikolai bowed his head as he said, *"Thank you,"* through the mental link.

"Come here, lad," Avgust said.

Though Nikolai couldn't pinpoint what it was, something told him to remain with Ulrik. He was trying to find the words to tell his King when Ulrik put his hand on Nikolai's back.

"We'll meet tomorrow for the burial of his parents and

to see those responsible brought to justice," Ulrik declared.

Nikolai looked up at the King of the Silvers. Ulrik remained calm, but his voice brokered no argument. His father would've liked Ulrik. As young as Nikolai was, he understood the great dragon Ulrik was—and that Avgust was afraid of him.

With a curt nod, Avgust shifted, and all of the Ivories flew away. Nikolai watched them, not at all concerned that he was no longer with his clan.

When he looked back at Ulrik, the King of the Silvers was once more in dragon form. *"If you wish to go with your clan tomorrow, I understand. But,"* Ulrik said, *"if you want to remain with me, you'll be in my household. I'll train you to fight, and in magic, as well as all the ways of a dragon. You'll be a member of my clan always. But after what I witnessed from you this day, I suspect you have another path that will eventually return you to the Ivories."*

"I want to stay with you," Nikolai said.

"Then we should get you fed. Ready?"

Nikolai's wings ached, but he gave a nod. If the King of the Silvers were going to offer to mentor him, he was going to be the best dragon he could be—for his father and for Ulrik.

He quickly launched himself into the air, his little wings flapping hard and fast. And when Ulrik joined him, smiling, Nikolai felt pride as the fear of earlier began to lessen. The tears for his parents would come later when he was alone. For now, he was in the company of greatness with a future ahead of him that stretched as far as the horizon.

"You're doing great, lad."

Nikolai beamed. *"I willna let you down."*

CHAPTER ONE

Dreagan Manor

I willna let you down.

The words he'd spoken to Ulrik reverberated through Nikolai's head like a bell tolling. He blew out a frustrated breath and sat up. Tossing aside the blanket, he swung his legs over the bed as he hung his head.

The few hours of sleep he'd managed were filled with dreams of his years with Ulrik. The Silvers had accepted Nikolai, though they hadn't made his life easy. Their actions, in part, were what strengthened him.

The day Nikolai challenged Avgust for the right to rule the Ivories, there was only one who had stood by his side—Ulrik. The King of the Silvers had begun as a father figure, but soon became a brother in the truest sense of the word.

Nikolai held out his hands, palms up, and looked at them. The last time he had seen or spoken to Ulrik was right before they stripped the Silver of his magic and banished him.

It didn't matter how many millennia passed, the burden of standing against Ulrik still weighed heavily upon

Nikolai. It's why he had taken to his mountain with the others and woke only one other time.

He'd still be asleep if Con hadn't forced him to wake. The fact that Nikolai would most likely have to fight the man he called brother only worsened the situation.

Squeezing his hands into fists, he fought back the tide of regret. He drew in a deep breath and rose to his feet. Striding into the bathroom, he turned on the water in the shower.

He couldn't remember a time when there hadn't been tension running through the manor, but it was getting worse. Every Dragon King knew that the battle between Ulrik and Constantine, the King of Kings, was coming any day now.

No one wanted to see Ulrik dead, but if he won, then the vows made by each of them to protect the mortals would pit them against Ulrik, who wanted nothing more than to wipe the humans from the face of the earth.

In order to prevent that, Con would have to kill Ulrik.

Nikolai stepped beneath the hot spray of water and braced his hands on the wall. He'd sided against Ulrik once. It had been the right choice, but there wasn't a day that passed where Nikolai didn't wonder if he should've chosen differently.

This time, the choice would be out of his hands. This time, the battle between Ulrik and Con would have lasting effects on every being in the realm—mortal and immortal alike.

If only that were all the Kings had to worry about, but unfortunately, it was only a small piece of a very large pie filled with nothing but enemies who were focused on everyone at Dreagan.

Nikolai put his face in the water and closed his eyes. The Dark Fae were a serious problem for the mortals because they fed off their souls by having sex with them. To make matters worse, there was talk that Ulrik had joined forces with them.

At least that was the theory. Sebastian claimed that Ulrik wasn't responsible for everything, that Ulrik's uncle, Mikkel, was the one the Kings should be hunting.

Nikolai leaned back and began to wash. He recalled Ulrik having an uncle, but not the name. Nikolai hoped Sebastian was right. Regardless, Bast had left for Venice without Con's approval in order to uncover proof about Mikkel.

That was a week ago. There had been no word from Sebastian, and Con had departed for Venice the night before to locate Bast.

The only good thing was now that MI5 no longer had a presence at the distillery, the ban on the Dragon Kings shifting had been lifted. It felt amazing to take to the skies again.

Nikolai ran a hand through his hair to get the shampoo out. Then he turned off the water and grabbed a towel to dry off. He walked out of the shower and frowned at the pile of clothes that he'd forgotten to hang up the previous day.

He tossed aside his towel and began putting away the clothes in his closet. As he did, he grabbed a pair of jeans and put them on. He then made his way to the chest in his bedroom. After he put away a stack of clothes, he paused and looked at the painting above his bed. It was the first thing he'd done for himself after he discovered what his power was.

He stared at the idyllic mountain scene with lakes so pure you could see straight to the bottom. Flying together in the bright blue sky were his parents. It was the only thing that hung on his walls other than his sword.

As he made up his bed, there was a soft knock on his

door. He didn't look up as he bade whoever it was enter while he bent, tidying the comforter. The door opened, but it took him a second to realize that no one had spoken. When he straightened, he was shocked to find Esther North standing there.

The British beauty was still in the doorway, her hand upon the knob as her gaze locked on the various drawings that were scattered about his room, hung on lines he had strung, or sitting on easels.

Her lustrous brunette tresses hung free about her shoulders. She wore an oversized gray sweater that hid her curves and dropped past her hips over a pair of black leggings. Fuzzy white socks that had a kitten face atop them, complete with a pink nose and whiskers, encased her feet.

The longer she stood there staring, the more he was able to gaze at her striking features at his leisure. The MI5 agent had captivated him from the very beginning when a Druid got into Esther's mind to control her with magic.

The Dragon Kings managed to undo the Druid's work, but there were side effects. The memories of the time Esther spent with the Druid were missing. It made Esther a liability, but she was allowed to remain because of one very important factor—she was Henry North's sister.

Henry, also MI5, worked with the Dragon Kings to track the activities of the Dark Fae in an attempt to figure out their next move. It was uncommon for the Kings to trust humans, but Henry was an exception.

And so was his sister.

Nikolai knew Esther's face. His power allowed him to conjure every detail about her from just one look. From the small, nearly hidden scar on her left wrist from some childhood accident, to the confident way she held herself.

He knew her hair wasn't just brown. It had strands of

the softest shade of walnut, darker tones that deepened into chocolate, and lighter streaks of amber. He knew the curve of her face, and how she lifted her chin when she was angry. He knew the lines in her brow from the expressive way she spoke. He knew her mouth and how her bottom lip was slightly fuller than the top.

He knew her round eyes and the deep shade of brown along with the band of black that encircled her irises. He knew the slope of her breasts, the indent of her waist, and the flare of her hips. He knew the way she preferred to wear muted colors to help her blend in with a crowd.

It had taken but one look to put all that to memory, but he found his gaze going to her again and again as if he couldn't get enough.

That fact was only one reason he kept drawing Esther. The other was that he had no choice.

She filled his mind like no other had before.

CHAPTER TWO

Esther was shocked. And that wasn't an easy thing to do.

Her eyes moved from one sketch of her to another, each depicting different areas of Dreagan she had been to—the manor, the distillery, or strolling through the snow in the Dragonwood.

There were even pictures of her walking the caves inside the mountain connected to the manor. The drawing she stared at the longest was the one where she had stood at the entrance to the cavern where four of Ulrik's largest silver dragons were kept, sleeping within a cage.

The look on her face was one of awe and curiosity. Though she remembered feeling fear at the idea of Ulrik killing Con and releasing those dragons to wipe out humanity.

But in many of the instances, she knew Nikolai hadn't been there. How then had he drawn them? His power of projected thermography allowed him to see something once and paint it, draw it, or weave it. But if he hadn't been there . . . ?

As her eyes moved from one side of the room to the

other, they clashed with a bare-chested Nikolai. Her mouth went dry as she stared at his chiseled form.

The Dragon King had a way of making her forget whatever she was thinking every time she looked into his baby blue eyes. But that's not what her gaze lingered on now. It was his tattoo. She knew every Dragon King had one, but this was her first time seeing Nikolai's, and it was stunning.

Starting at his right wrist was the tail of the dragon that snaked up his arm to his bicep where the body of the animal began. The back claws looked as if they were digging into Nikolai's arm as its wings were tucked.

The dragon turned and leaned over Nikolai's shoulder. The head of the beast was on Nikolai's chest with its mouth open as if roaring. One of the dragon's arms was outstretched as if reaching for something. It was the intricacy of the tat along with the mix of red and black ink that would ensure it was never duplicated in any way.

It was impossible not to ogle his washboard abs. Drops of water had fallen from his hair to his wide shoulders before they wound their way down his amazing chest. She bit her lip, her blood heating when she noticed that his jeans were unbuttoned and hanging precariously on his narrow hips.

Unable to look away, she followed the trail of hair from his navel until it disappeared into his pants. She swallowed, not quite sure how to feel about her blatant, carnal reaction.

As she raised her gaze, she noticed that his hands were clenched so tightly his knuckles were white. That caused her eyes to jerk upward and clash with his.

His features were strong and perhaps a bit harsh, but she found them disarmingly so. From his jawline to his wide lips to his hollowed cheeks.

She wanted to run her fingers through his subtle cinnamon red locks. He kept the hair around his face shorter than the rest that was full of body and thickness. Even now with it wet, the strands held a wave as they fell to the back of his neck.

It took her several minutes to remember what she was doing in his room, she was so consumed by him and the lascivious thoughts that ran through her head. Of all the men at Dreagan, it had been Nikolai who caught her eye, even as she fought against it.

He was one of the quiet ones. She'd noticed right from the start how he stood to the side, observing everything and everyone. She'd mistakenly assumed he was like her and trained for such things.

The real reason was because of his power. Everything he witnessed was filed away in his brain to be sorted through later.

The longer they stared at each other, the more aroused she became. She knew she should speak, but she couldn't think of anything to say. Which was a first. The one thing she never lacked was words.

"Esther."

Her name had been passed down through generations of Norths. She'd always hated it. Right up until Nikolai said it in that deep, husky brogue that made her stomach flutter and heat burn through her veins. Her name had never sounded sexy until that moment.

She parted her lips in an effort to take in more air. It was a mistake to be there. She knew that now, but even as she told herself to leave, her feet wouldn't obey.

"You drew pictures of me." She inwardly kicked herself. The words had come out jumbled, not in the perfect sentence she'd put together in her mind.

Nikolai's chest expanded as he took a deep breath and released it. His hands unclenched. "I have."

"Why? How?"

After all the training she'd received on interrogation techniques, that was all she could come up with? What the bloody hell was wrong with her?

"It happens when I have a deep connection with someone," he explained.

"A deep connection?" She glanced at the pictures. "You can see me wherever I go?"

A muscle ticked in his jaw. "No' everywhere."

"I think you do." Pulled by some unknown force, she made her way to a group of drawings. She pointed at one. "I was at the distillery Monday." She moved to the next. "Tuesday, I walked the Dragonwood." Then the next. "Wednesday, I was helping out in the gift shop."

"I doona see everything," he said.

She dropped her arm and looked at him with raised brows. "I can show you a week's worth of drawings that say otherwise."

It was a crazy notion that filled her mind, but when he remained silent, it gave her cause to believe that it just might be possible.

"All I can think about is that Druid who got into my head," she said. "I don't know exactly how much time I'm missing, and the fact that I can't remember anything terrifies me."

"Esther—"

"I was sent here to kill Kinsey," she said over him. "I didn't even know what I was doing. Had we killed each other as those responsible for controlling us wanted, none of you would even know about the Druid."

He crossed his arms over his chest, a frown marring his forehead. "Aye, that's true."

"We have an edge here. We should take this opportunity while we have it. I have to find this Druid, but more than that, I have to know what I did in the time that was stolen from me. What if. . . ." She trailed off because the

words were too difficult to think, and nearly impossible
to say. "What if I killed someone else?"

"What if you didna?"

"Wouldn't you want to know the truth if you were
me?"

He dropped his arms and sighed. "Aye."

"I came to look at the drawing you did of the Druid
again, but after seeing the others you've done, I think
you're the only one who can help me."

He ran a hand down his face as he looked at the floor
for a long time. When he lifted his gaze to her, he gave
her a single nod. "How can I help?"

"It began in London. That's where we need to go."

CHAPTER THREE

Nikolai leaned back against the wall in Con's office as he watched Esther and her brother, Henry, bicker about her proposed plan. There were many reasons not to go to London, but Nikolai wanted to help Esther.

And he wanted to be alone with her.

Con wore a weary expression as the siblings' argument moved into the second half of the hour. The King of Kings rolled the chair back from his desk and rose. Con then walked to stand beside Nikolai, his arms crossed over his chest.

"Are you sure about this?" Con asked.

Nikolai knew it was only a matter of time before Esther wore her brother down. She had valid arguments, and despite Henry's urgings to find another way, Esther's options were limited.

"Aye," Nikolai replied. "Especially after Sebastian's and Gianna's arrival last night. The Druid needs to be found and stopped before she does more than wipe memories. If I can help Esther trace her path before and after she met the Druid, there's a chance we can find her."

Con ran a hand through his wavy blond hair. "The

Druids from MacLeod Castle have all tried multiple ways to locate her. Isla has warned that the Ancients are in a frenzy because of this Druid."

"I doona suppose Broc had any luck locating her now that we have a face?"

"The Warrior's power of finding anyone, anywhere seems to be limited with this foe. Isla and the others suspect she's put up spells blocking discovery."

Nikolai turned his head to Con. "Then I'm our only hope right now."

"Just as I get everyone back under one roof, someone wants to leave again," Con muttered.

"I doona *want* to do this. I have to."

Con cut his black eyes to Nikolai. "That doesna mean I have to be pleased about it."

"We'll find out who this Druid is."

"Once you do, alert me. I'm going to bring her here. Then she's going to fix whatever she did to Bast's and Gianna's memories before she faces my wrath."

"*Our* wrath," Nikolai corrected him.

Con gave a nod. "Our wrath."

Neither of them brought up Sebastian's mission in Venice. Bast must have discovered something about Mikkel. If he really was Ulrik's uncle, then that could explain why the Druid had done whatever she did to Bast and Gianna.

The odd thing was, their memories hadn't been wiped of everything. The couple had all recollection of their time together, but what caused everyone to worry was that Sebastian had told Con he had proof about Mikkel. Now, however, Bast knew nothing about the man at all.

"Doona worry about Sebastian or his woman," Con said. "We'll look after them in case the Druid planted something in their minds as she did with Esther and Kinsey."

Esther suddenly got to her feet and very calmly told Henry, "I'm going."

"Please," her brother pleaded. "Don't do this."

"You would in my place," she said.

Henry then turned in the chair to look at Nikolai and Con. "Tell her this is a bad idea."

"I can no'," Con replied.

Nikolai might be an orphan, but he'd had sibling love for Ulrik, so he could understand what Henry felt. "All we'll be doing is retracing Esther's steps leading up to her encounter with the Druid to help her find her memories. She willna be in danger."

"Simply being my sister puts her in danger," Henry mumbled.

Esther took Henry's hand in hers. "Because you chose the right side."

"Look what that has gotten you," he said angrily.

Esther's gaze briefly met Nikolai's. She looked at her brother and smiled. "It's going to be all right. Whether I get those memories back or not, I'm free of the Druid's magic."

Nikolai knew she was lying. While she'd convinced him to help her, she had allowed him to see just how troubled she was about the missing time. It haunted her. The dark circles under her eyes and her gaunt frame were proof of how drastically it distressed her.

But she was doing what she had to for herself, and to calm her brother's fears.

Con leaned close to Nikolai and whispered, "I see how you look at her."

He didn't pretend to misunderstand what the King of Kings referred to. Instead, he said, "There's nothing wrong with looking."

"But you're taking her away from here. Alone. Can you honestly say you'll keep your hands off her?"

"Nay," he answered without hesitation.

"As I assumed."

Nikolai waited for the berating to start, or at the very least, a warning against such behavior. While Esther and Henry talked privately, Nikolai turned to Con. "You've nothing else to say?"

"Do you think I've been blind to your suffering all these eons? I knew why you chose to remain asleep rather than join us through the years. If you can find some happiness, I'll no' prevent it."

Nikolai had never told Con of his worry or fears with regards to Ulrik. Then again, Con and Ulrik had been as close as brothers for many thousands of years before Ulrik took Nikolai in. If anyone knew Ulrik better than Nikolai did, it was Con.

"That surprises you," Con said with the hint of a smile. "Regardless of what anyone thinks, I doona want to fight Ulrik. Just as you didna want to side with me when he was killing the mortals."

"I should've stayed by his side."

"You did what was right. The way Ulrik taught you."

Nikolai looked away. "He's suffered alone for so long. I should've been with him."

"Ulrik wouldna have let you, or me, or anyone near him to see his pain. You know that."

"Perhaps. But maybe I shouldna have given him a choice."

Con nodded and clapped a hand on his shoulder. "You carry guilt for a choice Ulrik forced upon you. You remained true to your vow as a Dragon King. Be proud of that."

"I see the anger in your eyes when you talk of him sometimes."

"Aye. I'm furious at him for attacking the humans, for no' listening when I tried to talk to him, and for giving me no choice but to send our dragons away. I become enraged each time I think about him making me strip him of his powers and banish him."

Nikolai knew many of the other Kings felt the same. And in some ways, he did as well. "I want to talk to him."

"I'm sure you'll get the chance. With our spy, he'll know where you're going and with who."

"When are you going to tell us who the spy is?"

Con issued a long sigh. "Verra soon."

"You're no' going to stop them now?"

"Why? You want to talk to Ulrik?"

Nikolai gave a snort as he shook his head. "I suppose I should thank you."

"Doona thank me when you'll likely be fighting to keep Ulrik away from Esther."

"Let me worry about that."

Con raised a blond brow. "Make sure you bring her back in one piece. Henry has enough to deal with."

Nikolai's gaze slid to Henry. The mortal had been kissed by Rhi, a Light Fae. Since both the Light and Dark Fae were irresistible to humans, Henry had fallen madly in love with Rhi.

The problem was that everyone knew Rhi was still head over heels in love with her Dragon King lover, who had broken her heart long ago. Rhi was doing her best to steer Henry in another direction, but he was having none of it.

"It's all set," Esther said triumphantly.

Nikolai met her dark gaze. "When do you want to leave?"

"Now, but we can wait until morning. I'm going to pack." She bent and kissed Henry's cheek before walking out of the office.

Con gave Nikolai a pointed look before returning to

his desk. Just as Nikolai was about to push away from the wall, Henry stood and faced him.

"My sister is important to me. Very important."

The threat hung heavily between them, but Nikolai wasn't angry about it. He walked to Henry and said, "I know how strong-willed Esther is, and I'll rein her in."

"No one has ever been able to do that."

"I'm no' going to let her get hurt. If I see the Druid, Esther willna get anywhere near her."

Henry blew out a breath and briefly closed his eyes. "I want to come with you two, but Esther has refused."

"We need you here," Con told him.

Henry glanced at Con. "Right, right. When it comes to my sister, I sometimes forget other things."

"We'll be back before you know it," Nikolai said.

Henry narrowed his eyes. "If anything happens to her, I'll hold you responsible. I may not be able to kill a Dragon King, but I'll find a way to do it."

Nikolai didn't reply as Henry turned on his heel and strode from the room. Only then did Nikolai look at Con and say, "He would've made one hell of a Dragon King."

"Aye. It's too bad it's no' meant to be."

"That it is."

"Keep Henry's threat in mind. He's resourceful," Con warned.

Nikolai grinned. "Indeed."

"And I meant what I said earlier. If there's something between you and Esther, perhaps you shouldna fight it."

"Or maybe I should. If we're no' compatible, it'll make working with her awkward. No' to mention that she lives here now."

Con picked up his Montblanc pen and asked, "What would Ulrik tell you?"

"To stop overthinking things."

"You always did remain in your head too much."

It was something both Ulrik and Con had told him many times. Could they be right?

"And toss off that guilt you've been wearing," Con added.

Nikolai shot him a wry look before he walked out of the office. It was true, he had let his remorse rule him for far too long. He had a precious package in his care now, and he wasn't going to let anything happen to Esther.

Ulrik had taught him strategy and battle skills, and now was the perfect time to implement them. Whether it was Ulrik, the Druid, Dark Fae, or even Mikkel who came after them, Nikolai would be ready.

He returned to his room and began to pack. Once all his clothes were sorted, he gathered sketchpads and pencils as well as a smaller version of his drawing of the Druid to bring with them.

He'd be lying if he said he wasn't excited to set off on this trip. He'd remained set apart from his brethren for too long. His guilt had done that to him.

Perhaps helping find clues to the Druid would allow him to feel a part of Dreagan once more. Because soon, he would have another choice to make.

He hadn't become a Dragon King to sit on the sidelines. He was powerful and dangerous, and it was time their enemies realized that.

It was time Ulrik realized that.

CHAPTER FOUR

Dating Doom

There was no rest for the weary. Esther had discovered that long before she joined MI5, but it wasn't until she became embroiled in the magical war being played out right alongside the mortals that the statement truly made sense.

She was more than fatigued. She was disillusioned, exhausted, and petrified. The last part she kept tightly hidden away. It was something she didn't like to think about herself, so she refused to share it with anyone else.

A glance at her watch showed another hour and a half before they reached London. She leaned to the side and looked toward the front of the helicopter where Denae, a fellow MI5 agent and now mate to a Dragon King, helmed the chopper, getting her pilot's license after Kellan bought the chopper. Next to Denae was her mate, Kellan, who was also Keeper of History for the dragons.

The two were talking—even smiling—as they flew. Esther had been on some harrowing missions where she managed to laugh off the danger and grin in the face of evil because she knew she could bring in the suspect.

She no longer had such optimism. How could she when she was a mere human with no magical abilities? The Druid had gotten into her mind and *controlled* her. It was a kind of hell Esther couldn't seem to get past.

Kinsey appeared to be dealing with it much better. Perhaps it was because she had Ryder. Whatever the reason, Esther envied her. No amount of meditation, yoga, sparring with her brother, or attempting to forget helped.

The Druid was still there, a monster lurking in the dark parts of her mind, waiting to come out.

Esther glanced over at her companion for this trip. Nikolai hadn't looked up from his sketchbook since they'd taken off from Dreagan. She almost leaned over to see what he was drawing but decided against it.

After convincing Nikolai to help, she realized she knew next to nothing about the Dragon King. As a private person herself, she hoped their foray together wouldn't be awkward.

Of course, it didn't help matters that every time she looked at him, she saw him bare-chested with that amazing dragon tat over his arm and chest. The man—dragon—was mind-numbingly gorgeous. How was she supposed to concentrate being so close to him?

She had to get her mind off him. To think of something other than the Druid inside her head and the Dragon King who occupied the other half of her dreams filled with wickedly erotic images.

Esther removed her laptop from her bag and opened it. She held her fingers over the keys, trying to think of something to do. Then she recalled the blog everyone at Dreagan was talking about. She quickly typed in the website address to *The (Mis)Adventures of a Dating Failure.*

The most recent post was at the top titled: *Dating Doom.*

Another day, another bad dating decision. Yes, my love-lies, it seems I'm in a perpetual circle of Dating Doom. The fact that I named this calamity should tell you just how horrible it is.

Let me start by saying words you've read by me many times—There's this guy . . .

I tell myself I'm not desperate, that if I'm meant to be alone, then I'll be alone. There are times I appreciate being single, especially during the holidays when I don't have to fight with someone about which of our families we'll go see because both live too far away.

But there are other times . . . I don't need to tell you about those other times because we've all lived them.

My most recent dating disaster came after one of my old university crushes/friends friended me on Facebook. After I accepted his request, we soon struck up a conversation on Messenger. We were exchanging messages throughout the day, so I sent him my mobile and said we could move the exchange there.

FOUR hours went by without a word from him. I tried not to read too much into it since he had been answering almost immediately before.

I berated myself for pushing things, but then I realized that I hadn't done anything wrong. All I did was give him my number if he wanted to talk that way.

And wouldn't you know it, he sent me a text. For the next few hours, we spoke back and forth. But I'm a firm believer in actual conversation, not texting. Just as I was about to call him, he ended things for the evening.

First thing the next morning, he texted. The entire day, we texted constantly. He even mentioned wanting to get together. I, of course, said that would be a lovely idea.

Then nothing. Nada. Zip. Zero. Zilch.

I waited, debating whether to contact him. After all, he could be busy. After six hours, I sent him a text. It was something stupid and funny.

But he didn't respond.

I left it, knowing that when he wanted to answer me, he would. Yet it plagued me all night. Why, why, why was he asking me all these questions and even mentioning getting together if he was just going to stop replying?

It bothered me to the point that I actually lost sleep. Lost sleep! *Can you believe that? I was so angry at myself for it, that the next day I was in* the *worst mood.*

And I was so embarrassed about it that I wouldn't even tell my best friend what was wrong.

All of this over a guy!

That loud bang you heard just now? That was my head hitting the desk.

To make matters worse, I kept looking at my phone to make sure the texts got delivered. Then I started worrying that maybe they hadn't. I looked into text retrievals and even almost bought software to see if he had sent me a text that maybe got lost in cyberspace somewhere.

Then . . . I did something I shouldn't have. I told myself not to do it. Again and again, I told myself to forget him, forget all of it. I yelled at myself. I berated myself. But it did no good. I still texted him again.

As soon as I hit send, I got a sick feeling in my stomach. I wasn't desperate. That's what I told myself. Why then was I acting that way?

Because I was desperate.

No.

I am desperate.

I hate that feeling. It's not me.

Yet I know in the depths of my soul that there is some-one out there for me. I've always known it. Even as a little girl, long before I knew what true love was or became enamored with romance movies and books.

He's out there. But for some reason, I can't seem to find him. Once more, I'll try to convince myself that when it's meant to happen, it will. I'll stop looking into the face of every man I see on the street, wondering if he's The One.

During all of this internal dialogue, the guy returned my text. There was no explanation for the missing time, and I didn't ask. I despised myself for the loneliness that brought me so low. Though I'm not alone in this.

Both men and women alike have been doing the exact same things all because we want to find The One.

I think it was because I was forced to look inward at myself that my feelings for the guy changed. I continued to answer his texts, but when he didn't reply, it stopped mattering to me.

It's been two weeks since I last replied to him. I don't know whether he got my text or not. I don't care whether he sent one and I didn't get it. If he did reply and I didn't respond, he obviously didn't care enough to double check with me to see what was going on.

And if he just hasn't answered, well . . . that pretty much says it all, doesn't it?

I can honestly say that I don't care, though. For a few days, my emotions went through the ringer, but I came out of it finding a little bit of comfort.

He wasn't The One.

My One isn't going to give up so easily on me.

Yours won't either.

Esther slowly closed the laptop. The blog resonated with her. Not because she was looking for The One, but because she understood loneliness.

When she took the job with MI5, she'd known that meant giving up any hope for a husband and children. The adventures, and yes, even the danger, appealed to her more than a family.

That was before she'd encountered the Druid and found out who her brother had been helping. It was before she learned how easily her species could be wiped from the earth.

She looked at Nikolai to find him staring at her with his beautiful, lucent eyes like the palest blue glass. He'd shifted in his seat to face her, his sketchpad in his hand. She knew he'd been drawing her and she didn't care.

"Are you all right?"

She shook her head.

He set aside his pad. "I suspect this involves more than just the Druid."

"It does."

"Aye," he said with a sigh as he glanced at the front of the luxury helicopter. "Our world isna for those who lack conviction. It takes a verra strong heart and mind, both of which you have."

"Not so strong a mind. The Druid got inside, remember?"

Nikolai lifted a shoulder in response. "That doesna mean you're weak. It means they saw your strength and exploited it."

"Will you say the same thing if we run into a Dark Fae and I strip out of my clothes and beg them to fuck me?" She knew she was being crass, but she couldn't help it.

His eyes sizzled with some emotion she couldn't quite name. Then he leaned forward and said in a voice laced with danger, "They will never get near you."

If she thought finding him bare chested had made her weak kneed, then hearing the promise in his words along with the fervor of his gaze made her *yearn*. Nikolai was one sexy-as-sin, toe-curling, breath-stealing Dragon King.

It took her two tries before she was able to swallow. She'd run into some lethal men and women in her work with MI5, but there wasn't one of them that could compare to Nikolai.

His quiet, artistic nature made her forget one key fact—he was a Dragon King.

None of the dragons became King by chance. They were chosen because of their magic and power and strength. And each of them had to challenge—and win against—the King before them.

"Do you believe me, lass?"

She jerkily nodded her head, desire pooling low in her belly.

"Good," he said and sat back. He picked up the sketchpad and went back to drawing.

She, on the other hand, couldn't stop looking at him. There had been a promise in his words, but there had also been a note of vengeance, as well. If she'd held any worry before, it was long gone. She had a Dragon King by her side. She knew how lucky she was, and she wasn't going to let this chance slip through her fingers.

She took a deep breath and slowly released it as she looked out the window. The Druid's meddling made Esther forget the trained agent she was. It was a Dragon King who reminded her, and it would be a Dragon King she helped to end the Druid once and for all.

Esther might not have magic, but she had other skills. And the Druid was mortal. Esther would take out one of the Kings' foes. It was the least she could do after everything they had done for her and Henry.

She clenched her hands before flexing them. The time of hiding in fear was over. It was time to bust through the shadows and confront the monster.

CHAPTER FIVE

Somewhere on Ireland's west coast . . .

Eilish stood on the slope of the cliff among the circle of stones, feeling the pulse of magic begin deep within the earth before rising upward through her feet to fill her body.

She held her arms out at her sides, her palms facing downward parallel to the ground. With every breath, the magic recharged what had been taken from her in Venice. As soon as she thought of the city, she tried to turn her mind elsewhere, but she couldn't.

Sebastian, and his lover, Gianna, were firmly set in her thoughts. She didn't know how long she had before Mikkel discovered that she hadn't killed Gianna. It was the act of delving into Gianna's mind and erasing everything about Mikkel that had taken so much out of Eilish after doing the same with Sebastian.

Eilish's gaze remained on the dark blue waters of the Atlantic Ocean. The wind whipped around her as the sea churned. A storm was quickly approaching—worse than the tempest that was about to open up above her.

No sooner had the thought gone through her mind than the first raindrop landed on her hand. There was a pause, and then the skies released their hold. The roar of the rain was music to her ears.

For as long as she could remember, Ireland had called to her, begging her to return. She hadn't understood why until she learned that her father and the woman she called Mother had been lying to her.

Eilish had kept her magic from her father and stepmother even when they asked her if she had any abilities. It wasn't long after her eighteenth birthday that she boarded a flight to Ireland with one suitcase.

And never looked back.

The moment she stepped onto Irish soil, she felt the magic. All around her, she could hear the sound of the land. Before, it had been just a distant whisper, but now, it was a roar.

It hadn't taken her long to find other Druids, and even less time to realize her power far exceeded theirs. A month into wandering around Ireland, and she had her first encounter with a Dark Fae.

She'd had no choice but to use her magic when he attacked. After that, no other Fae—Dark or Light—bothered her.

It was difficult to believe that the humans could walk among those with magic and not know it. Magic was everywhere, but mortals were too focused on whatever electronic device they had or obsessed with obtaining some item they didn't need.

Eilish was beginning to think she didn't belong anywhere when she'd stopped at a pub for a drink and overheard two Dark Fae speaking about Dragon Kings. She'd listened intently, barely keeping her queries to herself. But their talk only produced even more questions.

She lifted her face to the rain and closed her eyes while magic swirled around her, in her, and through her.

Despite her abilities, she couldn't find the answers she searched for, longed for.

Mikkel dangled a missing piece of her past over her to get her to do whatever he wanted. She'd thought that by agreeing to work with him, she might find the answers to who her mother was, as well as learn more about the Dragon Kings.

Because she had no doubt they were connected to the dream that haunted her. It was always the same. There was a man, though she never saw his face. All she ever saw was the dragon tattoo.

Her delving had gotten her large chunks of information on the Dragon Kings, but it wasn't enough. She knew their names and their powers, but she didn't know their tattoos, and that's how she'd find the one who was supposed to kill her.

The peace of the stones was broken by the sound of footsteps. She knew it was Mikkel by the way the magic retreated from him as if revolted.

She dropped her arms and turned to face him. "What are you doing here?"

"I grew tired of waiting."

"I said I'd come."

"You'll come now," he ordered.

It was on the tip of her tongue to refuse, but the need to learn of her mother was too great. Instead, she walked up the incline. As soon as she left the stones, she felt bereft.

Eilish followed Mikkel to his car. It was impossible not to compare him to his nephew. Mikkel had told her very little about Ulrik other than that he wasn't fit to be a Dragon King any longer.

With just one meeting, she'd known exactly the type of man Mikkel was. He hungered for power the way most sought love. Mikkel cared nothing for life—any life other than his own.

His conceit was only overshadowed by his superiority complex. But he had a flaw. His temper. He couldn't control it, and when he gave in to that emotion, the carefully perfected façade he'd put into place crumbled into dust.

He might be handsome, but his soul was as black as night.

She climbed into the car, uncaring that she was soaking his leather seat. He glanced her way. She briefly met his golden eyes, but it wasn't him she saw. It was Ulrik.

Ever since the King of Silvers had come to her pub, Graves, and confronted her, he'd been on her mind. He hadn't threatened her, hadn't tried to bargain with her.

He'd simply wanted to know who she was.

Even when she gave him a warning, he'd merely smiled. As if he approved of her actions.

Ulrik was a walking contradiction of everything she thought she knew about Dragon Kings. Then again, her only source was Mikkel, so she had to take that into account. Still, the picture Mikkel painted of his nephew was nothing like what she'd encountered.

Mikkel was always strung tightly, as if waiting to attack. Ulrik was calm and composed, but behind his golden eyes, he was cold and calculating. He feared nothing and no one. Ulrik exuded a lethal combination of arrogance and power that everyone immediately recognized.

That's when she knew she was speaking to a true Dragon King, not a wannabe like Mikkel. Yet her alliance was already given, and she couldn't go back on it now, not when she was so close to discovering the truth.

She and Mikkel didn't speak as his man drove them away from the stones. Eilish didn't know where they were going, and she didn't care. She wanted to get back to Graves where she could rest her mind and body.

The fingers of her left hand curled inward to her palm. She felt the brush of the cool silver against her skin and the bite of the claws. The finger rings were the only thing her father had of her mother's. Eilish had worn them from the moment he gave them to her on her eighteenth birthday.

But they were more than jewelry. They were filled with magic, a power unlike anything she'd felt before. It heightened hers, making it more formidable.

She looked out the window when the car slowed before turning down a narrow drive. The road was bumpy as they slowly made their way. With every jolt, she could sense Mikkel's growing anger.

Finally, the car came to a stop. Eilish got out of the vehicle and raised a brow at the small cottage. It was the opposite of what Mikkel preferred. The fact that they were there showed her the precautions he now took.

Mikkel was the first inside the dark dwelling. She followed him and halted in the main room, the light from one of the guard's phones allowing her to see. Unlit candles were everywhere, and there wasn't a single piece of furniture to be found.

"Light them," he ordered.

She really hated being told to do anything. But she had to bide her time. Eilish gave a wave of her hand, and the candles flared to life, shrouding the room in a soft glow.

It would be a romantic setting if she weren't standing with a power-hungry maniac. She knew what he wanted of her, but she wasn't going to give in without gaining something herself this time.

"I've suffered long enough," Mikkel said. "Ulrik got his magic back. It's time I have mine unbound."

When the Dragon Kings bound Ulrik's magic, they'd ultimately bound that of all the Silvers—including Mikkel. He'd had a few seconds of becoming a Dragon King, enough for him to shift before his magic was bound. And then he was forced to remain in human form.

She walked around the room, looking at the candles. She glanced at him. "I understand."

"What are you waiting for?" he bit out.

Eilish halted beside the window where large pillars were lined up. She ran her fingers slowly through the flame of one and felt the sting against her skin.

"I'm not playing, Eilish."

She bit back a smile as she heard just a hint of his Scottish brogue in the words. A sign that he was losing control of his temper. "Neither am I."

"I know you're powerful enough to unbind my magic. Do it."

"No."

There was a long pause. When he spoke, she could hear the fury that shook his voice as he said, "You dare defy me?"

"Yep."

"Do it!"

She turned her head to him. "The Druid who freed Ulrik, where is she? If she's that powerful, why didn't you get her to help you?"

"Ulrik killed her."

Eilish wasn't stupid. She'd spent enough time with Mikkel to decipher his meaning. "In other words, you had Ulrik kill her because she was a threat to your plan."

"So?" he asked with a shrug.

"If you'd kept her alive, you would've had two of us."

He raised a brow, refusing to reply.

Eilish lowered her hand and faced him. "I'm not going to help you any more until you give me some answers about my mother. This carrot you've dangled in front of me these past months is losing its effectiveness."

"Is that all?" he asked with a smile.

Immediately, she was on edge. His response was the

opposite of what she'd expected. She gathered her magic, ready to defend herself.

"Fine," Mikkel said. "Your mother was Irish, and she had magic."

"Then she was a Druid?" Eilish asked.

He shrugged, shooting her an innocent smile. "You'll get more when you've done as I asked."

The world wasn't perfect, but what would she unleash upon it by allowing Mikkel his magic? Her thoughts came to a halt when she thought about what he'd recruited her for.

"When you first came to me, you wanted me to kill Ulrik."

Mikkel flattened his lips in frustration. "We've been over this."

"Then you asked me to kill Ulrik *and* Con. I've learned enough about the Dragon Kings to know that it's going to take someone of immense power to kill Con."

"Your point?" Mikkel asked.

"That's what you wanted Ulrik to do, but he's moved off that path." It was a guess, but by the narrowing of Mikkel's eyes, she'd hit upon the truth.

It was no secret that only a Dragon King could kill a Dragon King, but she had the power to touch dragon magic, which made it possible for her to take out a King. It wouldn't be easy, and in fact, she might die from it.

She'd agreed to kill Ulrik because Mikkel knew of her mother. It was only recently that he demanded she kill Con, as well. As if she would refuse. She'd agreed, but only because she had no other choice.

"Why don't you kill Ulrik?" she asked. Though she knew the answer.

Mikkel wasn't strong enough to take out his nephew, which meant he'd never get close enough to kill Con.

"Unbind my magic, Druid," he demanded.

She thought back to the story she'd heard Mikkel tell Gianna in Venice. It was the arrival of the humans that allowed the Dragon Kings to shift, but only the Kings. And Mikkel wasn't a Dragon King.

"I'm pretty sure you don't want me to do that."

He took a step toward her. "Why not?"

"You'll be a dragon since only the Kings can shift. Then the Dragon Kings will come for you, halting all your plans."

Mikkel peeled back his lips as he took a step toward her. Whatever he was going to say, he changed his mind. He then pivoted and stomped from the cottage, his men hurrying after him.

Eilish waited until the taillights vanished before she lowered herself to the cold floor and curled onto her side as she lit the logs in the hearth on fire.

CHAPTER SIX

The moment Nikolai stepped out of the helicopter beside Esther on the tarmac and the blades began to slow, he knew he'd done the right thing in agreeing to help her.

He looked back to see Kellan give him a nod. Nikolai returned it before he and Esther walked away. Her back was arrow-straight, her chin lifted, but he saw the thread of worry she valiantly attempted to hide.

They walked through the main building of the private airstrip where a vehicle waited for them. As soon as Nikolai spied the black Mercedes G-class SUV, he walked toward it.

"How do you know that's ours?" Esther asked.

"A hunch."

As soon as they got closer, a man stepped around the vehicle and smiled in greeting. "Mr. Nikolai and Miss North. I hope your flight was nice. I have everything ready for you. I just need your signature."

Nikolai grinned at Esther before he took the clipboard and signed. Once presented with the keys, Nikolai opened the back for their duffels before he made his way to the driver's side.

"Are Kellan and Denae coming?" Esther asked.

He gave a shake of his head. "They're running some errands while the chopper is being refueled and then heading back." He studied her a moment. "If you'd rather no' be alone with me, I can ask them to stay."

"It's not that," she quickly said. "It's being back in London where it all happened."

He didn't respond as she put on her seatbelt then raked a hand through her brown locks. She was fidgety, her nerves on edge.

"You doona have to do this."

She turned her head to him. "I do if I want to get on with my life."

"You willna be facing this alone. I'll be with you."

The small smile she gave him was reassurance enough. He put the SUV into drive and headed toward the flat Ryder had rented for them.

It had been decided not to use the house owned by Dreagan. There might be too many eyes watching it. Since they wanted to keep a low profile, Nikolai thought it a good idea.

Music played, filling the quiet of the vehicle as he made his way toward the flat on the east side of London. It was a comfortable silence as each of them was lost in their own thoughts.

Nikolai concentrated more on the driving since it was new to him. Thankfully, Ryder had programed the navigation with their destination, so Nikolai knew where to go even though he had looked over and memorized all the street maps of London.

He quite liked driving, though. Except when there was traffic. He really hated when he couldn't go as he liked. It took him a few attempts on the roundabouts before he caught on.

By Esther's grin, she appeared amused instead of

annoyed by it. She kept her gaze out the window, tapping her finger to the music.

Despite being asleep for so many millennia, Nikolai was caught up with current events thanks to visits from Con every decade or so. As King of Kings, Con had the ability to touch a sleeping dragon and fill their minds with anything he deemed necessary.

So while the Kings who had woken a few months ago didn't know how to use a mobile phone or drive a vehicle, they knew what each of them was and how they were operated. It made acclimating into whatever century they woke easier.

They reached the flat without any problems. Nikolai found a spot along the street to park, and they grabbed their bags before heading inside.

The apartment was on the small side, but with just the two of them, they didn't need a lot of space. He set his duffle down in the foyer and walked through the main floor before stopping in the kitchen. It was stocked with everything they might need.

He closed the fridge and turned to find Esther staring out the front window to the street. He leaned against the bar. "There are two bedrooms upstairs," he said. "Choose whichever you want."

"Thanks." She turned and walked toward him, running her fingers along furniture as she passed. "Henry told me this is the first time you've woken in a long time."

"It is."

She stopped on the opposite side of the bar. "He explained how Con keeps all of you aware of the changes throughout time while you sleep. That's how all of you adapt so easily. But do you ever feel out of place?"

"Aye. I see the rapid rate in which your race has advanced, and no matter how I look, I can see no place for my kind among you."

Esther cocked her head to the side. "What about you?"

"Do I look out of place?"

"On the contrary. You drove as if you've been doing it for years."

He came around the bar to stand next to her. "You asked me a question, but I can no' truly answer it without telling the reason."

"If you want to start, I can pour us some wine," she said, jerking her chin to one of several bottles on the counter.

Nikolai nodded in agreement. It wasn't his nature to share things with strangers or humans. Even as he reminded himself of that fact, there was something about Esther that made it irrelevant.

The same something that had propelled him to agree to help her. The same something he found incredibly attractive both physically and emotionally.

She opened the bottle and found two wine glasses. Once she'd handed him a glass, he lifted it, looking at the red liquid before taking a drink.

"Wow," she said after taking a sip. "This is good."

"How much do you know of our story?" he asked.

She leaned her forearms on the bar. "I want to hear it from you."

"Before mortals arrived, dragon clans made alliances and fought with others over land and the usual things." He turned and walked to the living area. "The Ivories were strong and powerful, and we just happened to have the Silvers bordering part of our land."

He lowered himself into one of the chairs as Esther trailed after him and chose the side of the sofa that put her close to him. She tucked her legs against her and waited for him to continue.

"I was newly hatched and just learning about the world when my parents were attacked and killed. My mum hid me, which is the only reason I'm alive today."

"Nikolai, I'm so sorry," Esther said, sorrow filling her dark eyes.

He waved away her words. "It was a verra long time ago."

"What happened? Why were they attacked?"

"It was. Ivories from my own clan. They wanted the land my parents had." He took a drink of wine, recalling memories of that fateful day. "My parents had started teaching me to fly that day, but I had yet to master it when the assault came. My mum hid me. I doona know how long I was there before Ulrik found me."

She raised a brow, surprised. "Ulrik?"

Nikolai smiled. "You know the Ulrik he is now, no' the King he once was. He saved me that day. He took me into his clan when he didna have to. My King wanted me to return, but Ulrik gave me a choice."

"And you chose him," she said.

He nodded slowly. "It wasn't just the kindness that appealed to me as a youngling. I saw what made him a Dragon King. Ulrik didna pass me off onto someone else as my King most likely would have. Ulrik became a father—and later a brother—to me. He taught me everything he knew, sharing his knowledge and skills.

"He always told me that I had a path that would divert from his one day. I didna understand until I felt my power and magic grow. The only way I can explain it is that I had a drive, an overwhelming desire to challenge my King. When I did, Ulrik stood with me."

Her eyes crinkled as she smiled. "You loved him very much."

"Aye. And when the mortals came, I stood beside him as we vowed to keep your kind safe. I watched as he wooed and fell in love with Nala. I was the second person he told of his intention to have her as his mate."

"Who was the first?" Esther asked.

Nikolai took a long drink, licking his lips when he finished. "Con. There were no two Kings closer than the two of them. So, when Con gathered us and told us about Nala's intention to betray Ulrik, I was outraged. I gladly took up the call to hunt her down."

"And you killed her."

He gave a single nod. "Gladly. I'd do it again. You doona understand the man Ulrik was. He was giving and kind and loyal beyond reason sometimes. He found joy in everything, and passed that on to those around him. There hasna ever been anyone as generous as he, and I doona think there ever will be."

"In other words, Ulrik was liked by all."

"Nay," Nikolai corrected her. "He was loved by all. It's why we all willingly killed her to protect him. We were so shocked and incensed by her actions that none of us stopped to think what Ulrik would've wanted."

Esther set aside her glass and linked her hands together in her lap. "I was told he was angry when he found out."

"There was shock first, then denial. His fury was last, and it was directed at everyone—dragon and human alike. I tried to talk to him, but he was too enraged. He walked away. I wanted to go after him, but Con followed him. Everyone else left while I remained. Watching."

She swallowed and leaned forward, eager for the story. "What happened?"

"Con attempted to explain things. Ulrik heard none of it. All he knew was that Con had led the others against Nala. They fought."

"What?" she asked, her eyes wide.

Nikolai looked out the window as his memories turned to seeing the two Kings he looked up to most fighting. "Ulrik needed to release some of his anger, and Con knew that. Con didna defend himself at first when Ulrik shifted and attacked, but it soon became apparent that if he didna want to die, Con had to shift and fight back. I'd never seen Ulrik battle with such rage before. He got the upper hand with Con. I thought I would see Ulrik kill him, but he held back on the final blow."

"So if Ulrik challenges Con this time, he'll win."

Nikolai swung his head to her. "I honestly doona know. Both are incredible fighters. Con didna expect such brutality from Ulrik that night, so he left himself un-guarded, which allowed Ulrik to come out on top. It's a mistake Con willna repeat, and Ulrik is smart enough to know that."

Esther blew out a breath. "So it really will be a toss-up between them, won't it?"

"Aye. Ulrik is a brilliant strategist and sees people's moves dozens of steps ahead. Con is known for keeping his cool, but he's just as good at tactics as Ulrik. They know each other's weaknesses and their strengths. Trust me when I say the battle will be the bloodiest thing you've ever witnessed."

She pressed her lips together and reached for her wine. After she'd taken a drink, she asked, "What happened after they fought?"

"Ulrik left. Con returned to Dreagan. That's when Ulrik took his Silvers and began to attack the humans. Other Kings joined him."

"Did you?" she asked.

Nikolai held her gaze. "I made a promise, and Ulrik taught me to hold to such things. So I remained with Con while Ulrik waged war. All I wanted to do was join him. No' because I believed the humans needed to be wiped away, but because he was my friend and needed me."

CHAPTER SEVEN

Remorse. It burned in Nikolai's blue eyes and caused Esther's heart to lurch. Everything she'd heard about Ulrik had been horrible. She considered him a terrorist, someone who had to be stopped at any cost.

Yet Nikolai was giving her another side of Ulrik's story, one she wasn't entirely comfortable discovering because it made her look at the Silver in a different light. Nikolai was painting him as a caring and loving individual. It didn't mesh with the monster that she knew.

Or thought she knew.

In fact, she couldn't be sure whether she'd ever met Ulrik. But that wasn't the point. Her view had been clouded on the facts laid out before her at Dreagan. Everyone knew Ulrik was responsible for the calamity befalling the Dragon Kings.

Or did they?

Mikkel's name kept coming up. There was a reason for that.

"What happened?" she pressed Nikolai, praying he finished the story. She had to know details others had left out, particulars that only someone who thought of Ulrik as a friend would impart.

"Ulrik and many Dragon Kings began killing. I was with Con and the others as we fought to protect the humans, but the more we did, the more it didna seem to make a difference. Every day, more mortals turned against us. When we arrived to help, they'd attack us."

"They were scared," she said.

He sighed loudly. "Aye."

When he remained silent, she said, "Henry told me that some of the humans killed dragons sent to guard them. That those dragons had orders from their Kings not to harm the mortals."

Nikolai squeezed his eyes shut and sat forward, bracing his forearms on his thighs. When he opened his lids, his gaze was trained on the floor. "Sadly, that's true. That's when Con told us that our options had run out. We pulled all the dragons to safety. I told my clan that if mortals attacked them, they should defend themselves, and I know I wasna the only King to do so."

"I'd have done the same. You had to look out for your people."

His lips twisted as he shrugged. "We focused everything on the Kings with Ulrik. Sebastian was one of Ulrik's closest friends, and he rejoined Con. One by one, Con convinced the Kings to return. I thought that might get Ulrik's attention, but it didna seem to have any effect. He kept attacking."

She finished her wine. There was a tightness in her chest as she listened, as if she were there in Nikolai's memories with him. "Did you talk to Ulrik then?"

"I couldna get close enough, nor would he answer my calls through our mental link. The Silvers who had once been my friends blocked me from getting to Ulrik." He raised his gaze to her. "They did it because Ulrik told them to."

"He knew you'd try to talk him out of what he was doing."

Nikolai downed his wine and set the glass aside. "We really had run out of options by that point. Dragons were dying, and we couldn't allow that. That's when we used our magic to create the dragon bridge to another realm and sent our clans over."

He grew quiet, and she knew he was reliving the memory of watching his dragons leave. It would be akin to her sending her family away, knowing she might never see them again. Just the thought of an event like that made breathing difficult.

And Nikolai had lived it.

"We all knew what had to happen," he said. "Especially when Con, as King of Kings, demanded the Silvers answer to him. All but four listened. The Silvers were the last dragons over the bridge. We had no time to mourn our clans, friends, or family. Instead, we had to trap the last remaining Silvers, making them sleep as we locked them away on Dreagan."

"Then you went after Ulrik." This was a part of the story she knew well, but she had a feeling her thoughts would change once Nikolai told his side.

He nodded slowly. "Ulrik was all alone, but he kept attacking the humans. When we caught up with him, he faced us like a cornered animal. Because that's exactly what he was. The King who had saved me and showed me love and compassion was gone. The dragon who was known for his laughter and generosity had vanished. The feral beast I saw was someone, *something*, altogether different."

The longer Nikolai's story went on, the harder it was

for Esther to look at him. Not because she didn't want to hear his words, but because his pain was seeping into her.

"The others urged me to talk to Ulrik because they thought he might listen to me. So I tried," Nikolai continued. "At first, Ulrik ignored me. Then he tried to attack me. I knew it was the pain of what had happened that warped him. He just needed time, but that was the one thing we didna have."

Esther rose and got the bottle of wine from the kitchen before returning and refilling both of their glasses. She set the bottle on the table next to the sofa and lowered herself to the floor, using the couch to rest her back upon.

Nikolai swirled the wine before taking a long drink. "The mortals were gathering into one large army, intent on attacking us. Ulrik saw it as an easy way to wipe them out. He tried to rally us, but it wasna working. We watched our dragons leave the realm and destroyed our dead so there was no trace of us. We were . . . distressed and full of despair. Con attempted to talk to him, but it was a waste of time. Ulrik refused to listen to anyone.

"I knew what was coming. It was the only option left to Con, and I didna want Ulrik to suffer such horrors. I shouted, I yelled, I roared. But Ulrik wouldna hear me. He tried to get away, to resume his attacks. That's when Con told us we had to take Ulrik's magic."

From the small amount of time Esther had been at Dreagan, it had become clear that while the dragons needed their magic to feel whole, they went out of their way not to use it. But to take it away. . . .

"I didna think Ulrik could become any more enraged," Nikolai continued. "Then I looked into his eyes as all of his brethren bound his magic, locking him in the mortal form he despised so much. If there had been any remorse or even forgiveness within him, we killed it then. He didna go down easily. He fought us, which only brought him more pain."

Unable to help herself, she leaned forward, closing the small space that separated them, and put her hand on Nikolai's arm. Their gazes met, and she clearly saw the anguish he lived with every day.

He moved his other hand to lie atop hers. "Ulrik was a Dragon King I thought I'd never see defeated, and yet I watched as he shifted into his human form. He tried, again and again, to shift back into a dragon, but it didna happen. That's when he dropped to his knees with his arms outstretched and his hands fisted as he bellowed his fury."

Nikolai paused then, swallowing several times before drinking more of the wine. "I saw the need for retribution in Ulrik's eyes. There was a promise for vengeance there that Con noticed, as well."

"Is that when Con banished him?" she asked.

"I doona know what Con planned to do after Ulrik's magic was bound. Maybe his intention was always to banish Ulrik. It matters no' now."

She licked her lips and tightened her grip on his arm. "It might've been better had Con killed Ulrik instead of letting him suffer."

Nikolai's forehead furrowed. "Could you kill Henry, even if you knew it would end his suffering?"

"I . . ." She realized that it was an impossibility. Henry was her brother, her family. Her blood. She'd do anything in the hope that he might recover, but she couldn't kill him.

"That's why," Nikolai said softly. "He was our dearest friend, our brother. No' a single one of us could've done the deed." His gaze dropped to the floor. "We all watched him leave Dreagan a broken King. It was difficult to view one of our own brought so low. Since we intended to sleep through centuries, the majority of the Kings sought out their mountains then. It wasna long until only Con and I remained."

She scooted closer to him. "And Ulrik."

"And Ulrik. I debated whether to go after him, but Con wasna sure it would be a good idea. He told me he hoped that by taking such drastic measures, it would calm Ulrik and make him see reason. But Con admitted that the opposite had occurred. For months, I refused to seek out my mountain as I waited in hopes that Ulrik would return to the King I once knew him to be."

"Did he?" Esther asked.

Nikolai shook his head and gave her a sad smile. "I was the first Con came to wake after several centuries. It was strange to see how quickly the world had changed, and how easily dragons had turned to myth. I used it to my advantage and searched for Ulrik, but I couldna find him. After many years, I returned to my mountain."

"You're carrying such guilt when you shouldn't." She rose up on her knees so that that their faces were close to each other. "You tried to help your friend, but he was beyond reasoning with. Sometimes, that happens. Ulrik made his decisions, and they had consequences.

As she finished her sentence, she grasped how close she and Nikolai were. She could see the silver band that encircled his iris as well as the streaks of blue so pale they were nearly white. They were eyes that saw everything. Magical eyes.

Dragon eyes.

She had the sudden urge to see him in his true form. The request was on the tip of her tongue, but she managed to hold it back at the last minute.

Being around Nikolai gave her the freedom to shake off the chains that confined her. Apparently, it also made her forget herself since both of her hands were touching him. One was on his arm from before, and the other now rested on his leg.

There was no use denying the attraction she'd refused to acknowledge while at Dreagan. She was drawn to Nikolai in a manner that alarmed her as well as aroused her.

She became very aware of his warmth that seeped into her palms. Silence stretched between them as her blood rushed through her. Her stomach fluttered in anticipation.

Then his gaze lowered to her mouth.

It became impossible to breathe. Her chest heaved as she fought to bring air into her lungs while desire filled her lower belly making her ache . . . for him.

His hand moved to the back of her arm. Time slowed as he applied the slightest pressure with his fingertips. She leaned forward slowly. Her eyes focused on his mouth, her heart skipped when his lips parted. She realized she was breathing through her mouth even as her head leaned to the side, anxiously awaiting the feel of his mouth on hers.

Her heart pumped wildly, the blood rushing in her ears. As his face loomed closer, her eyes slid shut.

The moment was shattered by the sound of her mobile ringing.

She snapped her eyes open and leaned back. Nikolai dropped his hand and reclined in the chair. Esther got to her feet and hurried to where she'd left the cell on the kitchen table.

When she saw that it was Henry calling, she wanted to scream. Instead, she looked at the ceiling and attempted to keep her voice calm as she answered the phone.

"Is everything all right?" Henry asked. "You sound peeved."

She was definitely perturbed, but she wasn't going to let her brother know that. "Just eager to start the process."

"I included something in your duffel that will help."

"You didn't think to mention this sooner?"

He laughed through the line. "Ah, little sis. Keep me updated. I know if anyone can figure this out, it's you."

She glared at the mobile when he hung up then she set down the phone and walked to her bag. As soon as she unzipped it, she found the cigar box.

"What's that?" Nikolai asked from behind her.

She turned and held the box between them then opened the lid and smiled. "It seems Henry remembered something that my father started me on long ago."

Nikolai reached into the box and pulled out one of the items. "Bar coasters?"

"I collect them from everywhere I visit."

Suddenly, Nikolai smiled. "We just need to follow the trail."

CHAPTER EIGHT

Dark Fae Court
Ireland

The time was drawing near. Balladyn knew it, wanted it. He'd been preparing for the day when he could take over as King of the Dark ever since Taraeth had made him his lieutenant.

As the current king eyed the assortment of humans who had been brought to him, Balladyn stood with his hands clasped behind his back, thinking of all the changes he would make.

At one time, Balladyn would've been right beside Taraeth examining the mortals who were writhing naked on the ground, the sex appeal of the Fae too much for them to resist. But that was before Rhi.

After loving her from afar for many thousands of years, Balladyn finally called her his. She was a secret he couldn't yet share. Mainly because in his anger at being turned Dark, he had caught her and tortured her, hoping to turn her, as well.

Balladyn then made the mistake of telling Taraeth all about it, as well as promising to return Rhi after her escape. By the time Balladyn had caught up with her, all his anger was gone. All he'd wanted was to hold her, to cherish her. He'd confessed his love, and to his shock, she returned his kiss.

Now that she was his, it irritated him that he had to keep their love a secret. Soon, it wouldn't matter. Once he was king, no Dark would dare speak ill of his Light Fae lover.

Because if they did, Balladyn would kill them.

Taraeth chose four of the ten mortals. Guards then took the chosen ones away to be prepared while the rest waited until Taraeth came for them.

Killing mortals was his way of letting off steam since Amdir had failed in his quest to break another Dragon King. In the end, Anson had been freed.

By Rhi, Con, and . . . him.

Though his intent had been to help Rhi, not the Dragon Kings. The line between the two was getting blurrier with each week.

But that wasn't something Balladyn wanted to think about right now.

"That's the third time you've declined the humans," Taraeth said as he turned to face him.

Balladyn bowed his head. "I appreciate your willingness to share, sire."

Taraeth sat upon his large throne and tucked the sleeve of his missing left arm to the side. "You've still not told me why you're abstaining."

"I like to hunt my own."

The king nodded in understanding. "It's from all those centuries when Usaeil prevented you from giving in to your baser urges."

"That's right," Balladyn lied, doing his best not to roll his eyes.

"I suppose I should say that you were right."

Balladyn raised a brow in question.

"About Amdir. I know the two of you hated each other."

"That we did."

Taraeth leaned forward. "You said his plan to break Anson wouldn't work. In allowing Amdir to go against our plans, I've lost a Dragon King as well as my favorite torturer. And pissed off Mikkel in the process."

"Tell Mikkel to bugger off. You are the king."

"Yes. I am," Taraeth said with a smile.

There was a shimmer on the opposite wall that had Balladyn frowning. He called forth his magic, and a ball of iridescent light filled his hand.

Taraeth sat straight as he too noticed the contortion of the wall. Balladyn recognized it as a Fae doorway being opened, and he was shocked that he hadn't even known one was there. Someone had locked it from the other side, preventing anyone at the palace from noticing it.

It was the king's subtle relaxation that put Balladyn on high alert. Taraeth knew who it was. Balladyn tucked that away for later and moved back into the shadows, though he kept the orb of magic ready.

The Fae doorway suddenly opened. A moment later, Usaeil, the Queen of the Light, stepped through. Her long, black hair was loose, part of it of hanging over her left shoulder as the strands curled at the bottom next to her breast.

Her silver eyes locked onto Taraeth as she strode toward him wearing a strapless, white jumpsuit with a gold belt wrapped around her waist. Gold stilettos didn't make a sound upon the plush red and black rugs scattered throughout the throne room.

"Well, isn't this a surprise?" Taraeth said with a grin.

Usaeil put her hands on her hips as she came to stand

before him. Then she smiled, winking at him. "Hello, Taraeth."

Balladyn was too surprised to move. Anger and disbelief coiled within him, making him glad he was half hidden. The Light and Dark hated each other, and that extended to their respective rulers. But Taraeth and Usaeil's greeting suggested otherwise.

And that both irritated and worried Balladyn.

"I didn't think you'd ever use that door again," Taraeth said.

"Necessity. Something we both understand."

Taraeth laughed. "Are you still masquerading as an American actress?"

"I'm damn good at it. You should see my latest film."

"Oh, I've no doubt you're an excellent actor, my dear," he said as he leaned his right elbow on the arm of the throne. "You've been fooling the Light for millennia."

Usaeil narrowed her gaze. "Your point?"

"I have none. Just stating a fact."

"Good," the queen replied with a lift of her chin.

Balladyn stared at Usaeil, hatred and rage rolling through him with such violence that he thought he might explode. It had been three thousand years since he'd last seen her. He'd served her faithfully and led the Queen's Guard into battle numerous times. Yet the first time he fell, she hadn't sent anyone back for him.

It was how he'd ended up in Taraeth's dungeon, being tortured for unending centuries until the darkness finally took him and he became a Dark Fae.

"Why are you here?" Taraeth asked. "I cannot imagine you've come to chat."

She jutted out one hip before she turned and walked to the red velvet sofa. Usaeil sat, stretching her legs along the cushion before flexing her stiletto-encased feet. "You know me so well."

It would have to be something important for Usaeil to visit Taraeth. She didn't look around the room, as if she never considered there might be someone with Taraeth. Their easy banter was worrisome.

Balladyn searched his mind and kept coming back to the Dragon Kings. Was Usaeil miffed about Con's rejection? Since Balladyn didn't know if Con had officially rejected the queen, he was reaching. He knew very little about what was going on with the King of Kings and Usaeil, other than that the queen had had their picture secretly taken. That picture was now plastered with headlines all over the world, with mortals wanting to know the identity of her secret lover.

Well, not Usaeil, but the actress she pretended to be.

Balladyn hadn't spoken to Rhi about it because he didn't like discussing the Dragon Kings with her. It brought back the years of pain he'd suffered as he watched her with her lover. Now, he wished he had mentioned it.

If anyone knew what was going on, it was Rhi.

Usaeil released a dramatic sigh. "There's someone else I need you to kill."

Balladyn didn't know what alarmed him more. The fact that the queen had come to Taraeth for this deed— or that it had happened before.

"If you weren't so determined to have the Light worship you, you'd take care of this yourself," Taraeth said.

There was a pit that began in Balladyn's stomach, a growing panic that he knew exactly who Usaeil had set her sights on. Yet, he prayed he was wrong.

Usaeil flicked back her long midnight hair and grinned. "You like to rule with fear. I rule my people differently."

"Fear does the job."

She shrugged, her boredom apparent as she glanced

at her perfectly manicured nails. "Will you do this or not?"

"I enjoy killing, so you know I will," Taraeth stated.

The queen immediately perked up. She flashed Taraeth a wide smile. "Wonderful."

While Usaeil played with her hair, Taraeth looked Balladyn's way. There was a secret in the king's smile that set Balladyn on edge. That pit in his stomach widened and soured.

"Who is the target?" Taraeth asked.

The queen swung her legs to the floor and cocked her head at Taraeth. "I'm almost hesitant to tell you since you had her once and lost her."

A bellow resounded in Balladyn's head. He glared at Usaeil as he raised the ball of magic. All it would take would be one hit to slow her, then he'd thrust his sword into her heart and ensure her death.

"Ah, Rhi," Taraeth said with a chuckle. He motioned toward Balladyn with his hand. "We've been searching for her."

As soon as Usaeil swung her gaze to him, Balladyn saw her face lose all color. Despite her claims to fame as an actress, she couldn't hide her fear. It rolled off her in thick waves. And he enjoyed it. Matter of fact, he wanted more of it.

She stumbled to her feet and moved toward Taraeth. "We had a deal," she whispered loudly.

"What deal?" Balladyn demanded as he walked to her with the ball of magic still in hand.

Taraeth hooked one leg over the arm of the throne. "She came and asked me to kill you."

Balladyn welcomed the fury that rose up swift and absolute. He gathered it against him and focused his gaze on the person who had destroyed his life.

"I gave you everything," Balladyn told her. "I went

above and beyond to get you everything you desired. What did I ever do for you to want me killed?"

Her lips trembled as her panic shifted into anger. "You know exactly what it was."

"Tell me!" he bellowed. "Tell me what I fekking did that would cause you to order my death!"

In her silver eyes, he saw the ugliness that she hid behind her mask of beauty. More importantly, he saw her darkness.

"You loved Rhi," Usaeil spat.

Her confession only incensed him more. "You wanted me killed because of Rhi?"

"Yes!" Usaeil yelled, her arms outstretched. "Everywhere I go, people love that bitch. I don't know why. She doesn't do anything to deserve such love. I'm tired of it."

Jealousy. His life was ruined because of jealousy? He couldn't wrap his head around it.

Usaeil fisted her hands as she lowered her arms. "Everything Rhi sets her sights on doing she accomplishes. The first female in the Queen's Guard was a major hurdle, but then to gain the love of a Dragon King when I. . . ."

She trailed off, but Balladyn zeroed in on her words. "When you couldn't get Con to look your way," he finished. He gave a shake of his head as he gazed at her with disdain. "You were responsible for Rhi's affair falling apart, weren't you?"

"So what if I was?" Usaeil asked with contempt.

Balladyn lifted the orb of magic. He wanted to shove it in her face, to watch the beauty of her visage melt away and show the true monstrosity that she was.

"Easy," Taraeth said as he stood and blocked Balladyn's way. "She wanted you dead, but I saw your potential. I kept you alive."

"About that," Usaeil began.

Taraeth jerked his head around and gave her a stern look before he returned his attention to Balladyn. "You've told me how you hated Rhi for not coming for you. You captured her and tortured her. You said she was becoming Dark. You have one last chance to convince her to come to us, or you'll have to kill her."

There wasn't an entity in the universe that could make Balladyn kill Rhi. Though he would gladly take out everyone else for her. He kept all that to himself as he stared at his king.

He knew without a doubt that the time had come to remove Taraeth so he could take the throne. There was no other choice for him. Or Rhi.

And once Taraeth was gone, Balladyn was going after Usaeil.

"I understand," he said calmly and dropped the magic.

With one last scowl in Usaeil's direction, Balladyn walked from the throne room to find the love of his life. As the door closed behind him, he heard Usaeil yelling at Taraeth, but he didn't care. There were more pressing matters.

"Rhi," he whispered, knowing his voice would reach her wherever she was.

CHAPTER NINE

Nikolai's mind was filled with lustful thoughts about the things he longed to do to Esther's body. He ran his hand over his lips as he thought of the near kiss with her the night before.

While she slept, he paced the flat. He studied more maps of London, he sketched, and he even turned on the tele. After only ten minutes, he shut it off and paced some more. Finally, he went to the cigar box and spread the coasters on the living room floor and began to systematically look up each location on Esther's laptop.

He felt her presence behind him long before she appeared. He stilled, his gaze lifting as he focused all of his senses on her. She was like a whisper of pleasure, a sigh of anticipation.

A breath of desire.

Con's urging to give in to what he craved came back to Nikolai. It would be so easy to reach for her, to let the fires of lust consume him.

It was the longing within him to do just that, which kept him from surrendering.

"Did you sleep at all?" she asked as she walked into the kitchen.

He heard her moving things around, and then he smelled the coffee grounds. "I doona need sleep."

"Lucky you," she said, yawning.

Incapable of stopping himself, he turned his head to her. He found her leaning against the counter with her eyes closed in a plaid sleep shirt that buttoned up the front and stopped at her shapely thighs. Her brown locks were mussed. Thick socks covered her feet with the long neck of an ostrich running up the outside of her leg to the animal's face that stared back at Nikolai with derision.

She looked positively adorable except for the dark circles under her eyes. He'd noticed them weeks ago. Now, they were more visible, but the exhaustion was taking a toll on her body, as well.

He watched as she cracked open one eye when the coffee beeped that it had finished brewing. She poured the caffeinated liquid into the largest mug he'd ever seen. Then, with it held between both hands, she sipped it, her eyes closed once more.

It was the Druid that kept her from finding rest. Or rather what the Druid might have made Esther do in the time that had been lost.

"You're staring," she murmured.

He leaned to the side, bracing himself on one hand. "Did you sleep?"

"The bed was very comfortable."

"That's no' what I asked."

She sighed and lifted her lids to look at him. "Sleep is . . . difficult to come by."

"Do you see the Druid?"

"I wish that wench had a name," Esther grumbled. Then she shook her head. "It's not really her. When I close my eyes, I see myself trying to kill Kinsey as she attempts to end my life. Then all the things I could've done that I can't remember run on a repeating loop, getting worse each time."

It was as he thought. "Does Henry know?"

"Sometimes it's better if my brother is unaware of such things."

Nikolai didn't agree with her, but it wasn't his family. "You're going to need rest."

"I'll be fine as soon as I'm recharged with a mug or two of coffee." She flashed him a wide smile, then changed the subject. "What are you doing?"

He glanced at the coasters spread around him. "Learning what I can about these locations."

"And what did you find?" She walked to the island and leaned on it, gazing at him curiously.

"You like out-of-the-way places. The smaller pubs that locals tend to frequent." His gaze moved to a pile of coasters. "Though you do sometimes visit the popular restaurants where there is a wait."

She walked to sit in the chair he'd occupied the night before during their talk. Tucking her legs against her, she leaned on the upholstered arm and sipped her coffee.

Pointing at a large stack of coasters off to the side, she asked, "What are those?"

"Places outside of London. I thought it best to focus within the city for now."

Leaning back, she eyed the pile. "I have a container for each year I collected the coasters at my flat. That cigar box is only a few months' worth. I started the box when I went undercover at Kyvor."

"A smart move." Especially since they now knew the Druid was working with someone at Kyvor.

It had been Esther, along with Kinsey, Devon, and Anson who exposed the corruption within the tech company and brought it down. Though everything pointed to

Ulrik, someone looking like Ulrik had been seen. That's what sent Sebastian on a hunt to track down Mikkel.

Now, the man who had run Kyvor, Stanley Upton, was locked away in the mountain at Dreagan. After an initial talk with him, he was left alone except to be fed, but it wouldn't be long before Con began another interrogation.

"What are you thinking?" Esther asked.

Nikolai ran a hand over his jaw. "Bast was certain we'd been wrong all this time. That it isna Ulrik attempting to expose us."

"You were one of those closest to Ulrik, do you remember Mikkel?"

"Con asked me the same thing. I didna spend much time with Ulrik's family. I met them on a few occasions, but they were in dragon form, no' human."

She watched him for a silent moment. "But you find it odd that someone looks like Ulrik."

"Aye," he replied. "As should you."

"I do. The fact is, I don't care which of them is to blame. It could be one or both. Regardless, they need to be stopped."

Nikolai moved to the sofa. "I'm holding out hope that it isna Ulrik."

"If it isn't him, why has he told Con he would fight him to be King of Kings?"

"I doona have an answer."

She tucked her hair behind her ear. "Perhaps it's because you're trying not to see what's right in front of you."

"You could be correct. I suspect we'll know soon enough."

"Yeah," Esther said with a nod. "We know the Druid is part of the scheme, so if we can find her, we'll put a kink in the plans of whoever is running the show."

He grinned at her enthusiasm. "So, where do we begin?"

"After I accepted the mission to go undercover at Kyvor, I devoted a few days to becoming my new persona. I moved into a flat and spent the next three weeks being seen by my neighbors. I conducted my life as if I were looking for a job."

Nikolai nodded as he listened. "How long did it take you to get an interview with Kyvor?"

"Less than a month. MI5 used their connections to get my application noticed. That's all it took to be brought in for the interview. Then it was up to me to make sure I got hired."

"Which you did," he said.

She curled her toes and smothered a yawn. "It wasn't as easy as I'd thought it would be. There were five interviews in all. I was passed over, but MI5 worked quickly to procure an even better position for the person who was offered the job. I was next on the list, but even then, it took them a week before they called."

He frowned at her words. "A week?"

"I was leery, as well. Turns out, I had a right to be. Somehow, they'd figured out I was MI5, which is nearly impossible. There were only four other people who knew about my mission."

"I assume you checked into that."

She nodded. "I called each of them individually with my fears after I was hired."

"So they would check each other out," he deduced with a grin. "Smart."

"Or foolish if more than one were working together."

"But you doona believe that."

She shrugged her shoulders. "The only other option is the Druid."

"Which is verra possible."

"It is," she replied bleakly.

Nikolai swiped his hand from left to right over the coasters. "Which place do we visit first?"

"That one," she said, pointing to the coaster with a white horse rearing up on its hind legs.

He picked up the coaster and read, "The White Mare."

"Give me twenty minutes, and I'll be ready," she said as she got to her feet, refilled her mug, and headed upstairs.

Watching her go, Nikolai wondered if finding Esther's missing memories would help her. What if the thing she feared the most were true? She would then have to live with that.

It was the unknown that was slowly eating at her. Nikolai knew exactly how that felt. How many times had he wondered what might have been if he'd only spoken with Ulrik.

Or sided with him.

Ulrik had once listened to his counsel. Nikolai should've tried harder to talk to him. He should've done a lot of things differently.

Nikolai made his way upstairs to take a shower. As he passed Esther's room, he saw that the door was cracked. He looked inside to find her sitting on the corner of the bed staring off into space. The despair that contorted her beautiful features pulled at him. If he couldn't help Ulrik, he would make sure Esther found the answers she sought.

Her head turned then, and their gazes met. She didn't try to hide her feelings, and he was glad she allowed him to see who she really was. Because she had kept all of it hidden away at Dreagan.

"I'm going to be fine," she said.

He wasn't sure if she was convincing herself or him. "I've no doubt."

She stood and began unbuttoning her nightshirt. Nikolai wanted to stay and see her bared to him, but he wasn't yet ready to test the attraction between them when they had just begun their mission. He turned away and headed to the bathroom. He turned on the shower. While the water heated, he braced his hands on either side of the sink and stared at his reflection.

The man he saw wasn't the one he'd once been. He was crushed under the weight of his grief and remorse, but that wasn't the man Esther needed. Though she would never admit it, she was vulnerable.

He would be her shield, the Dragon King who stood against all of her enemies. Then he would stand beside her as they slew them together.

Whether she knew it or not, she was helping him find his way back to where he belonged. He hoped he would be able to do the same for her. Because it was a desolate place out in the cold alone.

He stripped out of his clothes and stood beneath the spray of water. This was the first day of a long journey that posed threats at every turn. He smiled because he was more than ready to face them.

CHAPTER TEN

The act of looking back on a part of the past caused Esther to eye her life as an outsider would. And, frankly, she didn't like what she saw.

For two hours, they walked the streets around where she'd used the flat for her mission, searching for anything. Every once in a while, Nikolai would stop and stare at something before they finally made their way to the pub.

She flipped the new coaster over and over in her hand as she sat with Nikolai at a table in The White Mare, waiting for their drinks to arrive. Her gaze scanned the occupants of the bar, seeing those deep in conversation with friends, while others sat by themselves.

It had never bothered her to eat alone. Yet now, as she looked at those unaccompanied by others, she noted the loneliness in their eyes. For whatever reason, they were lost, whether it was intentional, or Fate had set them on that course, there was no hiding their forlorn and bleak expressions.

That hadn't been her. Had it?

Each table she looked at where the person was by

themselves, reading a book or on their mobile devices, it was all the same—loneliness.

The thump of the glasses being set on the table caused her to jump. Her gaze shot to Nikolai, who was watching her with his intent gaze. Always, his baby blue eyes were on her. They were never mocking or judgmental. Just observant.

"What do you see?" he asked in a soft voice after the server had left.

Her gaze briefly lowered to the table. "Have you ever had to do this? You know, go back over your life with a fine-tooth comb?"

"Nay, but I doona believe it would be easy."

"That's putting it mildly." She motioned with her chin to a woman who was sitting alone, her back to the room as she faced the wall, reading a book. "What do you think when you look at her?"

Nikolai lifted the ale to his lips and drank deeply. When he sat the glass down, he said, "I see someone who wanted a hot meal, not a sandwich brought from home. I see someone who doesna want to be disturbed as she selfishly seeks every second she can of her lunch break."

"You asked me what I see. I look around, and all I notice is dismal, awful isolation. I see those who are alone because they have no other choice."

"There's always a choice," Nikolai said.

She raised a brow, silently chiding him. "Sometimes, when I had to be alone, was when I was the loneliest. There are times people or events put others in a place where they have no one. Not a single friend or family member who is there for them. They want to reach out for help, they long for it, but there is no one there. Just an empty void, a constant reminder of how isolated you are."

His brow crinkled in a frown as his gaze studied her.

"Then there are the others. The ones who want to be alone. They are the worst."

"How?" he asked.

To share this would give him a glimpse into her world, a world she had eagerly rushed into. A world that changed everything.

Esther slowly released a breath. "Those are the people who have shut others out, who don't want or need anyone. They've either been hurt so deeply they can never trust again, or. . . ."

"Or?" he urged when she trailed off.

She swallowed as she was forced to look closely at herself and the life she'd led. "Or they've been taught not to trust anyone. Ever."

"You have to be wary in your line of work. Otherwise, you could be killed."

"I didn't romanticize being an agent, but I didn't grasp the reality of it either. Henry was right when he said I didn't tell him my plans to join MI5 because I thought he'd talk me out of it. I knew he would give me the cold, hard facts, and I didn't want to hear them. I thought I knew better than he did."

Nikolai sat forward in his chair. "He was doing what any brother would."

"That's Henry. He always does what's right. Perhaps I should've let him tell me how the first mission would be hard, but that I'd catch on quickly. Too quickly. Because then I'd be thrust into assignments I wasn't quite ready for."

"Obviously, your superiors thought differently."

She turned her glass around on the table as she looked at the dark amber ale. "In all the training and books they shove at you, they never tell you how deceiving everyone begins to take a toll on your soul. There are all kinds of classes and people telling you how you'll feel when you kill someone—because it's inevitable in our line of work. They have therapy and time off for that. But not for the deception or the loneliness." She raised her gaze to Nikolai. "I see all of that in Henry's eyes when I look at him."

She forced a laugh despite the tears that gathered at the corners of her eyes. "Only after years in the agency do you realize you don't fit in anywhere. I've led so many different lives, been too many people spouting too many lies. I no longer have a place."

"You have a place at Dreagan. With us."

"I'm grateful that I've been given a chance to put the pieces of my life back together again. Returning to London with Kinsey to take down Kyvor went a long way to helping me right things. But I don't belong at Dreagan any more than I belong anywhere else."

Nikolai slowly sat back, never taking his eyes off her face. "Someone once told me that Fate will chew you up and spit you out many times, taking you away from those you love and dumping you into places you never wanted to be. It's up to each of us where we choose to belong. We can either fight everything, or accept what we're given and make the most of it."

"Did you know Buddha?" she inquired with a grin.

A flash of sorrow filled his eyes. "I knew Ulrik."

"Ulrik told you that?" she asked in surprise.

Nikolai smiled as he nodded. "It was one of his favorite sayings."

"His words make me consider things differently."

Nikolai held her gaze, looking deep into her eyes. "Good. Because you belong with us."

The server interrupted their conversation as they placed their order. Esther wasn't that hungry, but since she wasn't sleeping, she definitely had to eat to keep up her strength.

After the waitress had left, Esther thought over Ulrik's words and the fact that they resonated with Nikolai so deeply, that thousands of millennia later, he still quoted them.

"You want to find Ulrik, don't you?" she asked.

Nikolai froze. He looked at her and nodded as he returned the glass of ale to the table. "Verra much."

She cocked her head at him. "What would you say to him?"

"There's so much. I doona know where I'd begin."

"You should be looking for him, not helping me."

Nikolai quirked a brow. "Who says I can no' do both."

"Oh," she said, taken aback. "Is Ulrik in London?"

"I doona believe so."

Confused, she raised both brows. "I don't understand."

"If we find the Druid, I suspect we'll also encounter either Ulrik or Mikkel."

"Or both," she added.

Nikolai nodded in agreement. "If it's Mikkel, then I can determine if Ulrik was involved."

"It's hard to believe he isn't. It's too much of a coincidence that all of these things are happening to each of you, and Ulrik challenged Con."

"True," Nikolai conceded.

She crossed one leg over the other. "And if we find Ulrik?"

"I'll get my chance to talk to him before Con or any of the other Kings arrive."

"You could do that now. The mental link all of you dragons have. You could call for Ulrik."

Nikolai moved his gaze to look over the occupants of the pub. "I've thought of that, but it willna work. Other Kings have tried it."

"They weren't you. They didn't have the bond you had with Ulrik."

Nikolai grunted at her words. "Aye. But if he holds the hate he does for Con, I doona imagine he sees me much better."

"You won't know until you try."

"Let's concentrate on you."

Esther wasn't done trying to convince him to contact Ulrik. After the story he'd shared the previous night, she was thinking about Ulrik in completely different terms than before. She let the conversation drop as their food arrived.

While they ate, Nikolai asked, "Tell me about the last time you were here."

It took her a while to sort through her memories since the Druid had messed everything up by being in her head. Which only irritated her.

Esther swallowed and said, "It was a Tuesday night, and the pub was crowded and very loud. There was something on the tele, but I ignored it. I sat in the back corner so I could see the room and anyone approaching."

"What did you order?"

"An ale and fish and chips."

He finished his bite then asked, "How long did you remain?"

"Over two hours. I didn't want to go back to the flat."

"Anything else you remember."

Esther closed her eyes and took herself back to that night. "A waitress got into an argument with a bartender. By the way they spoke, it was a lover's quarrel."

She opened her eyes and saw that Nikolai had his sketchpad out and was drawing. He didn't reply, so she went back to eating and observing those around her.

One of her favorite pastimes was people watching. She and Henry used to play a game where they would try and guess the people's lives. It was a silly thing, but it had brought them hours of entertainment.

As lunch passed, the pub began to clear, and still, she and Nikolai remained. She glanced over to see that he was on his second sketch. With nothing else to do, she continued to pick at her food.

It wasn't until she reached down for another bite that she noticed she had eaten everything. With a full belly, she leaned back and propped her feet up on the chair across from her.

The longer she sat there, the harder it became to keep her eyes open. Finally, after another yawn, she let her lids fall closed, intending to rest until Nikolai finished.

But in the next heartbeat, she was running through darkness, hollering for someone to help her. She kept her hands outstretched in front of her as fear held her tightly in its grip.

She knew this place. Knew and hated it. It was her mind, and the Druid had trapped her here. An empty, desolate place where she would forever be alone.

"Esther."

She jerked awake, her eyes snapping open to find Nikolai frowning at her. She sat up and smoothed back her hair. "I must have fallen asleep."

He stared at her a long time before he said, "It's time we leave."

CHAPTER ELEVEN

A Dragon King's magic was immense, his power vast. But Nikolai didn't fully appreciate the extent of either until he met Esther and found that his connection allowed him to see deeply into her life.

Once they were outside the pub, Esther turned to him and asked, "What is it?"

"Nothing."

"I don't like being lied to."

He put his hand on her back, urging her to start walking again. Then he said, "I want to show you what I've drawn."

"All right. But that still doesn't tell me why you wanted to leave."

"You were having a nightmare."

Her head swiveled forward, and she didn't say another word. He spotted an empty bench and steered her towards it. It wasn't the time to talk about what she saw while she slept, but it would come soon.

"Before I show you these," he said, holding his sketch-pad. "I need to explain."

Esther shook her head. "You already did when we were at Dreagan."

"That was a vague explanation. I expected you to ask more."

She shrugged and settled more comfortably on the bench. "I've come to learn that when magic is involved, it's easier to accept it than question how it works."

"Aye, but you saw my power as a way to help you, so any questions you would've had halted."

Her dark gaze slid away from him. "It's unnerving that you know me so well. I know very little about you."

"You know a lot more than most of the Dragon Kings."

Shock filled her face when her head jerked to him. "You can't be serious."

"I am."

"I know you're not as outspoken as Rhys, or as frank as Thorn."

He grinned at her attempt at lightheartedness. "I tend to stay in the back or off to the side in any group setting."

"Because you don't like them?"

"On the contrary. They're my family." He put his palm on the cover of his sketchpad. "My power of projected thermography puts me in a position to look at a scene, no' be involved in it."

Understanding filled her gaze. "So it's your power that unwillingly sets you apart."

"Exactly. But doona think that means I hold back my opinions. I tend to mull things over, weighing options before I voice anything."

"Did you pick that up from Ulrik?"

Nikolai looked out at the people walking past them. "I did. Ulrik was never hasty in anything. He cautioned me against such actions because once a choice is made, it is difficult to change it."

"Wise words."

"My power and the lessons I learned from Ulrik have made me verra private. It's no secret among the Kings that Ulrik raised me. But only Con and Kellan know the specifics I told you the other night."

She tucked her hair behind her ear. "Thank you for sharing your story. Now I understand things better."

"I told you about Ulrik because it's time others know the King he once was. And I shared it with you because I wanted you to know that part of me." He turned his head to her to find her eyes softening.

"Now is when I ask you about your power."

He glanced down at the pad. "You've seen the paintings, tapestries, and drawings around Dreagan. I only have to see something once, and it remains locked in my mind for me to pull from for eternity. I believed that was the extent of my powers until I developed a friendship with a dragon after I became King."

"How did it happen?" Esther asked.

"I was verra fond of her. I thought of her as my sister, though I didna realize she considered me something else entirely."

Esther gave him a knowing look. "She wanted you as a lover."

"And I didna see her that way. We had an amazing friendship, and I opened myself up to her as I had only ever done with Ulrik. That's when the images of her began to flash in my mind. I was never with her in them, so I knew they were no' memories. I then went to Ulrik to see if he might have an answer. He urged me to welcome my growing power and allow it to expand."

"I gather you did," Esther said.

He nodded, his thoughts turning grim as his memories continued. "I opened my mind and let my power take me. It didna take long for the images to come. They ran through my head like a movie. She was crying as she flew above my mountain. I saw her thoughts. The things she wished for. And longed for."

"What did you do?"

"I spoke with her and told her my feelings toward her didna run in any direction other than sisterly. She was heartbroken when she left. I didna see her again until the day she flew over the dragon bridge to leave this realm."

Esther sat still for a long time. Then she asked, "Did you ever have such a connection to Ulrik?"

"Nay, and I didna try it with anyone else."

"Then why me?"

He handed her the sketchpad for her to look through the pages. "I didna have a choice. The images were there, unbidden, and once I saw them, I was unable to stop. You intrigue me."

She raised a brow, her lips lifting in a small smile. "I'll take that as a compliment."

"As it was meant."

Her grin widened as he stared into her beautiful eyes. The smile died suddenly as a frown formed on her brow. "Should I ask what you've seen?"

"You saw the pictures."

"I don't imagine you drew everything you saw."

He hesitated. She was right. There were some he kept to himself. Like the image of her in the bathtub with her eyes closed and strands of hair clinging to her damp face.

Or the one of her standing in front of the window of her chamber at Dreagan with her arms wrapped around her, staring desolately out at the snow falling as she was bathed in moonlight.

Esther whispered, "Oh."

"I can no' help what is shown to me," he assured her. "Nor did I seek out the connection."

Or had he? Perhaps it was his fascination with her that allowed his power to penetrate to such a level once again.

"Do you know my thoughts?" she asked.

He gave a shake of his head. "I see your expression, and I can deduce things, but I doona know more than that."

"That is some consolation, at least."

This was what Nikolai had been afraid of when she walked into his bedroom at Dreagan and saw the drawings. When she looked at them as a means to uncover her past, he'd held out hope that she understood him.

"Perhaps I should return to Dreagan and send someone else," he offered.

"No one else has your power," she said, her frown deepening before she turned her head away.

He hated the misery that began to fill him. The emotion chilled his blood and soured his mood. "Aye, but you no longer feel comfortable with me. That will make working together impossible."

"You're right," she said as she met his gaze. "I should've asked more questions at Dreagan, but I didn't. It's disconcerting to know that you can see into my life like a snapshot."

"I'm sorry."

She held up a hand to stop him from talking as she struggled to gain control of her emotions while her eyes watered and she swallowed several times. "Did you agree to help me because you saw me as I made sure others didn't? Or did you see me crying? Weak? Vulnerable?" She paused, her lips trembling. "Scared?"

Nikolai shifted so that he turned on the bench to face her. "You had someone in your mind. They moved memories and took control of you. There's no reason to be ashamed of the emotions that came as a result of that."

"Kinsey isn't having the same issues."

"Kinsey is verra much like you. She puts on a brave face, but I know Ryder has been helping her deal with the aftermath of the Druid's attack."

Esther's chest expanded as she took a deep breath and released it. "I never wanted anyone to know."

"That's no' true."

She gave him a stern look. "Excuse me."

"You're a verra strong woman who has taken on much in your short life. But somewhere in the back of your mind, you knew I'd noticed what you struggled to hide when you saw the drawings in my chamber. You accepted that, and then asked for my help."

She swallowed and held onto the sketchpad tighter. "You're right."

"I doona think less of you for bending beneath such a heavy burden."

Esther smiled as she sniffed. "Thank you for that."

"It's the truth."

She licked her lips and briefly glanced away. "I want to continue whatever it is we've begun. I just don't want you to think I'm weak."

"I doona. Nor will I ever."

Her lips curved into a soft smile that made his heart miss a beat. The fact that she was prepared to stand beneath such an incredibly debilitating burden on her own made him admire her even more.

And it only made his desire grow hotter.

"Do you want to look at what I drew now? Or shall we wait?"

"Now," she said and wiped at her nose. "I don't want to lose any more time."

Nikolai put his hand on hers before she could open the pad. "You need to understand that even if we follow your trail, we might no' find the Druid."

"I've tracked enough people to know that there is a clue somewhere. We'll find it, and if we're really lucky, it'll lead us to something else, which will lead us to something else until we find her."

He loved her determination and the steel that ran through her. Reluctantly, he removed his hand. "Start whenever you want."

She didn't hesitate to open the pad. He watched her face as she perused his drawings. The rush of surprise, the flash of a frown as she looked at herself, and the acceptance of it all.

Her finger traced over a sketch of her sitting at the table alone in a pub with her food before her. He glanced down at the page to see what had brought such consternation.

Then he saw the look he'd drawn on her face. She looked haggard, weary. And so very alone.

For a woman who prided herself on hiding such things, it must be difficult for her to know that those emotions sometimes showed.

"This is exactly where I sat," she said as she pointed to the set of swords crossed behind her in the drawing. "I didn't tell you that."

He gave her a lopsided smile. "It was being in the pub as you spoke about your time there. I opened up my magic and let my power do the rest."

"It's amazing," she said, looking back down at the page. "You have the placement of my drink and even where I put the ketchup on the plate for my chips." Her gaze returned to his. "You saw into my past."

"Aye." Though he wouldn't tell her it wasn't as easy as he made it out to be.

Her smile was huge as it lit up her face. "We can do this. We can follow my trail, and I know it's going to give us the Druid one way or another."

The happiness surrounding her was as bright as the sun. No matter how difficult it got, he would do everything he could to get Esther the answers she sought.

More importantly, he was going to get her the Druid.

CHAPTER TWELVE

Milan, Spain

A chill of foreboding went through Rhi with such force that it caused her to stagger backward. Her heart pounded erratically as her blood turned to ice.

She hurriedly walked to the corner and ducked behind a shop before veiling herself. Only then was she able to lean back against the building, her hands gripping the brick for some semblance of stability.

Not far away on her left, she felt Daire's presence. The Reaper continued to follow her no matter what she did, but he steadfastly refused to drop his veil or talk to her.

Rhi.

Balladyn's voice echoed through her mind. It was no coincidence that she'd felt such a sinister threat, and he called for her seconds later. It also didn't help that she heard the urgency in his voice.

She had only to think of her island before she teleported there. Her gaze landed on Balladyn, who stood near the shore in his standard all black clothes with waves coming within inches of his boots as he stared out over the turquoise waters.

Dropping her veil, she walked toward him. He turned and saw her. He met her halfway, jerking her tightly against him. The anger that burned in his red eyes was only one indication that the threat she felt was real.

The reason he summoned her had nothing to do with their last encounter at the Dark Palace when she, Con, and Devon rescued Anson. This was something else entirely, something that greatly upset him.

"What is it?" she asked as she returned his embrace.

For long minutes, Balladyn silently held her. Then he released a sigh and leaned back to look at her.

"Just tell me," she stated when his face kept waffling between anger and remorse.

He closed his eyes for a heartbeat. "Usaeil visited Taraeth."

That same ominous feeling enveloped her again. She stepped out of Balladyn's arms. They had come a long way together. She'd grown up knowing him as her brother's best friend.

After Rolmir was killed, she and Balladyn had grown close, leaning on each other in their grief. And it was Balladyn who'd helped her through the horrible days following her Dragon King lover ending their relationship. Then Balladyn had fallen during the Fae Wars. It was one of the worst times of her life. When Usaeil had finally let her return to look for Balladyn's body, he was gone.

For thousands of years, Rhi believed him dead. It was only a short time ago that she'd discovered he was very much alive but now a Dark Fae.

It wasn't long after that when Balladyn captured and tortured her in an attempt to get her to turn Dark. She had broken the chains, but the damage was done. The darkness he'd wanted her to embrace now fought for control daily.

Perhaps that's why she'd stopped running from him. And then when he told her how he'd always loved her, she had reached for him and all he offered. Because she needed him.

"Say something," Balladyn demanded, breaking into her thoughts.

Rhi drew in a shaky breath, unsure if she wanted to hear what was next. The ice had yet to thaw from her veins despite the heat of the sun above her. She blinked against the bright light reflecting off the water.

Every mention of Usaeil made the darkness within Rhi churn, urging her to seek revenge. "What did Usaeil want? Did she see you? What did you say to her? And why are you looking at me as if everything is about to change?"

"Because it is," he answered ominously. His red gaze darted away for a moment before focusing on her again.

She gave a shake of her head even as he ran his hands through his long, black and silver hair. A shiver took her, the foreboding feeling once again telling her to prepare herself. "Start from the beginning. Tell me everything."

Balladyn's lips compressed momentarily. "She came to ask Taraeth to kill someone else."

Rhi's knees buckled, and she collapsed onto the sand. His words rang through her head, tolling like a bell. They couldn't be true, but she knew they were. "I couldn't possibly have heard you correctly. Did you say 'someone else?' "

"I did."

"You were there with Taraeth and Usaeil? You heard everything?"

He nodded slowly, his expression bleak.

Rhi sank her palms into the sand, curling her fingers

around the grains in an effort to keep herself still and hide her shaking hands. "Tell me she spoke to you."

"Oh, aye. She said I was supposed to be dead."

"No," Rhi said, shaking her head. But the truth hung between them like a silent entity.

Balladyn put his hands on his hips as he stood before her. "I was the one she asked Taraeth to kill the first time."

"That's it! I've had enough!" Rhi shouted as she jumped to her feet.

She'd wanted a piece of Usaeil for a long time now. The queen had been ignoring the Light, not taking the threat of the Reapers seriously, and then had tried to force Con into taking her as his mate. Now, this?

"No," Balladyn said as he grabbed hold of Rhi and pulled her against him. "You can't go to her."

Rhi searched his gaze. "Is Usaeil back at the Light Castle?"

"I don't know."

"Why don't you want me going to see her?"

Balladyn swallowed, his Adam's apple bobbing as he did. "I should finish telling you what happened."

"I think that's wise."

Yet, he hesitated. His chest rose rapidly.

"Balladyn," she urged softly. She touched his face and gazed into his red eyes. "Tell me."

"She was shocked that I was alive. And furious. When I confronted her about wanting me dead, she admitted that she'd had no choice but to get rid of me."

Rhi scrunched up her face in confusion. "Why? You were her best warrior. No other Fae has led the Queen's Guard like you."

"She said it was because I loved you."

Rhi's legs threatened to give out a second time. It was only Balladyn's arms that held her upright. She quickly found her footing again, though her mind couldn't register what she was being told. "I didn't know you loved me then."

"Aye, but she did."

"So? Was it because she wanted you?"

He gave a slow, single shake of his head.

When the truth hit Rhi with the soul-crushing force of a tsunami, she clung to Balladyn while trying to stop hyperventilating. The world was spinning faster and faster, and she couldn't get her bearings.

"I'm sorry, Rhi," Balladyn whispered.

He drew her closer, turning her head so that she rested on his chest. He smoothed his hand down her hair and simply held her. She squeezed her eyes closed. It was incomprehensible that the one person she'd turned to repeatedly for guidance and friendship was the one who had destroyed everything.

All those times Rhi had thought it was simply Fate, the blame lay with a single being—Usaeil.

How was it that Rhi hadn't seen the truth of Usaeil sooner? Had she been so blinded by loyalty that the facts had to literally slap her in the face for her to grasp them?

Rhi clenched her hands. How the bitch must have laughed while Rhi struggled to live without the love of her Dragon King. No doubt Usaeil rejoiced and celebrated in private, hiding her smile while consoling Rhi.

The darkness within Rhi hummed with excitement as the fury burned hot and bright. She didn't attempt to hold it back or tamp it down.

No, she welcomed it with open arms.

"You're glowing," Balladyn whispered.

She knew if she didn't control her rage, she could blow up the planet. Which might not be too bad if she could take out Usaeil in the process.

Balladyn kissed her forehead. "Hold that anger, love. You're going to need it. Not only did Usaeil seek out

Taraeth to kill me but she also destroyed your relationship with your King all while intending to have Con. Now, you're in the way of that."

"Don't," she warned, her voice shaking with indignation. She shoved Balladyn away. Her emotions were too raw to have anyone close. "You don't need to remind me what she's done. I know full well."

"Nay, you don't. She asked Taraeth to kill you."

Someone had to stop Usaeil. And Rhi was more than ready to step up. After everything the queen had done to her and her family and friends, Rhi had the right to go after Usaeil. First, though, she needed to calm herself.

Rhi held her hands before her and looked at them, concentrating while taking control of her rage until the glow finally dimmed and then stopped altogether. She dropped her arms to her sides and raised her gaze to Balladyn. "I'm going to kill Usaeil. Want to join me?"

"It's not time for that yet," Balladyn cautioned. "Don't let her know you're aware of her actions."

Rhi gave him a scathing look. "You can't be serious. Why?"

"Because I'm going to kill Taraeth and become King of the Dark. Then we'll face Usaeil together. We'll join our people into one race and rule them as one."

The idea was interesting, but she wasn't sure it could work. "The Light and Dark have always hated each other. They won't come together easily."

"They will when we show them what Taraeth and Usaeil have done. Our people will see us working together, and they'll follow," he said and bent to give her a fevered kiss.

She ended the embrace and met his gaze. "Take care of Taraeth soon. I don't know how long I can hold off from attacking Usaeil."

"Protect yourself," he said and vanished.

Rhi turned and looked at the spot where Daire stood veiled. "Is this why you've been following me? Did you know Usaeil would do this?" she demanded, stalking to him.

When she reached him, she shoved against his chest. Suddenly, he was no longer veiled. He looked at her with confusion.

"What did you do?" he asked.

Rhi moved her thumb over her fingers as magic ran just beneath her skin. She looked at Daire's tall form, her gaze skating down his long, black hair. As a Fae, he was gorgeous, but he had something other Fae didn't. He was a Reaper who answered to just one entity—Death.

"I was tired of you being veiled and pretending that we haven't met or talked. I told you my memories returned. You can tell Death to kiss my grits."

"You may get to tell her yourself." Daire's silver eyes flashed dangerously. "Now tell me how you removed my veil."

She shrugged. "I don't know."

"That's shite."

"It's the truth."

His nostrils flared as he drew in a breath. "Rhi, if what Balladyn told you about Usaeil is true, there is a lot of upheaval that's about to happen."

"Are you saying I shouldn't go after her?"

"I'm saying to be cautious. Usaeil hasn't been the Queen of the Light all these millennia for nothing. She'll expect you to come for her."

Rhi hated that Daire was right, but it forced her to consider other options. "And Balladyn?"

"We've long known he would take the throne from Taraeth. I'm surprised he waited."

"What about our two races being joined?" she asked, genuinely wanting to know his opinion.

Daire shook his head. "It'll never work. No matter how strong a ruler Balladyn is. Or if you reign by his side."

She thought the same thing. It was nice to know someone else had the same opinion.

"What now?" he asked.

Rhi felt as if she were about to explode. There was too much anger and frustration along with a driving need for retaliation and retribution within her for her to control.

As if sensing she was close to bursting, Daire moved closer and took her hands in his. "I can help."

Before she could agree, she began to breathe easier as her fury lessened. She looked down at their joined hands and realized he was pulling it from her. When she looked up at him, he smiled.

"One of the perks of being a Reaper."

"Tell me why you've been following me?" she asked.

Daire released her hands. "I do what Death orders. She's not shared her reasons with me."

"Does she know that I have my memories back?"

"She does."

Rhi raised a brow. "And?"

Daire shrugged. "Death keeps her thoughts to herself. She said nothing other than for me to keep following you. She said you would need me eventually."

"She was right." Rhi looked at her hands again. "My own queen wants to kill me."

He gave a snort. "Usaeil hasn't been your queen in a long while."

Rhi dropped her hands and lifted her gaze to him. "She's not acted like a queen either. Perhaps it's time the Light had a new ruler."

CHAPTER THIRTEEN

The truth will set me free.

That's what Esther kept telling herself in order to keep going, but in the back of her mind, she wondered if it were wise to stay on her current path.

She was free of the Druid's control, and she was safe with the Dragon Kings. But was that enough? Could she live with the missing time?

As she sat alone in the silence of the SUV, looking over Nikolai's sketches again, she didn't know what to make of things. It was harder than she'd expected to see how he observed her. Mainly because he drew with an impartial eye.

The one promise Esther made to herself when she went to work for MI5 was that she would always be honest with herself. It had been simple at first, but with each mission, it became more difficult to keep that pledge.

Somewhere along the way, her vow had ceased. She wasn't exactly sure when or how, only that with Nikolai's drawings, it was plainly evident that it had.

Before her assignment at Kyvor, she'd come back from a weekend holiday in Nice. A trip where she'd convinced herself she was happy with her life. That the exciting adventures of her job were just what she desired.

She flipped a page of the sketchpad and saw another angle of herself in the pub. No longer could she pretend that she'd been happy. Because the proof was right before her.

After the Druid's intrusion into her mind, everything had been stripped away. Leaving Esther naked and exposed to . . . everything.

The driver's door suddenly opened, inundating the interior of the SUV with the noises of the outside world. Esther winced at the sounds as her gaze jerked up to clash with Nikolai's.

He silently observed her for a heartbeat before he climbed inside the vehicle. "What is it?"

In the short time she'd spent with Nikolai, she should be used to how quickly he picked up on others' feelings, but it was especially tough since she'd been trained to hide such things.

Then again, he wasn't just anyone.

"Just trying to get accustomed to seeing myself through your eyes."

He looked forward out the windshield. "Perhaps we've done enough for one day."

"No. I'm fine," she insisted.

His head swung back to her. "That's no' what I see."

"We just began. Clearly, this is going to be challenging, but I can handle it."

"What are you no' telling me?"

She frowned and kept herself from looking away at the last second. "What do you mean?"

"You've been keeping something hidden for weeks now, and I know it's connected to the Druid."

"You're guessing."

He lifted one brow. "But I guessed correctly."

Esther looked out her window, inwardly kicking herself for not hiding things better. Although, she was beginning to think that no one could conceal anything from Nikolai once those eyes of his found you.

"The Druid did more than just control your mind, right?" Nikolai asked.

She reluctantly nodded. Then she looked at him. "I'll tell you, but you have to swear not to tell anyone else. I don't want Henry to know. He can't know."

"You have my word, but I doona know why you wouldna want your brother's help."

"Because Henry is a fixer. He's always set things right for me or those he was close with. He belongs in your world despite being mortal."

Nikolai's expression relaxed as comprehension dawned. "And you believe he'll feel inadequate because he willna be able to fix this?"

"Exactly. Henry is dealing with enough right now just being in love with a Light Fae."

Nikolai's lips compressed briefly. "Aye."

"He thinks I'm getting better, and I want him to continue believing that."

"If you imagine that you've fooled Henry, you're gravely mistaken. He knows you're hiding something."

She didn't bother to ask Nikolai how he knew that. The answer was obvious. Nikolai saw it as he saw everything else. "I still don't want him to know."

"It'll be up to you what you tell him, though I doona think continuing to lie is the way to go," Nikolai said.

He had a point, but she'd consider that later. She took a deep breath and made her fingers relax after she realized she had a death grip on the sketchpad. "Some of my memories are out of order. At first, I thought it was just my mind working itself out after the Druid's intrusion, but I'm beginning to believe the damage is much more than that."

"How?"

Fighting the urge to fidget, she took in a deep breath to calm herself. "When the Dragon Kings stopped Kinsey and me from killing each other, we were then locked in our minds."

"I heard Kinsey describe some of it."

"It's ten times worse than you can imagine." She looked away as she thought of the nightmares that continued to plague her sleep. "The Druid turned my own mind on me. I couldn't trust myself. I was alone in the dark, the echoes of my voice the only thing I heard."

She felt her heartbeat rising as she spoke. "It was like I was in a building with a maze of hallways and numerous doors. I ran in every direction, but there was nothing. I tried door after door, banging on them until I couldn't feel my hands, but they wouldn't budge. It felt like I was trapped for an eternity, but none of that compared to the other."

"The other?" he urged.

Her eyes slowly returned to look into his. "I wasn't alone. There was something in my mind with me, trying to kill me. If Tristan hadn't helped me, if I hadn't heard his voice in my head, I'd be dead."

"Is that what you see when you sleep?"

She nodded. "I can't be trapped in my mind again. I won't survive it."

"It willna happen."

"You can't guarantee something like that."

Nikolai shot her a lopsided smile. "I'm a Dragon King."

He announced it as if it explained everything, and the simple fact was that it did. She did her best to give him some semblance of a smile.

"It's going to be all right," he promised. "We're going to track down the Druid, and we're going to get everything sorted properly."

This time, her smile came easier. She liked that he kept saying "we." As she looked into his baby blue eyes, she had the urge to run her hands through his auburn hair. Whether it was his promise or his willingness to help, she felt comfortable and safe with Nikolai.

"Where to next?" he asked as he started the engine.

She turned to the cover of the sketchpad and flipped it so she could write on the inside. Then she quickly wrote down every place she recalled visiting in order.

"After the pub, I went back to the flat," she told Nikolai. "I read over everything we had on Stanley Upton. No, wait." She gave a shake of her head to clear it. "That's not right. I called in to MI5 to do my nightly check-in first. Didn't I?"

"I have an idea."

She looked at Nikolai, hating that she couldn't remember the order of her memories. "What?"

"Do you trust me?"

"Yes."

He simply smiled and pulled out into traffic. It wasn't long before she saw that he was taking them back to the flat. Once parked, he motioned for her to follow him.

Esther wasn't happy to return to the house. She wanted to keep retracing her movements. Yet she trailed Nikolai into the flat because he asked her to trust him.

Inside, she removed her coat and walked with him into the living area. She looked at him, waiting for some kind of revelation.

He pointed at the sofa. "Lie down."

"I'm not going to sleep," she stated.

"I never said anything about sleeping." He held out his hand to her. "Come."

She swallowed before reaching for his hand. As soon as her palm met his, his fingers curled around her and gently tugged her close. His skin was warm, his strength comforting. She walked to him, looking up into his face.

It was impossible to be so near him and not think of the previous night when they had nearly kissed. His hand glided up her arm, causing her to shiver from the trail of heat he left in his wake.

When his other hand reached up and smoothed her hair back from her face, she found herself drowning in his gaze. Her stomach fluttered when the pad of his finger skimmed along the top of her ear as he tucked her hair.

"Close your eyes," he whispered.

With her heart pounding, she let her lids close. Every other sense came alive. She smelled the lingering scent of ale from their time in the pub, but it was his scent that caused her breath to hitch. The smell of charcoal and paper along with a hint of some spices she couldn't quite pinpoint.

She heard his slow, even breaths. Wherever he touched, she melted against him, wanting and needing more of his seemingly endless calm and power.

"Release your mind," he urged. "Let down the barriers you've erected."

"I can't."

He quieted her with a finger against her lips. The action surprised her so much that it halted any more words. Then she forgot about talking when he moved closer. Her heart thumped against her ribs as their bodies came into contact.

Her mind halted as her body hummed with desire. It was instinct that had her releasing his hand and setting her palms on his hips.

"I'm right here," he whispered. He wrapped an arm

around her, his hand splaying on her back. His mouth brushed against her ear. "I've got you."

She wondered if he knew how romantic his words sounded. Though he didn't mean them that way, her mind and her heart had already decided otherwise.

"Relax," he said. "Let your thoughts wander."

He couldn't be serious. The only thing she was thinking about was ripping off his clothes and having another look at his impressive chest. But she knew he was right. She took a deep breath and attempted to forget her craving for him. It wasn't easy, but not once did she sense that he was frustrated. He simply held her, waiting for her to accept what needed to be done.

She was scared, but the only way to take back control was to trust Nikolai. So she let the tension ease from her body and opened her mind.

"What do you see?" he murmured.

She answered with what she saw. "You." He was all around her, filling everything.

His warm breath fanned her neck. "Then you know I'm with you. I'll no' leave. Go deeper. Think back to the night you visited The White Mare."

The more he spoke, the more his seductive brogue lulled her. She did as he asked, the memories rolling past as if she were scrolling through pictures on her mobile until she found the ones she sought.

"You've finished, and you're leaving the pub," he said. "What did you do?"

Esther was able to look at her memories as if they were a movie. "I went to the flat, though I took my time."

She saw the desolation on her face that Nikolai had sketched. And walking into the quiet flat had made things even worse.

"Then what?" he asked.

"I called Stuart and did my nightly check-in with MI5."

Nikolai held her tighter, and for just a moment, she was sure she felt his lips against her jaw. As much as she wanted to linger on that, her memories were calling.

And she had to follow.

CHAPTER FOURTEEN

"I've got you," Nikolai repeated.

He breathed in Esther's jasmine scent. His eyes closed as her body sank against him. When he saw the distress in her gaze as they sat in the SUV, there had been only one option.

In order for her to be able to proceed with their task, she had to face her fears. He was taking a chance because there was a real possibility the Druid was somehow still inside Esther's head.

Yet he was going with his intuition. Tristan had searched both Kinsey's and Esther's minds to make sure the Druid no longer had a hold over them. The Dragon Kings had always been the beings with the strongest magic on the realm, but that didn't mean they would always be. This Druid proved that mortals could push back.

Nikolai lowered his head, his lips brushing Esther's neck. He gave in to the temptation and pressed his mouth against her jaw. Then, before he did more, he opened his eyes and lifted her in his arms, cradling her as he sat on the sofa.

If this experiment went south, he was prepared to subdue Esther until reinforcements could get there. He'd thought about telling her his plans, but he knew she might fight him, and he needed her compliant.

Her cheek rested against his shoulder, and he leaned his head against hers. Touching her, holding her was sublime.

So many days of looking at her from afar, yearning for her. Aching for her. Now that she was in his arms, he begged the outside world not to intrude. It was a wish he knew would go ignored, but it was one he had to ask anyway.

"Nikolai."

Her voice held a note of panic. He tightened his arm around her. "I'm here. Doona be afraid. What did you do after you phoned Stuart?"

"I cleaned my gun then read over the file on Upton again."

Nikolai used his free arm and reached for the sketchpad and pencil he'd left nearby. He flipped it open and jotted down what she was saying. "Then?"

"I went to bed. I got up at five the next morning and went for a run. After, I got ready and went for another interview."

Now that he'd opened her mind, it would be easy to discover just where she'd encountered the Druid. If they were really lucky, they might even get a name.

"Good," he told her. "Did you eat lunch out?"

As her breathing quickened, he set the pencil down. He frowned as he watched her face contort into an expression of fear. Her fingers dug into him as her body stiffened.

"Esther," he said. "I'm with you. You're safe."

She began to tremble uncontrollably. "Not safe. Never safe."

He knew he had to get her calm quickly. "Turn away from whatever is there. Open your eyes and look at me."

Her eyes moved back and forth frantically behind her eyelids. She no longer showed any signs that she heard him. Since they weren't at Dreagan, he couldn't just yell for Tristan to get into her mind and help her.

"Esther," he said, giving her a shake. "Wake up. Come back to me. Esther!"

Her eyes suddenly flew open. The next second, they welled with tears as she buried her face in his neck. Nikolai wrapped his arms around her, feeling the tremors wracking her.

"It's all right," he soothed.

She gave a shake of her head. "There's something in my mind. It's horrifying."

"Doona think about it." Nikolai could've kicked himself. He'd really thought his idea would work, and for a moment, it had.

What prevented it from going forward?

Then he knew—the Druid. Her magic reached far into Esther's mind. The problem was, they had no idea what all she'd done to Esther.

He remained holding her for another twenty minutes before she finally stopped shaking. Even then, he was happy she hadn't moved away from him.

He'd fought the Dark Fae and mortals many times, but he couldn't fight whatever was in Esther's mind. As a Dragon King, that infuriated him. She was being threatened and terrorized. He'd promised to protect her. What a fucking fine job he was doing.

More than anything, she needed sleep. Humans couldn't go extended periods without rest, and it was taking a toll on her whether she wanted to admit it or not. Yet he couldn't make her sleep and face whatever was in her mind. It could be nothing but fear, but then again, knowing that a Druid had tampered with Esther's mind, it could be something much, much worse.

"I'm sorry."

Startled, he leaned back to look at her. "You've nothing to apologize for."

Deep brown eyes gazed at him. "My next memories are faded. I know I went somewhere to eat, but I don't know where."

"We've got clues in the coasters. We'll use those."

"That could take days. Weeks even."

He gave her a smile, hoping to ease her anxiety. "I'll stay as long as you need me."

"Thank you."

It took everything for him to loosen his arms when she climbed off his lap. Nikolai wanted to pull her back down, to continue holding her. Once she was gone, he felt bereft, his arms empty.

"I need to take my mind off things," she said.

He nodded, watching her as he tried to figure out what he should do. "Of course."

She then moved to the opposite end of the sofa and grabbed the remote. As soon as the television was on, she began flipping channels.

Nikolai gathered his pad and pencil and got to his feet. She didn't look his way as he moved to the kitchen table and sat. There, he opened his pad and held his pencil above the paper.

Images flashed through his mind. He settled for something he'd drawn hundreds of times—dragons. As his hand began to move, making marks on the page, he opened the link in his mind and said Tristan's name.

Almost immediately, Tristan's voice sounded in his head. *"Aye? Is everything all right?"*

Tristan was their newest Dragon King. He'd fallen from the sky a few years earlier, and it had taken some time before they realized Tristan had once been Duncan Kerr, twin to the Warrior, Ian Kerr. There were few memories Tristan had of his life as Duncan, but despite that, he and Ian remained close.

"*I'm no' sure. When you delved into Esther's mind to free her from the Druid, what did you see?*"

Tristan sighed. "*Magic. The Druid weaved it throughout Esther's mind. With Kinsey's, it was just in a certain part, but it's as if the Druid took special care with Esther. Why do you ask?*"

"*Esther says there's something in her mind.*"

"*Something? Like what?*"

"*She willna say,*" Nikolai said. "*I doona think it's because she's afraid to say it. I think it's because she doesna know what it is. But whatever it is, she's terrified of it.*"

Tristan paused before asking, "*How so?*"

"*She's no' sleeping. She also says some of her memories have been rearranged.*"

"*Now that doesna surprise me,*" Tristan said with a snort. "*The difference in what was done to Kinsey's mind versus Esther's is significant.*"

Damn. Nikolai had been hoping to hear something different. "*So there's a chance the Druid did move memories around?*"

"*Aye.*"

"*Why didn't you say something before?*"

Tristan's voice lowered as it tinged with anger. "*I did. I told Esther, but she made me promise no' to tell anyone else. I was hoping you'd figure it out and ask me.*"

"*She admitted the same to me, but she forgot to mention that you spoke with her about it.*"

"*It would take me months of sorting through Esther's mind to determine exactly what the Druid did.*"

"*Then do it,*" Nikolai demanded.

"You sound like Ryder. As I already explained to Esther, Kinsey, Ryder, and even Con, the Druid left scars upon Esther's and Kinsey's minds. Each time I go in there, I make things worse."

Nikolai paused in his drawing as he closed his eyes. The news was bad. And all the time, he'd thought Esther was improving. *"In other words, things are steadily going to get worse."*

"I'm afraid so. I can no' tell if the Druid planted something in Esther's mind to keep her away from memories that would lead Esther to the Druid or something else."

"How can this be fixed?"

Tristan let out a long sigh. *"Only the Druid can do that."*

"We're fucking Dragon Kings!" Nikolai shouted. *"Our magic is stronger than any others'."*

"Aye, but we're talking about a mortal's brain. It's a delicate place. One wrong move on my part, and Esther will no longer be the person we know."

Nikolai opened his eyes and looked at her sitting on the sofa. She was engrossed in some show. *"Does she know the risks of you entering her mind?"*

"We tried it, briefly, a few weeks ago. It didna go well."

"What happened, exactly?"

"I attempted to break through some of the Druid's magic that remained. Before I began, I had Esther call up a memory and tell it to me in detail. Each time I got near the Druid's magic, more and more of Esther's memory began to fade or change."

"Shite," Nikolai murmured. He ran a hand down his face. The news kept getting worse and worse. *"Henry should know."*

"I think he suspects. He made a comment about her lack of sleep the other day."

"I'm her only chance then."

Tristan made a sound at the back of his throat. *"Unfortunately, brother, we're all counting on you."*

Nikolai knew that, and it didn't bother him. What settled in his gut like a stone, was knowing that he was Esther's last shot. It focused him, clearing away any outside noise.

"I can come down there to help," Tristan offered.

"We're good for now."

"Well, if you find the Druid, I'll be one of the first to meet you. I saw firsthand what she did to the girls, and it wasna pretty."

Nikolai drew in a deep breath before he released it. *"Thanks, Tristan."*

He disconnected the link and looked down at the page to see that the dragon he'd begun to draw had shifted midway so that half the drawing was the dragon, and the other half was Esther's face in profile.

More troubling was that the dragon he'd drawn was him.

CHAPTER FIFTEEN

There was something inside her mind. Esther was sure of it. So sure, she knew if she went to sleep, it would take over.

Each time she closed her eyes, she felt it on the fringes of her subconscious, waiting for her to drift off so it could take over. It sounded ludicrous, but there was no denying it.

Her eyes stung. Each time she blinked, it felt as if sandpaper rubbed along her corneas. All she yearned to do was close her lids. But if she did, she wasn't sure what might become of her.

Before arriving in London, she'd known things in her mind had changed. Tristan confirmed it. Now, however, she didn't trust her memories. She wasn't sure what was real or what the Druid had added, changed, or removed.

It was better that Esther wasn't at Dreagan. Not only did Henry not need to see her like this, but the Dragon Kings also had enough to deal with, without worrying about what she might do. That was what she kept coming back to.

The Druid must've known there was a chance the

Kings would stop the first attack. In doing so, it would make sense that Esther remained wherever her brother was.

Which would make her a prime candidate to become a Trojan horse.

She'd already been stopped. The Kings would believe they'd caught it all, so they would never think she was the cause.

Esther's stomach rolled so viciously that she hurriedly stretched out on the couch to keep from being sick. Some might think her idea farfetched, but then again, when it came to magic, anything was possible.

She hoped her theory was wrong. She prayed her fears were all in her head, manifesting because of lack of sleep, but she'd rather be safe than sorry.

The movie she was watching had done nothing to help take her mind off things, but it filled the silence. She realized Nikolai was worried, and she knew he wanted to help. The problem was, she couldn't help herself. How did she expect him to do anything?

Slowly, her stomach settled enough that she was able to sit up again. Her gaze lowered to the cigar box. She got on the floor and reached for the container. But she hesitated in opening the lid.

She knew without looking up that Nikolai was watching her. She'd felt his gaze several times over the last hour. It was his voice that had pulled her out of the fear that nearly locked her within her mind.

Within the confines of his arms, his warmth surrounding her, and his sexy voice guiding her, she'd placed all her trust in him. Now, he waited patiently for her to gather herself and face it all again.

The problem was that she didn't think she was strong enough to do it.

Finally, she lifted her eyes and met his gaze. His pale

blue eyes held no censorship, no anger. She couldn't imagine being here with anyone else. But it wasn't because none of the other Kings understood her.

It was because Nikolai saw deeper than anyone else. He saw past her walls, through the false bravado, and beyond the various people she'd become while undercover, to see the woman huddled in the darkness.

He didn't judge her. And while he protected her, he allowed her to find her strength once again. For that, she would always be indebted to him.

That's where things should stop, but they didn't. The attraction was thick, fervent. She'd felt his response when he held her earlier.

The hands soothing her hadn't been those of a friend. It was the embrace of a man who fought against a rising tide of desire. It was a battle she'd lost before they left Dreagan.

It was a fight she continued to lose every second she was with him.

Nikolai rose from his seat in the kitchen and walked to her. He knelt before her, his hands at his sides. A muscle clenched in his jaw as he stared at her before he lowered himself to the floor.

"What is it?" he asked.

She wanted to scoot toward him and lay her head on his shoulder. Instead, she motioned to the cigar box. "We assumed that I took a coaster from everywhere I visited."

"It's a habit, as you said."

"True, but what if the Druid stopped me from doing it? We could be going to all this trouble for nothing."

An auburn brow lifted high on his forehead. "So you'd give up?"

"I'm not saying that. I'm merely pointing out a possibility."

"There are millions of possibilities. We have a path

before us. Let's continue on that until we have a reason to deviate."

It sounded simple and easy, but she knew searches like this rarely were. "I think we should be prepared for other options."

"I agree. You were so sure of the coasters yesterday. What happened?"

She looked away, hating the fear that clawed through her like a rabid animal. "I don't trust my memories."

"Because of what's inside your mind?"

Again, there was no condemnation, and it brought out a flood of emotion in Esther, enough that it choked her. She knew it was the lack of rest that was causing her feelings to swing so drastically from one side to the other. She nodded, unable to speak.

"And you can no' see what it is?"

When she had herself back under control, she licked her lips and returned her gaze to him. "It's like a shadow. I can feel it."

"Does it verbally threaten you?"

"It never speaks. But it's always there. Like it's waiting for me to let my guard down so it can take me."

Nikolai propped one foot on the floor, his leg bent as he rested his arm on his knee. "Soon, exhaustion will win out, and you'll sleep whether you want to or no'."

"Believe me, I'm aware." Her stomach chose that moment to growl. She glanced at the clock, surprised to find that it was already dinnertime. "Can you cook?"

His face crinkled in disgust. "If you want burnt toast."

She laughed. It felt freeing to push away the darkness with some mirth. Perhaps she should do it more often. "I think we're in trouble then because I don't either."

"I thought all women knew how to cook," he said with a grin.

"Unfortunately, my poor mum attempted to teach me several times, but I can't even boil water."

"What a fine fix we're in." He twisted his lips before flashing her a heart-stopping half-smile. "Looks like I'm getting takeout."

She gave him a sassy wink. "Now, I can order take-out like a pro."

"You do the ordering, I'll pick it up."

"Consider it done," she said as she reached for her mobile phone. As she did a search and scrolled through places to eat, she asked, "Anything you don't like?"

"No' really. I do have a particular fondness for Thai."

She was somewhat shocked by his admission. She'd figured Nikolai would stick to regular English fare, but she was pleasantly surprised. "I know a place just down the block. It's good."

Once he'd made his choices from the menu, she called and placed their order. Twenty minutes later, they were on the floor, eating.

Esther opened the cigar box and began shifting through the coasters again. "I don't know where to go next."

"So we just pick some and go tomorrow. I'll do some drawings and see what we can come up with."

It was really their only option, and until that ran out, she should see where it took her, just as Nikolai suggested. "Just random coasters?"

"Or we can group them by location."

"Random," she said.

He grinned as he swallowed and reached for his bottle of ale. "Because you doona like conformity?"

"Because, sometimes, random can surprise you."

"Then random it is."

She wiped her mouth on her paper napkin and set

aside her food once she was finished. "We each pick three."

"All right. You pick first," he said.

Esther dusted off her hands and reached into the box, shuffling the coasters around. After feeling as if the world were crashing down upon her just hours ago, the light-hearted mood did wonders to help her.

She smiled at Nikolai as she pulled the first coaster out and read, "Callooh Calley. It's a contemporary pub with a very *Alice and Wonderland* feel."

"If you say so," he said with a chuckle. Then he reached in and pulled out a coaster. "The Dove."

"Ah. It's a pub along the Thames with a very colorful history."

"How far away are these two?"

She had to think a moment, and once more her memories began to blur. "I don't think they're close. Why?"

"I would've thought it would be easier to eat in the same places."

"I always had a different routine every day, and I rarely went back to the same pub within the span of a month."

He lifted the bottle of ale and finished it. "Understandable. So you went all over London?"

"I did."

He chuckled as he got to his feet and began to gather the food. "This is going to be fun, then."

"Fun?" she asked as she helped put the empty containers into the trash bin. "You think driving around London is fun?"

"Aye."

She shook her head and smiled despite herself. "I think I'm going to go soak in the tub. It might help the tension in my shoulders."

He gave a nod, and she went upstairs to start the bathwater. After setting the water temperature, she removed her boots and sweater. It wasn't until after she'd taken off her shirt and stood in her jeans and bra that she heard the floor creak.

She looked in the mirror to see Nikolai in the hallway. His gaze darted away but quickly swung back to her. The desire she saw made her knees weak.

One of her first lessons in MI5 was seduction. Even before becoming a spy, she'd used it to her advantage many times.

Tonight, the seduction flowed both ways. She met Nikolai's gaze in the mirror and unbuttoned her jeans. While her gaze remained on him, his drifted down as she shimmied out of her pants. When his eyes returned to the mirror, need burned hot and palpable in his clear blue depths.

Esther turned to face him. Then she unhooked her bra and let it fall to the floor before she slid her panties down to puddle at her ankles.

In three strides, Nikolai was before her, his hands grasping her face. His breathing was harsh, his touch tender. A tremor went through her as she recognized that it was longing that rushed through her.

A need so great, so visceral, that she knew every decision, every path she'd taken thus far had led her right to this moment.

Right into Nikolai's arms.

Their lips met, the heat of the kiss melting away any reservations she might have had.

CHAPTER SIXTEEN

Esther's sweet, incredible taste was like a brand upon Nikolai's soul. A thrilling, intoxicating experience that he prayed would never end. There was nowhere he'd rather be than in the arms of a woman who had ensnared his very being.

The soft moans coming from her only made him crave her more. Her strength and vulnerability beckoned him. It was a summons, a call that he couldn't ignore. It transcended time, weaving through centuries as if they were milliseconds.

In that moment, it all became clear. She was his mate, the other half of him that he'd never thought to find. The part of him he worried was forever lost.

He ended the kiss and looked down into her brown eyes. The sight of her lips swollen and wet from his kiss made his balls tighten, and his cock jump.

"Don't stop," she begged in a voice roughened with need. "I've wanted your kiss for too long."

Every detail of the moment was seared onto his brain, but it was one picture he would never put on canvas.

The steam from the water caused a light dew upon

her skin, the mirror and window fogged, and the all-consuming heat, need engulfed him.

This picture was for him alone, something to look back on in wonder and happiness.

He let his fingertips caress down the silky skin of her shoulder and over her arm to her side before sinking into the indent of her waist and then the flare of her hip. When he reached her thigh, he altered his route and moved to her shapely ass, cupping it.

She sucked in a breath, her pulse at her throat jumping. He'd often imagined her naked, and now that he had her that way, he was going to take full advantage of it.

He leaned down and kissed her slowly before he straightened and let his gaze and hands wander over her amazing body.

With a smile, he put his hands on either side of her neck and stroked down the column to her shoulders, his gaze following his hands. He touched her collarbones before drifting lower to her breasts.

He held the weight of them in his palms, his blood heating as her nipples hardened. Unable to deny himself, he thumbed both until the peaks were straining, and her chest rose and fell rapidly.

His fingers stroked around each breast before coming together in the center and gliding down to her navel. He dropped to his knees when he took hold of her hips. Her hands delved into his hair as she held his head, and her gaze, heated and blazing with desire, watched him. Her lips parted. The hunger within her was evident in the way her pupils dilated.

Wordlessly, she waited. He held her gaze as he splayed his hands from hipbone to hipbone. Then he slowly lowered them until he felt the first brush of her trimmed, dark curls.

He looked down at the triangle of hair and had to see

more. With just a touch, she widened her stance. As much as he yearned to sink his finger inside her, he made himself stroke down her outer legs before coming up on the inside. He then stopped just short of touching her.

A glance upward showed her biting her lip as desire ruled her. He understood because it governed him, too. They were two halves of a whole, two parts of a body that had finally found each other.

"Nikolai," she whispered breathlessly.

He rose up, yanking her against him as he savagely took her lips. She clawed at his clothes, ripping his shirt in her effort to get it off. In order to get free, he had to break the kiss, but as soon as the garment was gone, he had her in his arms again. Except her gaze was locked on his dragon tattoo.

Chills spread over his skin as her fingertips ran up his right arm where the tail and a part of the dragon body were. Her caress then followed the dragon as it bent over his shoulder with wings tucked. She swirled her fingers along the head that came to rest on his chest with its mouth open on a roar. Then she trailed her hand along the outstretched claw that looked as if it were reaching for something.

When her gaze lifted to him, and she laid her hand flat on his tat, he groaned and lowered his head. Their tongues dueled and mated as their hands roamed over each other's bodies.

It wasn't until she moved to unbutton his pants that she tipped backward. He reached for her and found himself tumbling with her into the tub. Water splashed over the sides, smacking against the tile floor.

But not even their fall could break their kiss. They rolled and twisted until the rest of his now soggy clothes were removed.

She straddled his waist, continuously kissing him as

she shut off the taps. He took hold of her legs and stood. Stepping out of the tub, he walked, dripping, to the bedroom and halted beside the bed.

His body demanded to be joined with hers, to solidify the connection that brought them together. To claim her, mark her.

As his.

He lowered her onto her back and straightened. She reached for him, trying to bring him back for another kiss, but he had other ideas.

Holding her legs wide, he gazed at the swollen flesh of her sex. He glided his fingers over her woman's lips and groaned when he felt how wet she was.

He brushed his fingers against the soft petals of flesh before pushing inside her slick heat.

Esther knew when she left Dreagan with Nikolai that she would surrender herself to him. This moment had been inevitable.

She craved it, hungered for it.

For *him*.

With him, there was none of the fear, anxiety, and doubt that plagued her. In Nikolai's arms, she was a woman who longed to be mastered by his touch. He was the embodiment of masculinity, the epitome of virility.

Her hips rocked against him as his fingers pumped inside her. She felt every fold of herself parting, opening for him. Accepting him.

She cried out when he used his other hand and began slowly circling her clit with his fingers. The combination of thrusting and teasing soon had her on the edge of climaxing.

The more she tried to hold back, the harder he worked. It wasn't long before she was spiraling down the abyss of pleasure and calling out his name.

With her body still wracked by the orgasm, she felt his hardness between her legs. She reached for him, tugging him down so their lips could meet once more.

Being with Nikolai freed her from restraints she hadn't known she wore. He unleashed lust and sexuality within her, calling to an animalistic side that only he could match.

His pulsating length brushed against her. No longer would she wait to feel him inside her. She needed him. All of him.

Her hands roamed over his thick shoulders and the chiseled sinew of his chest and abdomen. She could feel the strength in his hands, the power that he kept concealed. But it was there, waiting to be released.

With her palms against his warm flesh, she caressed over his narrow waist and trim hips to an ass that made her mouth water. She dug her fingernails into the tight muscles and arched her back.

"I need to be inside you."

His voice roughed by need made chills race over her. She smiled before wrapping her fingers around his thick arousal and pumping her hand a few times. When his eyes closed, and he let out a moan, she smiled. It was good to know that she could make him feel the same heat he brought out in her.

Guiding him, she brought his cock to her entrance. The tip of him entered her slowly, moving back and forth, but he refused to give her more. She tried to shift to feel him deeper, but he held her firmly.

Just when she thought he wouldn't give in, he drove hard and deep, filling her. She barely had time to process the feeling of him stretching her before he began to thrust.

They were lost in a dance as old as time, tangled in lust that was thick and erotic—bound by desire.

She clung to him as their bodies moved sensuously, evocatively, as ecstasy waited for them. Their limbs were intertwined, his hand was fisted in her hair, and all the while, they drew closer and closer to the pinnacle of desire.

Desire tightened in her belly with each stroke of his arousal inside her. She was wholly unprepared for the second orgasm when it struck.

She found herself floating on a wave of incomprehensible pleasure that only expanded when Nikolai climaxed. They stared into each other's eyes, their bodies, souls, and hearts firmly joined.

They remained locked together until their breathing evened out. Then he stroked his fingers down her cheek. He pulled out of her and shifted to his side. She rolled over to face him.

He held up a hand, and she pressed her palm against his. Then he entwined their fingers together. There was no need for words. What was between them went much deeper than anything that could be voiced.

She couldn't remember a time when she'd felt like the girl she used to be before MI5. Everything had been stripped away, leaving her bare and exposed. She wasn't afraid for Nikolai to see her. In fact, he was the one who gave her the courage to stand tall.

At Dreagan, she hadn't liked the person she'd become. It was easier now to see her flaws and accept them. The greatest gift of all was that Nikolai helped to show her the path so she could be herself once more.

No more false personas, no more lies. Good or bad, she was who she was.

Their joined hands rested between them. She kissed the tops of his fingers and smiled. His answering grin made her heart skip a beat.

There would be quite the mess to clean up later in the

bathroom, but she didn't care. It was a memory that the Druid's magic couldn't touch, one that would forever reside in her heart.

Just like Nikolai would.

She wasn't yet ready to tell him how she felt. It hung wordlessly between them, but something so profound had to be spoken eventually, or it could fade away. She would tell him, but not now. Not when her life was such a mess.

He needed to know that she could stand on her own. Magic had brought Esther low, but she would rise again. She would win and find the Druid.

Esther realized there was a chance her memories may not return. She still held out hope, but she always liked to think of worst-case scenarios. Unfortunately, not getting her memories back wasn't worst-case.

That would be if the Druid managed to get in Esther's head again.

But she refused to think along those lines now. She was in the arms of a Dragon King, a sexy-as-hell immortal who was possibly the world's best kisser.

There was no way she would allow such morbid thoughts to intrude on their interlude. The glow of pleasure still filled her, and she would cling to that and Nikolai.

His smile grew as he pulled her closer. He rubbed his nose against hers before tilting his head and brushing his lips over her mouth.

Within moments, they were once more locked in a passionate embrace. Desire had them firmly in its grip, and it wasn't done with them yet.

And that made Esther very happy.

CHAPTER SEVENTEEN

Dreagan

Con turned from the window of his office when his door opened. He looked at Asher and Kellan as they strode into the room. He knew what they wanted, but he let the two state their business.

"We want to confront the spy," Asher said.

Con nodded for them to proceed then walked to his desk chair and sat.

Kellan ran a hand through his long, caramel-colored hair as he sat in one of the chairs before Con's desk. "I thought you'd be more excited to get this taken care of."

"I am," he urged.

Asher leaned his hands on the back of the other chair and said, "We should stop her now. You said we would confront Alice after the mating ceremony. Well, it's time."

"You already knew who the spy was before we came to you," Kellan announced, his words tinted with a hint of irritation.

Asher narrowed his green eyes at Con. "You knew and sent us on this chase?"

Con leaned back in his chair. "I did my own investigation and discovered the name right before you delivered the file to me."

Kellan's celadon gaze was penetrating as he stared. "When have you had time for this between running Dreagan, aiding Sebastian in Venice, dealing with Usaeil, and helping all of us strategize against the Dark Fae and Ulrik?"

Con shrugged. As Keeper of History, Kellan had the ability to focus on one Dragon King and learn things. It always left Kellan drained, so he rarely did it, which was why Con wasn't worried about him looking into things.

But now that Kellan's attention had been brought to him, no doubt the King of the Bronzes would start searching. Con hoped Kellan didn't because there were things he didn't want shared with anyone.

"What are you no' telling us?" Asher demanded.

Con looked between the two. "I'm no' ready to confront her just yet. Alice is feeding Ulrik—"

"Bast thinks it's Mikkel," Kellan interjected.

"Or Mikkel. Regardless, she's feeding them information," Con amended. "Let's see if we can use this to our advantage and get her to pass along something in our favor."

Asher grinned as he straightened, crossing his arms over his chest. "I do like the thought of that."

"You're juggling too many balls," Kellan said. "One is going to drop if you doona begin to deal with them."

"You doona think I'm taking the correct actions with all of my . ... balls?" Con asked, a brow lifted.

Kellan's lips flattened as his chest expanded when he took a deep breath. "You know that's no' what I'm saying."

"MI5 has been taken care of for the moment," Asher said. "Thanks to Vaughn and his legal skills. But that still leaves our spy, Alice, the Dark, Ulrik—or Mikkel, or both—the Reapers, Usaeil, the mortals—particularly the one you have in the dungeon—no' to mention the wooden dragon and the magic mixed up in that. And lest we forget, the Druid who continues to wreak havoc among us."

Con didn't bother to add what he knew about Rhi and Balladyn, and how the pair could disrupt things. Anson and Devon had been too caught up after their return from the Dark Palace to mention anything about Rhi and Balladyn. Yet.

It was coming.

Kellan threw up his hands in defeat. "Say something."

"What would you like me to say?" Con asked. "We have a ton of enemies, and they keep coming out of the woodwork. We deal with it."

Asher dropped his arms to his sides. "That's the thing. You're no' allowing us to handle *any* of it. You're doing it all."

It was on the tip of Con's tongue to tell them that it was his job, but he didn't. He swiveled his chair and got to his feet, returning to look out the window and the snow-covered mountains that surrounded them.

"I plan on taking care of Usaeil verra soon," he told them. "I willna be alone. Rhi will be with me."

The chair creaked as Kellan moved. "Are you sure that's wise?"

"It was Rhi who brought me the picture. There's also . . . history between the two of them."

"Like what?" Asher asked.

Con felt a disturbance in the air and turned to find Rhi standing to his right. At the sight of her pale face and clenched fists, he frowned. But it was the devastation and outrage he saw in her gaze that alarmed him. Something was wrong. Very wrong.

The Light Fae looked at Kellan and Asher before her silver gaze returned to Con. Her lips parted, and she tried to speak, but no words came. Con slowly walked to her. Rhi was doing everything she could to remain composed and keep a tight rein on her anger, but she was losing control rapidly.

"Easy." He spoke softly, keeping their gazes locked. As he drew closer, he saw her shaking, her eyes bright with fury. "You can control it."

She squeezed her eyes closed as she began to glow. Con glanced at his men. Asher ran out to warn the others about Rhi's struggles.

Con's choices were limited. If he didn't get Rhi contained and she lost control, she could blow up the entire planet and everyone on it. Several tense minutes went by before the glowing began to ebb, as did her shaking. Finally, she opened her eyes.

He gave her a nod. "You did it."

Before she could speak, the sound of footsteps approached. Rhys burst through the door and made his way to Rhi. Con watched the interaction between the two friends as Rhys made sure Rhi was all right.

She rubbed her hand along her forehead and then down the side of her face. She took a deep breath and released it before she looked at Con. "We need to confront Usaeil now."

"What's so important?" Kellan asked.

Rhi never took her eyes off Con, and he realized she continued to struggle to contain her rage. "Usaeil went to see Taraeth."

Con didn't need to ask how Rhi knew that. The answer was clear—Balladyn.

Rhys frowned as he regarded her. "How would you come by such information? Tell me it didna come from that fucker—"

"Enough," Rhi interrupted him as she glanced his way. "Yes, it was Balladyn."

Con waited until her attention was back on him before he asked, "What was the reason for Usaeil's visit?"

"You ask that so calmly," Rhi replied with a derisive snort. She gave a shake of her black hair. "The hatred between the Light and Dark runs so deeply that nothing will ever conquer such a divide. The fact that Usaeil went to Taraeth is troubling. More distressing, was that she had her own doorway into his throne room."

"She's been there before," Rhys replied in shock.

Con now understood why Rhi was fit to be tied, but he also suspected it was the rest of the story that would upset him more. "We're fortunate Balladyn shared this information with you."

"He didn't have a choice." Rhi closed her eyes and shook her head. "I still can't believe it."

Con nodded to Kellan, who quietly closed the door to keep others out. Then Con asked, "What did Usaeil do?"

When Rhi opened her eyes, they were awash in tears. For the Fae to show such emotion in front of him meant that Usaeil had done something truly atrocious. It also meant that the Fae Queen was one ball Con would be taking care of very soon.

Rhi's lip quivered, whether from anger or sadness, he didn't know. Then she said, "Usaeil asked Taraeth to kill Balladyn when he was a Light."

"Well, fuck," Rhys said in disgust and turned away to lean against the wall.

Kellan gave a shrug. "But Balladyn isna dead."

Rhi laughed, the sound hollow and filled with rage. "Taraeth turned Balladyn Dark instead. Usaeil discovered that today."

"Balladyn was one of her best warriors," Rhys said. "Why did she want him gone?"

A great look of sadness fell over Rhi's face, causing her shoulders to droop. "Because he loved me."

Con had a bad feeling he knew exactly what Usaeil wanted with Taraeth this time. Of all the things he expected of the Light Queen, betrayal of her warriors wasn't one of them.

Yes, Usaeil could be spiteful, petty, vindictive, and mean. But to have the Captain of her Queen's Guard targeted for death by the Dark?

It was unconscionable.

It also meant that, for Usaeil, there was no boundary she wouldn't cross.

Both he and Rhi made the mistake of believing they knew Usaeil. It was evident that they were dealing with something else entirely.

He looked into Rhi's silver eyes and drew in a deep breath. "What did the queen want of Taraeth today?"

"For him to kill me," Rhi replied.

Rhys's anger was explosive as he let loose expletives that would make a sailor blush. Kellan wasn't any less quiet with his ferocity over such a statement.

Con held Rhi's gaze and gave her a single nod. He wasn't able to speak, to give Rhi any kind of reassurance, because if he opened his mouth, everything he had kept tightly held in check with regards to Usaeil would be unleashed.

It was time Usaeil was put in her place, but he feared that she would not stop even then. It would take drastic action in order to halt the Light Queen—something that would affect all of them.

Never was Con more aware of his mistake in regards to Usaeil than in that moment. But it was one he was more than willing to correct—at any cost.

"She betrayed me," Rhi said.

Her voice was soft, barely discernable over Rhys's and

Kellan's rants, but Con heard her just the same. There was something more, something that Rhi didn't want to say. It was there in her words, in her eyes, in the way she was barely holding herself together.

Con closed the distance between them so that he stood near enough to make her tilt her head back to look at him. "Whatever it is you're hiding, tell me now. If we're going to face her, it has to be done with everything out on the table, so to speak."

"I don't think you should be there," Rhi said.

He gave her a flat look. "I'm going to confront Usaeil. You'll no' change my mind."

It took him a moment to realize that his office had grown quiet once more. Out of the corner of his eye, he saw Kellan and Rhys watching them.

"Please," Rhi said. "Leave her to me."

Con shook his head. "She brought me into this, remember? Just tell me whatever it is you're afraid to say. It can no' be any worse than learning she wants Taraeth to kill you."

Seconds ticked past as Con patiently waited for Rhi to make her mind up. He was beginning to think she would refuse to tell him whatever it was when her chest expanded as she inhaled deeply.

"She actively split me and. . . ." Rhi trailed off, unable to finish. She looked away. "Usaeil hounded me, telling me how the Fae would never accept a union between a Fae and a Dragon King."

Kellan's face crinkled in confusion. "That doesna make sense since she helped Shara and Kiril come together."

Con lifted a hand to quiet Kellan as he brought Rhi's gaze back to him. He'd been annoyed at Usaeil by the picture of them together, furious over the price on Rhi's head, and now he was bordering on homicidal at this latest news. But he kept it all well hidden.

For now.

Until the moment he had Usaeil in his sights.

"And?" he urged.

"Don't," she whispered.

He stood silently, waiting for her to say whatever was so horrible that she couldn't form the words. "Rhi."

"Inen took over as Captain of the Queen's Guard when we believed Balladyn had been killed in battle. It's Inen's duty to take care of things that Usaeil doesn't agree with. Sometimes, it was as trivial as the way a Light acted in court. Other times, it was much more drastic," Rhi said.

Rhys asked, "How do you know this?"

"Balladyn used to tell me," Rhi answered. "Inen was sent away a lot. None of it involved me, so I didn't care. At least, I didn't think any of it involved me. You see, Inen recently told me that one of those assignments was to Dreagan."

Con felt the gaze of the Kings on him. He didn't reply because there was nothing he could say. But murderous didn't even come close to describing the furious rush of emotions that consumed him.

"Finish," Kellan urged Rhi.

Rhi turned away from him, but Con didn't blame her. Because he knew what she was about to say.

She lifted her face and looked at Kellan. "Inen was sent to make sure that my affair was ended that day."

"No," Rhys whispered in disbelief.

Kellan looked away, and it was the flash of pain on Rhi's face that was like a punch in the gut to Con. She'd forgotten that while Kellan wasn't all-seeing, he knew a lot. And he'd known about Inen's visit to Dreagan.

Con knew the questions that were about to be turned on him, but he wouldn't answer any of them. Seeing the past dredged up would only hurt everyone. There would be a time he answered for his crimes, but now wasn't that day.

Rhys took a step toward him. "Con."

"Now isna the time," Kellan said, a hand on Rhys's arm to stop him.

Con met Rhys's accusing gaze. The sheer ferocity in his friend's gaze told Con exactly what Rhys wanted to do to him. And frankly, Con didn't blame him.

"That's everything," Rhi said into the silence and turned her face to him. "All the cards are on the table."

Con gave her a nod. "Then it's time we find Usaeil and put an end to her plotting."

"She won't stop," Rhi said.

Con looked at Kellan and Rhys, who were glaring at him. "I'm no' going to give her a choice."

CHAPTER EIGHTEEN

A new day, a new start. Those were the words Esther spoke as the sun reached the horizon. Nikolai didn't mention how she had only dozed off and on for a few minutes throughout the night.

There had been a period where he thought she might sleep. She'd been curled against him, her breathing soft and low. But then he felt her eyelashes against his skin as she blinked.

Since he couldn't force her to sleep, he would stand beside her until her exhaustion took her. That's the one thing he feared, because then she would have no defense if the Druid was still in her mind.

Nikolai waited for Esther in the kitchen as he stared at the six coasters they'd chosen the night before. He could hear her moving around upstairs as she finished dressing. There was a light rain falling with gray clouds giving the day a somber look.

But the weather was quickly forgotten when Esther came downstairs wearing a vibrant smile. She walked straight to him. He turned in the chair and parted his legs as she wound her arms around him before she leaned her head down and kissed him.

"I smell coffee," she said.

He shrugged, unable to keep the grin from his lips. "I know how much you enjoy it."

She laughed as she walked to the pot and poured herself a large mug. "I do like it, but it's moved into the need column. The shot of caffeine is what allows me to face each day."

"And here I thought that smile you wore was because of me."

Her eyes crinkled over the rim of her mug. She lowered it and gave him a wink. "It's definitely you this morning."

"That does bolster my confidence since I thought I was losing to a beverage."

To his delight, she laughed. There was a rosy glow about her that morning, a color to her cheeks that hadn't been there before. Her hair was down once more as she parted it to the side and kept tucking it behind her ear. She wore a raspberry-colored sweater and dark jeans that tucked into her saddle brown riding boots.

"It's raining," she said with a glower out the window.

He rose and walked around the island to stand next to her. "Shall we spend the day before a roaring fire making love? Only rising to get nourishment?"

"That sounds like perfection." Her sad smile prefaced her next words. "I wish we could. There's nothing else I want."

"But we have a Druid to find," Nikolai said.

Esther nodded. "Can I take a rain check on your offer?"

He gave her a quick kiss. "The day is yours whenever you want it, as many times as you want."

"Thank you." She set her mug down and rested her head on his chest.

"Doona worry. Every day we search, we get closer to finding the Druid."

Esther leaned her head back and looked at him with a determined gaze. "Yes, we do."

"Ready?"

"It's a bit early to set out. The pubs won't be open yet."

He shrugged and released her as he walked to the foyer where their coats were hung. He grabbed hers and held it open for her. "Aye, but I thought we might do something a wee bit different today."

"Like?" she asked after she'd taken another drink of coffee and let him help her into her coat.

Nikolai put on his leather jacket. "We know you visited the pubs because you have the coasters, and I'll draw you inside each of them. But I got to thinking last night. We've no' thought about you outside of the establishments."

"Meaning that I could've spoken to someone on the streets," she said with a smile.

"Aye. Or even ran into them."

She cocked her head to the side. "Can you do this? It's not tiring or anything?"

"I wouldna suggest it if I couldna do it." It pushed the boundaries of his powers, but it was something he should've done long ago. Now he would have to test things out in order to help Esther.

And the slight discomfort that came with it was manageable if he could get her the answers she so desperately needed.

"Then let's get going."

He followed her out, ignoring the rain that quickly dampened his hair. The sound of her laughter reached him as she dashed to the G-class. He unlocked the doors with the key fob so she could get out of the weather. Her wide smile as she watched him walk around the SUV made him wish they could remain in the flat and have the day to themselves.

They could, but it would not only be putting Esther's troubles on hold but also those at Dreagan. Because the Druid had become an enemy to every Dragon King and his mate, as well as anyone associated with Dreagan.

There was no telling when she would strike again, and since the Druid had an affinity for messing with other's minds and memories, the sooner she was found and taken out, the better.

Once inside the Mercedes, Nikolai started the engine, as Esther immediately turned on the heater and the seat warmer. She laughed again, rubbing her hands together.

"Stop," she said as she shook her head.

He frowned. "What?"

"You keep staring at me."

"I can no' help it. You're radiant."

She glanced away, her embarrassment clear, but she was also pleased by the way her dark eyes shot him a seductive look. "It's been a while since I've wanted to smile."

"So all you needed was sex?" he teased.

Her smile faded instantly. She leaned over in her seat toward him. Then she took his face between her hands. "It wasn't sex. It was you."

He held her gaze for a long minute before he pulled her forward and kissed her slowly, showing her how much her words meant. And how much she meant to him.

When he ended the kiss, he caressed her cheek. "Then I'll continue to keep you smiling."

They sat back and put on their seat belts. Nikolai then pulled out onto the road and headed to the East End to their first stop.

"I love Dreagan," Esther said suddenly.

He glanced her way and nodded, unsure where she was going with the statement. "It's a beautiful place. There's nowhere like it on the entire planet."

"That's true."

"I hear a *but*."

She shrugged as she looked out the windshield. "There are just so many eyes there. I feel like everyone is watching me, especially Henry."

"Your brother is just worried. But there are a lot of people on the estate. It can get overwhelming."

"Not for you. You can go to your mountain for privacy."

She had a point, one he hadn't considered before. "And you've nowhere to go?"

"My room, but even then, Henry or one of the mates comes to check on me if I stay there too long."

"So go to my mountain."

Out of the corner of his eye, he saw her head snap his way. He quickly met her gaze before returning his attention to the road. "My offer surprises you?"

"It's your mountain."

"Aye. To do with as I please. I'm offering it to you. No one will bother you there."

She gave a snort. "Right. Henry will."

"Nay, he willna. As you said, our mountains are our sanctuaries. I'll let the others know where you are, and you can remain as long as you want."

"Will you visit?"

"If you'd like." He grinned in her direction. "Once you find a cavern, I'll bring things in to make it more comfortable. It's no' relaxing to sit on the hard ground for long."

She chuckled and tucked her hair behind her ear again. "You don't feel it in dragon form?"

"It's different. Dragons were made to lie upon the

earth. A human body rarely finds any sort of ease sitting on a rock or the cold, hard ground."

"I probably don't need to ask, but which form do you prefer?"

"Dragon," he answered without hesitation. "I like having the option to shift, but I'm a dragon first and foremost."

She nodded absently. "I can understand that. If I had the ability to shift into another animal, I'd always want to return to my true form."

He turned onto Rivington Street and found a place to park not far from Callooh Calley, the bar from her coaster. He turned off the ignition.

"You forgot your pad and pencils," Esther said.

He reached down and took out a fresh sketchpad from the door. "I have them everywhere."

"Good," she said and turned her attention toward the pub.

He could sense her nervousness. "What is it?"

"I like this bar. A lot. I've been here several times."

"Then I'll draw you each time."

She turned her head to him, a slight frown puckering her brow. "You make it sound so easy."

"It is. All you have to do is be there."

"And relive memories."

He lifted one shoulder in a shrug. "It helps, but it isna needed."

"That's good because I'm not sure how much I trust what my mind holds."

"Does it help when you see my sketches?"

"It did yesterday."

He glanced at the pub. "Make yourself believe that it will again. Doona give in to the doubts that plague all of us."

She lifted her brows and nodded. "Sound advice."

He opened the sketchbook and found one of the pencils

in the pocket of the door. Then he turned all of his senses on Esther.

Long minutes passed with nothing. Anger and fear spiked, but he pushed them aside and let his power and dragon magic fill him. Then the world he saw began to blur along the edges of his vision as mist rolled in.

When the mist cleared, he saw the same street, but from another time. The sun was shining brightly as passersby huddled in their coats and scarves. The door to the pub opened, and he expected to see Esther, but two men walked out.

Then he spotted her. She strolled down the street. She was about to cross at the corner of an intersection when she looked toward Callooh Calley's. After a bit of hesitation, she proceeded down the sidewalk to the pub.

Nikolai let his gaze move over each individual to put them to memory. Then he began to draw picture after picture.

Now that he'd seen Esther at the pub, he was able to track her through the prior weeks and months with his power.

He'd never drawn so fast before, hoping to get each vision he saw down on paper so he could move on to the next.

The fact that she liked the pub and visited often gave him some concern after she'd mentioned how she always switched up her routine. Except she didn't. Callooh Calley's was a constant.

If he found that, most likely the Druid had, as well.

CHAPTER NINETEEN

Esther was still coming to terms with seeing her life through someone else's eyes. It was unsettling but also fascinating.

As she watched Nikolai draw her heading into the pub, she recalled that day. It had been one of those where she felt disconnected from everyone and everything. It was why she'd changed her mind at the last minute and headed to Callooh Calley's.

The atmosphere was eclectic, and every month, a bartender would get artistic freedom over the pub with decor and drinks.

The detachment she'd felt that day came through differently in the way Nikolai drew her. Through his eyes, the loneliness she'd seen in The White Mare drawings was there, but with it was a dose of melancholy.

Though the sketch showed her amidst people, she appeared as though she were the last person on Earth. As if she had no one to turn to, no one to trust. And the fact was, that was her life as an MI5 agent.

He drew page after page, each one with her wearing a different outfit, showing how many times in the last year she visited the quirky pub. They sat there so long, that the heat evaporated from the SUV. She lifted her hands to her mouth, cupped her palms, and blew through her thumbs in an effort to warm them.

"I sometimes forget about the temperature," Nikolai said as he looked at her.

She smiled, shrugging. "You're a Dragon King who doesn't feel cold or heat. You don't need to sleep, and you can go extended periods without food. I'm not jealous at all."

Her comment caused him to laugh loudly, his eyes crinkling as his lips turned up in a wide smile. "No' a single mention of magic either."

"Well," she said widening her eyes. "That *is* part of the package."

He rubbed a hand along his jaw. "Shall I start the engine so you can turn on the heater?"

"There's a coffee shop not far from here. Want to go in there?"

"I need to be where you've been."

She frowned in confusion. "But you drew me all over Dreagan and you weren't there."

"Aye, but Dreagan is full of magic and doesna have any distractions. What I'm doing with you, I've never done before."

That took her aback. "Never?"

"There wasna a need for it. I doona know how far I can push my magic, but I want to make sure I doona miss anything."

"I see. Well, then we need to stay here."

One auburn brow quirked upward. "Are you sure?"

"Yep. I'm just going to run and get some coffee since I didn't get to finish mine at the flat."

He reached for the door handle. "I'll come."

She put a hand on his arm and waited until he looked

at her before she said, "I've got this. I'll just be down the street. You can see the shop from here. I'll be in and out quickly."

"Aye."

She winked at him and exited the vehicle. Looking both ways to check for traffic, Esther crossed the street and jogged to the coffee shop. The rain was an irritating drizzle that wouldn't stop. It had been difficult for her to look out the window of the SUV when it was covered in droplets of rain. But it didn't seem to bother Nikolai. She fought not to reach over and hit the windshield wipers to clear it.

Raking a hand through her damp hair, she entered the shop and took a deep breath, inhaling the aromatic smell of coffee. There were five people ahead of her, giving her time to look through the menu.

When it was her turn, she stepped forward and placed her order. As she was paying, the hairs on the back of her neck stood on end.

It could have been her training with MI5, or it could be because of everything she'd discovered about Dragon Kings and magic, but there was no doubt that something was behind her.

She moved over, waiting for her coffee to be made and turned just enough that she could see the other people in line. At first glance, nothing seemed out of the ordinary.

Then her gaze clashed with a man who stood staring at her. He looked normal with dirty blond hair and hazel eyes, but she didn't let his looks fool her. For all she knew, he was a Dark Fae using glamour to hide his red eyes and black and silver hair.

It was the *way* the man looked at her. As if he were starving, and she was the meal he'd been chasing. Now Esther wished she hadn't stopped Nikolai from coming with her.

138   DONNA GRANT

Her heart banged against her ribs as her nerve endings sizzled. It was the same any time she was in this situation, but now there was another added layer—the Druid.

Though her mind told her to run, she remained inside the shop. Whoever this man was, the more people that were around, the less likely he was to do anything. At least that's what she hoped. However, that probably wouldn't hold true if he were a Dark. They didn't care who saw them.

The Dark Fae and their movements were Henry's passion. It's how she'd learned so much about them. And she'd been thankful she hadn't run into one.

Since the Fae—both Dark and Light—drew humans to them like a bee to pollen, she felt the tension loosen in her shoulders as her gaze moved away. She didn't feel anything sexual toward the man, which meant he wasn't a Fae.

Two things stopped her thoughts in their tracks.

One, she knew that the Fae sometimes lived among humans so they could turn their sexual appeal on and off at any time.

Two, she recalled how the Dragon Kings had learned that anyone who made love to a King no longer felt the same attraction to the Dark. And since she'd just had sex with a Dragon King. . . .

Her eyes snapped back to the man. That's when she paid special attention to the people around him. Everyone was staring at him. The woman in front of him leaned back against him, rubbing her hand along his cock. The man behind him was dry humping him.

The Dark's malicious smile made her blood run like ice. She was frozen in fear, just like on her first mission with MI5. She didn't know what to do. The Dark had magic, and she had nothing to fight him with.

"Order for Esther!"

She jumped at the sound of her name. Turning, she wrapped her hands around the large latte and glanced back at the Dark.

His hand was now on the woman's breast in front of him, fondling it. And everyone was watching him. The desire was intense and tangible as it filled the small shop. She was in real trouble here, but more importantly, so was everyone else.

Henry had told her the Dark Fae were gathering in Ireland. The few that Anson spotted in London had ignored the humans. It looked as if this one hadn't gotten the memo.

She lifted the cup to her lips. While trembling on the inside, her hand was steady as she sipped the hot liquid. She held the Dark's gaze, waiting to see what he would do. It was no surprise when he disengaged himself from the others and walked to her.

"What a nice treat for me," he said in a thick Irish accent.

She gave him a bored look. "You're a long way from home."

"You've no idea. Or . . . perhaps you do."

Esther merely blinked in response.

"I thought you might be a Halfling at first since you didn't respond to me, but the longer I watched you, the more obvious it became. You should be like all the others. I could have them naked with a snap of my fingers."

"Good for you," she said.

He leaned his head to the side and looked her up and down. "You've been with a Dragon King."

"I don't know what that is. What kind of drugs are you on?"

His smile was slow as it spread over his face. "You're good, mortal, but not nearly good enough. You know what I am, and you know exactly who and what the Dragon Kings are."

With that, he dropped his glamour. She swallowed as she took in his hair that fell to mid-back, more silver than black. His red eyes flashed dangerously and made her think of blood.

"Leave," she told him.

He laughed softly and shook his head. "Why would I do that when I've found something interesting? Is your King near? Will he come if you scream?"

"If I go with you, will you leave the others alone?"

He looked over his shoulder at the customers who were rubbing against each other in an effort to ease the ache his presence caused. When he looked back at her, he raised a black brow. "What do you offer?"

"Me."

"You?" he asked with a laugh. "Why would I want you?"

She twisted her lips. "If you don't know, I'm not going to tell you."

"Oh, you'll tell me."

"Do we have a deal? We leave now, and you don't harm anyone in here."

He rubbed his fingers over his chin as he considered her offer. Then he nodded his head. "It's a deal."

She started past him to the front door when his hand wrapped painfully around her arm. Her head whipped around to him.

He didn't say anything as he dragged her after him out the back.

Esther wanted to scream her frustration. The front was her way of alerting Nikolai. It was the sole reason she'd made the deal with the Dark. Had she done the wrong thing? God, she really hoped not.

She tripped over the threshold as the Dark stormed out the back door to an alley. The drizzle was gone, replaced by rain that was coming faster with every second.

A shiver raced through her. She wasn't sure if it was because of the Dark or the cold. Or both. Not that it mattered. Her situation had gone from bad to worse. And all this time, she'd thought the worst that could happen was the Druid in her head.

The rain instantly drenched her hair and jeans. Thankfully, her all-weather coat kept her torso and arms nice and dry. Too bad the cold, wet denim was ruining her warmth.

His fingers bit into her arm as he kept yanking her after him. She was already half jogging to keep up with his long strides, and every time he tugged on her, she lost her balance and fell behind.

She might be a mere mortal with no power or magic, but she was a damn MI5 agent with skills. Anger seethed within her, turning the fear into a rumble of resentment.

"I'm going to kill you," she said through clenched teeth.

The Dark laughed as they turned a corner, but his mirth died as they came to a halt. Esther looked through the rain to find Nikolai blocking their path. Undeterred by the torrent of rain, he stood with his hands clenched at his sides, his head lowered, and his gaze locked on the Dark. His wide stance was that of a warrior, one who had his target in his sights—and was about to strike.

It was the wrath she saw in Nikolai's blue eyes that made her heart beat faster in arousal. She smiled at him.

"You're about to get your ass kicked," she told the Dark.

With the Fae focused on Nikolai, Esther used the distraction to her advantage and kicked him in the side of the knee. She heard the bone pop as his knee bent at an odd angle.

She then jerked her arm free and elbowed the Dark in the face. Before she could rejoice in getting the upper hand, he shoved against her chest and sent her crashing into the wall behind her.

Her head slammed against the brick, dazing her as pain exploded. She blinked several times to keep from passing out. Finally, everything began to come into focus.

That's when she saw Nikolai and the Dark circling each other.

CHAPTER TWENTY

Bloodlust pounded through Nikolai's veins as he stared at the Dark through the pouring rain. There was a crushing, overwhelming need to obliterate the Fae standing before him for daring to harm Esther.

Nikolai had known something was wrong when it took Esther too long to get her coffee. In the next instant, an image of her popped into his mind as she stood in the shop staring at a Dark Fae.

Without hesitation, Nikolai was out of the SUV and tracking them. When he stopped at the alley and saw the way the Fae had his hand around Esther's arm, his vision went red with rage.

The only other time he'd felt even a taste of such anger was when he challenged Avgust to rule the Ivories. This was different because Esther was his mate. He'd suspected it at Dreagan, but he was certain of it now. And he wasn't going to let a Dark interfere with that.

"I knew one of you fekkers was around," the Dark muttered with a sneer as they circled each other.

Nikolai bared his teeth. "I thought the Dark were gathering in Ireland. What are you doing here?"

The Fae made a sound in the back of his throat. "I decide where I go and when."

"Taraeth willna take kindly to that."

"He can suck my cock. And so can you, Dragon King."

Nikolai flexed his fingers. He fought not to shift and take out the Fae that way. He wasn't on Dreagan land, and he needed to remember that. He was in the middle of London, surrounded by millions of people. Witnesses.

"I'll pass," Nikolai retorted.

"How do you know so much about the Dark?"

Nikolai shrugged. "I thought you knew the Kings were more intelligent than you."

Just as he expected, his comment enraged the Dark. With a growl, the Fae pulled back his hand as an orb of magic formed. Nikolai waited for the Dark to throw it, and once he did, Nikolai leaned to the side to avoid the magic.

Then he rushed the Fae, ramming his shoulder into the Dark's gut. The other male gasped and slammed his joined hands down on Nikolai's back, pushing dark magic into him.

Nikolai jerked upright and straightened his fingers, tightening them into a blade-like extension of his arms. Then he whacked them down on either side of the Dark's neck. Before the Fae could move, Nikolai kicked him in the solar plexus.

The Dark fell back hard on the concrete and rolled away. Nikolai went to him, ready to knee him in the face, but when the Dark got to his feet, he launched two balls of magic.

This time, Nikolai wasn't able to duck either of them. One landed on his left shoulder, the other in the center of his chest. The smell of burning flesh and muscle filled his nostrils, even as the pain brought him to his knees.

He heard a yell and looked up to find Esther on the back of the Dark, her arm wrapped around his throat as she tried to choke him. Nikolai gritted his teeth and forced himself to his feet. Esther didn't stand a chance against a Fae, no matter what fighting skills she possessed. Magic always trumped non-magic.

Nikolai hurried to the Fae and grabbed the Dark's fists, preventing him from forming any more magic balls. The Dark peeled back his lips and bellowed his rage, right before he threw his head back against Esther.

Nikolai watched as her hold went slack, and she fell to the ground once more. In order to put some distance between her and the Dark, Nikolai turned and threw the Fae behind him.

The Dark rolled several times before he jumped to his feet. Nikolai wanted the Fae to focus on him and forget all about Esther. Not to mention, there was the possibility of other mortals stumbling upon them and catching them fighting.

The Dark swiped the back of his hand along his lip to wipe away the trickle of blood. He grinned at Nikolai. "I bet you wish you could shift. Instead, you have to fight like the fekking humans. You're not even using your magic."

"Because I doona need to kill you," Nikolai said as he stalked to the Fae.

"The burns on your chest say otherwise. Do they hurt?" he mocked.

Nikolai took a deep breath and sent magic at the Fae's knees, shattering them.

The Dark screamed in pain as he fell to the ground. He glared at Nikolai. "I thought you said you didn't need magic?"

He stepped on one of the Dark's hands and held the other down with his magic. "I doona, but I wanted to use it so you'd know how it felt to be deceived right before you died."

The Dark's anger was visible as his face went red and spittle flew from his mouth as he said, "I'm taking the bitch with me."

Nikolai moved, pinning the Fae's arm with his knee as he put both hands on the Dark's head. He spotted the ball of magic forming in the Fae's free hand, but that didn't stop Nikolai. He crushed the Dark's skull in the next heartbeat.

"Bloody hell."

He turned his head to the side at the sound of Esther's voice behind him. Nikolai got to his feet and faced her. "Are you hurt?"

"My pride more than anything. The headache I have will go away eventually. You were . . . magnificent."

Her eyes were bright with approval and excitement. He started toward her, pulling her into his arms when she met him halfway.

"That was too close for comfort," he murmured against the top of her wet head.

"I knew you'd find me."

He didn't want to think what could've happened had he not. Nikolai dropped his arms and took her hand to walk her back to the SUV. The rain completely drenched them both, but he wouldn't fall ill. She, on the other hand, could.

"The bar should be open now," she said through chattering teeth.

He glanced down at her, concern filling him when he saw that she was shivering. "We're headed to the flat so you can change."

"I'll be fine. This isn't the first time I've been soaked in the cold, and I doubt it'll be the last. We're here. Let's do this."

"It willna take us long for you to change."

"My coat is waterproof. It's just my jeans, and they will dry along with my hair."

They reached the Mercedes then, but she pulled out of his arms and walked to the pub. Nikolai opened the SUV door and grabbed his leather jacket.

Looking down at his ruined shirt and healing body, he sat inside the SUV and removed the garment before turning to the back seat where he saw the duffel bag. Inside were several sets of clothes.

"Thanks, Con," he said as he pulled out a new sweater and tugged it on.

Then he ran his hands through his hair and grabbed his pad and pencil before following Esther inside. He was going to watch her closely. The minute he thought she might be sick, he was getting help.

He walked into Callooh Calley's and knew immediately why Esther liked it. She'd been right when she called it eclectic.

The walls were dark and went well with the dark wood floor and brick-accented walls. The leather chairs and tufted benches along with the dark wood tables made for an inviting atmosphere. But it was the strategic lighting that played upon the sexiness and playful ambiance.

He followed Esther to one of the benches that lined the wall. She motioned for him to take it while she chose the chair on the other side of the two-person table.

"Upstairs has sofas and seating stools of various colors," she said as she removed her coat and rubbed her hands together.

He watched as she shook out her hair. "Order something warm to eat."

"Yes, sir," she said with a grin.

It would take him a moment to calm down since he was still in fight mode. So much for Henry's theory that the Dark had orders not to touch a mortal. The Fae Nikolai killed had every intention of harming Esther.

"It's fine." She reached across the table and put her hand atop his. "The Dark is . . . gone."

Nikolai let his eyes move over everyone in the bar. "There could be others. I should've been looking for them."

"Don't," she warned. "It's done and over. We survived."

He raised a brow. "I still have wounds that are slowly healing that tell a different story."

"And I have a headache," she said with a shrug. "We can dwell on the fact that he cornered me, but I'd rather celebrate that I got him out of the coffee shop without hurting any of the people inside. Not to mention that you saved me."

He blew out a breath. "That was quick thinking on your part."

"I'm good like that," she said with a wink.

"You're right, we did survive, but at what cost?"

She frowned and leaned forward. "I don't understand."

"How many other Dark saw us? How many now know that I'm here and that you are with a Dragon King? There's also the chance that a mortal saw the fight and will report it to the authorities."

"I'll call Stuart and get him to take care of it."

Nikolai shook his head. "You can no' take a leave of absence from MI5 and then call them the first time something doesna go right. You're going to have to choose whether you're returning to the agency or no'."

"I know." Her voice held a note of defense as she released his hand and sat back.

"Notify MI5 if you wish, but I'm also going to talk to Ryder. Henry needs to be alerted about what I discovered. It will change his theories about the Dark."

She lowered her eyes to the table. "Of course. Everything circles back to Dreagan and Henry."

"It circles back to my family and my home."

Her gaze met his. "I'm not trying to make light of what happened, and I totally get you notifying Ryder so he can keep an ear out if the police are looking for you."

"But?" he asked.

"After the Druid took over my mind, Henry coddled me, smothered me. I want and need to do this on my own with you. No interference from my brother."

Nikolai leaned forward and held out his hand, palm up. After a moment's hesitation, she put hers in his. He curled his fingers around her hand. "I'll make sure Henry remains on Dreagan, but he needs to know this information. He's made it his mission to track the Dark for us, and he's done well."

"As long as he remains at Dreagan."

"He will," Nikolai promised.

She gave him a smile, which soothed him and helped erase the last vestiges of bloodlust. They ordered, and in minutes, he was sketching once more.

Before he realized it, he had drawn over a dozen pictures of Esther inside the bar. Most times, she was alone. Other times, men were hitting on her. She always chose the same seat, the very one they sat at now. The deeper he looked into her past, the more aware he was of how lost and alone she'd been.

No wonder Henry cossetted her—Nikolai had the same urge.

CHAPTER TWENTY-ONE

Though Esther would never admit it to Nikolai, she wished she would've changed out of her wet jeans. There was nothing worse than sitting in cold, damp denim that wouldn't dry.

They remained at Callooh Calley's for two hours. She soaked in the heat of the place and downed a bowl of soup and three mugs of coffee, none of which did anything to warm her. Then they moved onto the next pub, The Dove, and then the next, and the next.

Each time was the same. They sat in the bar for about twenty minutes talking before Nikolai asked her questions about her time in the pub. Then he'd spend the next hour or so drawing, lost in whatever he saw.

Esther took that time to think about the attack with the Dark. She didn't let on just how terrified she'd been. Of the monsters she'd faced, all of them had been mortals with only strength, cunning, and money to get them free from authorities.

She'd learned to use her size and quickness when confronted in a fight. And she was damn good at it. Her brain, like her body, had been trained to perceive the moves her quarry might make and put herself in a position to stop them. Likewise, she used her connections with MI5 to prevent her targets from using their money to escape.

But none of that was a match for magic.

She'd known that after the Druid, so why she thought she stood a chance with the Dark Fae, she'd never know. She'd expected magic from the Fae, but she hadn't been prepared for his strength. He'd thrown her as if she were a toy doll and not a full-grown woman.

Now, as she and Nikolai walked from the seventh bar that day, she found herself mentally exhausted. All she'd done was sit. And think.

But it had done a number on her. That, combined with her lack of sleep, was wearing her down just as Nikolai had warned her it would.

She'd known it would happen. Had expected it, as well. But none of that compared to the reality of the situation. She was used to her mind being sharp and quick. The slow, sluggish thinking was infuriating, as well as scary.

As Nikolai pulled the SUV onto the road, she looked out the window at the darkening sky as dusk fell. The rain had finally stopped, but everything was still coated with water droplets as if to warn them that more rain was on the way.

"I think we should call it a day."

She glanced at Nikolai and nodded before returning her gaze out the window. "Sure."

"You hungry?"

"I've eaten everywhere we've gone today. I don't think I could look at food at this point."

They rode the rest of the way back to the flat in silence. She didn't ask him if he'd contacted Ryder yet because she knew he had. Just as her brother knew about the incident with the Dark by now.

When they reached the flat and exited the Mercedes, she welcomed Nikolai's arm around her as they walked inside. She changed out of the damp jeans and into some sweatpants. When she came back downstairs, Nikolai had moved the sofa, chairs, and tables. All of his drawings were on the floor.

"My life in pictures," she mused from behind him.

He leaned back on his haunches and smiled at her. "You didna ask to see any of these while I drew, so I thought I'd spread them out and give you a wide view to compare with your memories."

"Good idea." She moved next to him and got down on her knees.

Her gaze went to the first half-dozen sketches. They were the ones from when they'd arrived outside Callooh Calley's. She hadn't paid attention to them at the time. Now, she examined each one carefully.

She barely took notice of herself, preferring to study everything around her. She went through each of the sixty-four sketches before she sat back.

"Do you see it?" Nikolai asked.

She looked at him with a frown because she didn't. Damn her slow brain. "No."

"First, tell me if all of these match your memories."

"Actually, they don't. These," she said and pointed to fifteen sketches, "I don't remember at all. Not the clothes, going to the pub, or anything."

Nikolai lifted one of the fifteen and held it up as he faced her. "Look close."

"What am I looking for?"

"You'll know when you see it."

She threw up her hands after several minutes of studying the drawing. Then he added a second sketch to the first. She took a deep breath and looked again.

That's when she saw it. Or rather *him*.

Once she saw the man, it was the only thing her eyes picked up. He was in a long, dark coat, something worn by millions of other men. But it was the fact that he was half hidden and looking right at her that caught her attention.

Esther moved to her hands and knees to reexamine the other sketches. To her dismay, the man was in nearly every one.

She sat back, dazed. "I was trained to notice people following me. In fact, I looked for that very thing every day."

"I think you knew he was there."

Her head turned to Nikolai. "What makes you say that?"

"A hunch."

"Then why can't I remember it?" No sooner were the words out of her mouth than she realized why. "The Druid."

Nikolai twisted his lips as he nodded. "Aye. The Druid."

"Just one more piece of the puzzle that doesn't fit. This exercise was supposed to help me, not make things worse."

"It is helping," he said. "You're discovering more of what was taken from you, which is a piece of the puzzle. You doona believe it fits, but I think it's integral to leading us to the Druid and learning how long they've been watching you."

She wrinkled her nose in disgust. "You're talking about Kyvor."

"If they were on to you from the beginning, it's because there was a leak in MI5."

"Not possible," she quickly added.

He continued, "Either that, or you encountered the Druid almost immediately without even knowing it."

Esther shifted to the side and swung her legs around to cross before her. "That's a possibility."

"Do you remember exactly when you went to Kyvor?"

She jumped up, ran to her coat, and pulled out her mobile. "That, I do know. I contacted Stuart for dates to test against my memory."

"And?" Nikolai prompted.

"The Druid didn't touch my memories about when I interviewed with Kyvor. But she did alter my perception of how long I was there."

Esther grabbed one of the pencils and sat down. She flipped over one of the sketches and jotted down the dates and times of her covert assignment with Kyvor. The day she went undercover, the day she first interviewed with Kyvor, and the day she was offered the position.

"When you and Kinsey were here a few weeks ago with Anson trying to bring down Kyvor, you two hacked into their computers."

Esther nodded. "That was all Kinsey and Ryder. I merely stood by and watched."

"Did she find anything on you?"

"We did a quick search, but we didn't have time to really find anything when everything went sideways with Devon and Anson. Then Harriet got away. At least Con caught Upton."

Nikolai rubbed his hand over his jaw. "Thanks to Devon. She helped expose Kyvor's true motives to the world."

"Rachel was quick to do a piece on Kyvor right after. She was waiting in the wings to write up her expose, which helped to topple them completely."

He grinned, making her heart melt. "We did it as a family. You, Kinsey, and Devon got things moving. Rachel used her talent as a journalist to put the final nail in the coffin."

A family. He'd said it several times. Hell, even Henry called those at Dreagan family. However, this was the first time that she felt a part of it, even though she had been in the midst of the takedown of Kyvor from the beginning.

"Perhaps we should question Upton," she said.

Nikolai gave a shake of his head and pulled her onto his lap. He wrapped his arms around her as she leaned her head against his shoulder. "Con can handle that. We're no' finished here yet."

"What are the odds that we find anything?"

"Look at what we uncovered today."

She blew out a breath. "It wasn't a lot."

"It was something," he stated.

"You're right. It was. I just expected more."

He rubbed his hand up and down her back. "We'll find it. We just need to be patient. Besides, I'm no' ready to return to Scotland yet."

She smiled and lifted her face to his. "What do you suppose we could do with the time we have tonight?"

He looked at the fireplace, and a second later, a fire roared to life. She laughed and wound her arms around him as the heat quickly filled the room.

"I could get used to this," she said.

"You make it sound as if it willna continue when we return to Dreagan."

She pulled out of his arms and began to gather the sketches. This was a conversation she wasn't ready to have, but ready or not, it was out there. She had to face it now.

"It didn't happen while we were there. Why would it continue when we return?" she asked.

He rose up on his knees and took the sketches from her. He tossed them aside and looked into her eyes. Her gaze was locked with his, causing her to drown in a pool of blue.

"Listen to me," he whispered. "I've battled my attraction to you from the verra beginning because you were fighting the demons the Druid left behind. No' because of Henry or because I didna want you."

She swallowed and opened her mouth to speak, but he quickly spoke over her.

"Now that I've had you and marked you as mine, I doona intend to ever let you go."

"Ever?" she asked.

A brief frown flickered over his face. "You're no' ready for what I have to say on that."

"I am," she insisted. Now that he'd spoken about it, she had to know what he meant. All of it. Because . . . what if he meant she was his mate?

That was insane, right? She was only at Dreagan because of a Druid. They never would've met otherwise. She never would have known his passion, his power, or his tenderness.

"Nay, you're no'," he said, breaking into her thoughts. "Know that I want you. I crave you."

She felt the desire tighten in her stomach. "Show me," she demanded.

With a grin, he pulled off her sweater and slid his hands around her back as he bent to take her lips in a scorching kiss.

CHAPTER TWENTY-TWO

Cork, Ireland

The birds were loud, and the breeze cool. The disorder within Ulrik was at odds with the calm, serene countryside of West Cork.

He stood on the bank, looking out over the water that was still as glass. Behind him, the mountains rose up, the craggy rocks pushing through the vivid green grass to give the setting a majestic view.

Though it could never rival Scotland. The only reason Ulrik remained in Ireland, residing in the ancient cottage nestled amid a grove of trees surrounded by lush foliage was because of Eilish.

Any day now, she would come for him on orders from Mikkel. His uncle's hunger for power had been there all along. Only Ulrik hadn't seen it.

Before the war with the humans, all Ulrik had cared about was having his family close. He'd been too naïve to see who Mikkel really was. And now, Ulrik was paying the price.

He briefly thought of going to Con and alerting him but there was no point. The King of Kings wouldn't believe him. And to be honest, if Ulrik were in Con's shoes, he wouldn't believe him either.

Mikkel was an issue Ulrik would have to deal with on his own. It wasn't that he wanted to kill the only link to his family, but after everything Mikkel had done, there was no other option.

Ulrik was the rightful King of Silvers. Though he hadn't had to battle his father for the position, it was no less his. His strength of power and magic had propelled him into the position whether he wanted it or not.

That might was the reason Mikkel didn't dare confront Ulrik outright. Mikkel didn't have what it took to be a Dragon King. It was why he'd been passed over to begin with.

In a battle between the two, Ulrik would slaughter Mikkel within minutes. So the coward had found a loophole—a Druid.

Ulrik wasn't sure Eilish could kill him, but he wasn't going to take any chances. Mikkel thought she could, and so did the Druid. Which was enough to put Ulrik on edge.

The easiest solution would be to kill the Druid, but for some reason, Ulrik couldn't do it. He'd thought of several ways to end her life, and each time, he found a reason not to. None of which helped his dilemma.

And he didn't want to think about why he didn't want the Druid's life to end.

Movement out of the corner of his eye had him turning his head in time to see Balladyn appear. Ulrik wasn't so sure he liked the idea of a Fae having easy access to him. Then again, if he were supposed to be working with the Dark Fae, he would have to trust Balladyn.

Just as Balladyn had to trust him.

Ulrik faced him. The Fae was dressed in all black and strode angrily toward him. "What is it?"

"We've got a problem," Balladyn stated.

"And that is?"

Balladyn halted before Ulrik, his nostrils flaring as the long length of his black and silver hair lifted in the breeze. "Usaeil."

"The Light Queen? What does she have to do with anything?" Ulrik asked, puzzled.

"You mean besides asking Taraeth to kill me years ago and going to the King just now to put out a hit on Rhi?"

No matter what Ulrik thought of his fellow Dragon Kings, Rhi was a friend. "No one is going to harm Rhi."

"My thoughts exactly," Balladyn confirmed.

Ulrik nodded as he realized the implication. "You're ready to take out Taraeth."

"Aye. It's the only way I can protect Rhi."

"I suppose you've told her."

"I did."

Ulrik knew Rhi most likely went to Dreagan immediately. "Becoming King of the Dark willna save her."

"I'm well aware of that. Which is why I'll kill Usaeil."

At this, Ulrik smiled. "Want some help?"

"You'd meddle in Fae affairs?"

He shrugged as he looked at Balladyn. "She's no' exactly a model of decorum if she's having the Dark murder her people. I think it's time for a regime change for the Light, as well."

Balladyn smiled. "You want Rhi to take over."

"I'm no' the only one. You've thought of it, too."

"I have, but I don't think she'll do it."

Ulrik shrugged and scratched his cheek. "She may no' have a choice. If Taraeth isna there to give the order for the Dark to kill Rhi, Usaeil will have to do it herself."

"If I know Rhi—and I do—she's already preparing."

"She may no' wait for the queen to come to her. Rhi has yet to confront Usaeil about everything you've told me is going on at the Light castle. Add in the photos Us-aeil had taken of her and Con, and Rhi will no' be alone when she decides to do something about the queen."

A flush of resentment stained Balladyn's cheeks. "You mean Con will be with her."

"Or Rhys." Ulrik didn't mention Phelan. He'd discovered the Warrior was half Fae on one of his secret trips to see the Silvers.

Rhi had gone to great lengths to conceal Phelan's identity from all Fae, and since Phelan was heir to the Light throne, it was a smart move. It was a secret Ulrik would keep as well.

"Soon, Rhi won't have reason to keep turning to the Dragon Kings," Balladyn bit out.

"Doona be a fool. You know she'll always have a connection to us. Discounting it or pretending it isna there will only push her away."

A vein protruded in Balladyn's temple as he glared at Ulrik. "I'm going to be enough for her."

"She has friends at Dreagan. Doona ask her to ignore them. She willna do it."

"You act as if you know her better than I, when I'm the one who has known her the longest."

Ulrik lifted his hands, palms out to calm the Dark. "Your judgment is clouded by your love. I can see things clearer than you, and if you want to remain with Rhi, you will have to accept her link to Dreagan."

"You're probably right," Balladyn said and blew out a resigned breath. "I thought she was over her dragon lover."

"She may be." There had been a time Ulrik thought Rhi might get past her longing for her King, but he wasn't so sure now. He'd personally pushed her to let go of that love, but she hadn't done it. Nor was she likely to.

Just as her King would never be free of it.

Balladyn shot him a wry smile. "We both know the truth."

"You love her," Ulrik said. "She's with you, so give her your strength, friendship, and love. Stand with her in all things, and she will be forever loyal."

The Dark nodded and clasped his hands behind his back. "If I see Mikkel after I kill Taraeth, I'm going to remove your uncle from this war."

"Take the chance if you get it, but I have a feeling you willna find him once he learns of Taraeth's demise. Mikkel distrusts everyone, and he wants me dead. He'll be getting everything into position to ensure that he takes my place as King of the Silvers."

"Are you going after the Druid?"

Ulrik drew in a breath and released it. "I thought about talking to her, convincing her that Mikkel is the wrong dragon to ally with."

"But?" Balladyn asked.

"I've already spoken to her. I've manipulated and bribed enough humans and Fae to know when one willna switch sides. Eilish is one of those."

"I looked into her pub, Graves. It's not widely known among the Dark, but there are some who visit it. They've told me she has banned any beings from harming the mortals who live in the village. She backs that up with quick and painful retaliation for anyone who doesn't abide by that rule. She's powerful, even against the Fae. That's not something we see in Druids."

Ulrik had deduced as much when he visited Graves himself. "There's a reason she's loyal to Mikkel. I just need to discover what that is. If he's promised her something and I can get it before he does, then the tide may turn in our favor."

"Then you'd better start looking. Once Taraeth is dead, Mikkel will come straight for you."

"The coward won't do it on his own. He's sending a Druid in his place."

Balladyn wrinkled his nose. "You're the only Dragon King I can tolerate. Doona let him take control."

"No' my intention."

"How does the Druid plan to take you out if only another King can kill a Dragon King?"

Ulrik looked back out at the water. "I've been wondering that myself. Mikkel seems too sure of the outcome, and he doesna act like that unless he has proof. Even if Eilish can no' kill me, she might weaken me enough for Mikkel to finish me off."

"Just don't let any of that happen."

"No' in my plans," he said and glanced at the Dark.

Balladyn grinned then. "Mikkel may be more of a match than you expect if he gets the rest of his magic unbound."

"That willna happen if the Druid is as intelligent as I think she is."

That caused Balladyn to lift a brow. "How so?"

"My uncle is so wrapped up in thoughts of being a Dragon King that he's forgotten one thing. I already have my magic. *I'm* the Dragon King."

"Which means he'll be a dragon unable to shift," Balladyn said with a grin.

Ulrik smiled. "Precisely."

"And if the Druid isn't that smart?"

"She is."

Balladyn raised both brows as he chuckled. "So Mikkel will continue to be limited in what he can do."

"For now." Ulrik had a plan that would ensure his uncle returned to his true form. "By the way, any more word on the Reapers?"

"Nay, though Rhi's obsession with them has been bothering me."

Ulrik pulled his hair back at the base of his neck and then tugged a strip of leather from his pants pocket to wrap around the strands. "Does Rhi know more than she's letting on?"

"I think so, but she won't tell me what that is yet."

"If what you've shared about the Reapers is true, then there's a reason she's keeping it from you."

Balladyn ran a hand down his face as he sighed loudly. "I've thought of that."

"One thing at a time. Deal with Taraeth. That will force Usaeil to make a move if Rhi doesna beat her to it."

"And you?" Balladyn asked.

Ulrik was silent for a long minute. "I could talk to Eilish again. Or . . . I could find a weapon that will give me ultimate power over the Druids, my uncle, and the Dragon Kings."

"You're talking about *the* weapon."

"I am."

Balladyn narrowed his red eyes on Ulrik. "You've known where it is the entire time?"

"I have."

"Both you and Mikkel promised it to Taraeth."

Ulrik stared at Balladyn. The Dark's next reaction would determine if Ulrik could trust him.

Balladyn lifted one shoulder and grinned. "If you rule the Dragon Kings, you'll want to be rid of the mortals on this realm. The Dark can help with that. What need do I have of the weapon?"

Ulrik smiled in response. "We do make a great team."

CHAPTER TWENTY-THREE

Icy shards of apprehension immobilized Esther. She recognized the darkness around her, sensed the threat just out of sight.

The last thing she remembered was Nikolai holding her with the fire warming their naked bodies after hours of making love. She'd only closed her eyes for a second, but that's all it took for sleep to claim her.

She swallowed and pinched herself to try and wake. It was a useless endeavor, but that didn't stop her from trying again and again.

"Nikolai," she whispered.

The sound would never reach him. She was on her own, locked in her mind and about to face terrors she'd run from ever since waking from the Druid's hold.

She lifted her hand and saw it clearly. There was a light above her as if spotlighting her for whatever waited in the recesses of her psyche. Yet everything else was black as pitch, the dark so deep that she instinctively recoiled from it. Not that it did any good when it surrounded her.

Esther had walked into meetings with people armed

to the teeth. She'd dined with a known terrorist, and even partied with a man who was involved with human trafficking. All of those people were among the most evil of humanity, but the fear she'd felt around them was nothing compared to what gripped her now.

She was a joke, telling everyone how strong—both mentally and physically—she was. That her training had prepared her for anything.

The instruction had done nothing to prevent a Druid from controlling her thoughts and actions. It hadn't readied her for magic or the supernatural. It did little to show her how to defend herself against her own mind—or whatever creature was there, waiting for her.

But she wasn't a Dragon King. She couldn't remain awake indefinitely.

"Bloody brilliant," she mumbled.

How did one plan for battle with oneself? One way or another, she was going to find out just how tough and resilient she was.

She took the first tentative step, her knees literally knocking together. How Henry would love to see her so terrified after all those pranks he'd played while they were growing up. What she wouldn't do to have someone with her. Nikolai or Henry. Hell, she'd even take Con. Yet she had no choice but to face whatever was to come alone.

"You can do this," she told herself.

The encouragement might have worked if her voice hadn't shaken so badly, but it was hard to motivate yourself to move forward when all you wanted to do was curl up in a ball and pretend that none of it was happening.

Standing around wishing she would wake up wouldn't solve her dilemma. If she wanted to survive, she had to do something.

She thought of Nikolai and how he'd stood steadfastly

beside her. His stillness and silence were a peace she hadn't realized she needed. He was a calm in the storm that was her life. The tree with roots that went so deep, nothing could ever move him. And he offered for her to hang onto him.

It was Nikolai who allowed her to take a breath and calm her racing heart. He might not be standing beside her in her mind, but she knew he was holding her, encouraging her. He gave her the courage to take another step—and then another and another.

The light above stayed with her, shining just enough to emit a glow so that she saw a few feet in front of her. Esther felt as if she walked for miles and saw nothing but more of the inky blackness.

She didn't know how long she walked before she realized that the monster she'd sensed earlier felt as if it were right behind her. She didn't stop, though. Her feet kept moving even as she trembled in dread.

It was there for her. She knew it with a certainty that she couldn't explain. What would happen when it finally reached out for her? Would she be tortured? Would she be wracked with pain?

Or would she simply cease to exist?

The questions multiplied a thousand times over until she couldn't take it anymore. She halted and whirled around, only to come face-to-face with herself.

Except this Esther wasn't plagued with fear. She stood calmly, bright eyes locked with hers. How wrong was it that she'd been afraid to sleep because she might encounter . . . herself?

"I've been waiting for you," Esther II said.

Esther still wasn't sure what to make of what was happening. "Why? Who are you?"

"Call me E2."

Esther blinked and scratched the side of her nose

where an inexplicable itch suddenly developed. "All right. E2, why have you been waiting for me?"

"For a long time, I was locked away, unable to show you."

Esther was getting frustrated with the lack of answers. "Show me what?"

"Who you are."

"I know who I am."

E2 smiled and tilted her head to the side as she raised a brow. "Do you?"

"Of course."

"Then tell me."

Esther wondered if she were going insane. She talked to herself often to fill the silence when she was alone, but she'd never actually imagined a clone of herself standing in front of her, demanding things.

She studied the way E2 stared at her. Was that really how her hair looked as it framed her face? Maybe it was time for a new style. And she really needed to relax, if E2 were any indication.

"Are you afraid?" E2 asked.

"Yes."

"Don't be."

Esther shrugged. "I'm an MI5 agent."

"Are you still?" E2 inquired softly.

Damn her. Esther had been debating leaving the agency, but that was because she didn't feel as if she belonged anymore. "Yes."

"Truth," E2 commanded.

Esther shrugged. "I don't know anymore."

"What else are you?"

"I'm Henry's sister and the daughter of Jack and Lucy North."

E2 gave a nod. "You are Henry's sister."

Esther frowned at the way she obviously left off

being the Norths' daughter. "Are you telling me I'm not Jack and Lucy's daughter?"

"You said you knew who you were. I hope it's more than what you shared with me."

Esther was really beginning to not like E2. At all. "I'm a sister, a friend, a warrior, and a truth seeker."

"Yes," E2 said with a bright smile. "You are a Truth-Seeker."

Esther took a step back. The last part had come out of nowhere. The words had formed and were spoken before she realized what they were.

"Explain," she urged E2.

"The truth is waiting for you."

"I'm ready."

E2 shook her head. "Not quite. You still hold too much fear."

"Because I'm in a world with magic and dragons and Fae! I don't stand a chance against any of those."

E2 merely smiled. "You're a TruthSeeker. Seek."

"Seek what?"

"You'll know it when you find it."

Esther grabbed E2's arm when she went to turn away. "Are you here because of what the Druid did to me?"

"Yes," she replied. "The Druid inadvertently unlocked a door and let me out. I've been trying to talk to you ever since."

"So you weren't a monster?"

E2 shrugged. "That depends on who you listen to."

Esther was taken aback at the candid response. "What do you mean?"

"Learn to listen to your heart. The answers you need are here," she said, touching Esther's chest. Then she touched Esther's temple. "And here."

"I feel like I'm talking to Yoda. I just want answers. I want my memories to stop being jumbled."

"You're doing some of it yourself."

Esther flattened her lips and glared. "And my missing memories?"

"Only the Druid who took them can replace them."

"Oh. That's awesome," Esther said with a roll of her eyes. "I'm trying to sort through my memories in order to find her. I can't do that when they're all jumbled up and switched around."

E2 simply looked at her. "You're a TruthSeeker."

"So you keep saying. I need to seek," Esther said and nodded.

When she blinked, E2 was gone. Esther turned in a circle, but there was no doubt she was alone. It took a second to see that the darkness had vanished, as well.

She stood in the middle of a crossroads with large corridors and other hallways in front of, behind, and on either side of her. There were seemingly thousands of doorways, as well.

Now this place she recognized. It was her mind, and behind each doorway was a piece of her life. But where did she begin? Which portal was the one she needed to uncover the Druid?

Did she want to know what E2 had meant when she hinted that Esther wasn't the daughter of the Norths? Or perhaps she should try and find out what a TruthSeeker was. She needed answers to all those questions and more.

The light above her began to dim. She felt herself being pulled awake, and she fought to remain asleep to find those answers. In the next second, her eyes opened, and she looked up at Nikolai. His pale blue eyes were filled with concern as he searched her face.

He smoothed his hand over her hair. "You were screaming in your sleep, and I couldna wake you."

"What was I yelling?"

"Seeker."

The longer she was awake, the more the event with E2 seemed like a dream. Except she knew it wasn't.

"What happened?" Nikolai asked.

Esther shrugged and reached for him, burying her face against his neck. "I don't know."

"But something happened?"

"The monster I thought was in my head was me."

There was a beat of hesitation. Then he asked, "You?"

"Another version of me," she said and lowered herself back to the floor. "She said she's been locked away, but the Druid accidently released her."

Nikolai raised an auburn brow. "What else did she say?"

"That I'm Henry's sister, but she alluded to the fact that my parents might not be my parents."

"Hmm," he murmured.

Esther licked her lips. "She also said I was a Truth-Seeker."

"What's that?"

"I don't know, but I want to find out."

Nikolai's lips lifted in a half-grin. "Then let's get started."

CHAPTER TWENTY-FOUR

TruthSeeker. The word ran through Nikolai's head over and over. He'd never heard anyone called such a name before, yet somehow, he knew that the term was uniquely Esther's.

Waking to hear her screaming and thrashing about had frightened him. And when he couldn't wake her, he'd feared the worst. Finally, she'd opened her eyes, and the clarity he saw in her brown depths made him believe everything she divulged.

While they had breakfast, she told him of E2 and everything that had happened while Esther slept. What Nikolai kept tripping over was how E2 said she'd been locked away.

A mortal might look at such a situation and say that Esther had multiple personalities, but he knew that wasn't the case. In fact, E2's imprisonment had the stink of a binding spell.

Once Esther went upstairs to get ready for the day, Nikolai opened his mental link. *"Ryder."*

It was a few minutes before Ryder responded. *"Aye? How's it going? Any more Dark attacks?"*

"Nay. I need you to quietly look into Esther's family."

Without missing a beat, Ryder asked, *"How far?"*

"As far back as you can go."

"I'm still looking into Faith's family and her connection to the Druids, and I've gone back really far. You want me to do the same for Esther? I'll do it, but I'd like to know why."

"Esther finally fell asleep last night, and she encountered herself, a version she calls E2. E2 told her that she was a TruthSeeker, and that the Druid released her unintentionally."

"Well, shit," Ryder said. *"That's no' good. A binding spell?"*

"Maybe. E2 also hinted that Henry and Esther might be adopted."

"I doona need to tell you how badly this can go."

Nikolai looked up at the ceiling toward the room above him where Esther was dressing. *"She needs answers, and I'm going to help her find them."*

"What about her missing memories?"

"E2 told her that the Druid was the only one who could replace them."

"Does that mean you are going to halt following the trail of the coasters?"

Nikolai held one of the coasters in his hand. *"We'll keep pursuing that avenue for now. But I doona want Henry alerted to any of this."*

"I agree. He has enough to handle at the moment. But if I find anything that leads to any of E2's claims being fact, it will change a lot."

"It'll change everything. Have you ever heard of a TruthSeeker?"

Ryder sighed loudly. *"I've no', but I know someone who might."*

"Kellan," Nikolai guessed.

"If any of the Kings have come in contact with a Truth-Seeker, he'll know."

They ended the conversation, and Nikolai severed the link. He was already thinking about what to do if Kellan came up empty-handed. Nikolai's next options were either the Fae or the Druids.

He really didn't want to ask Shara, Kiril's Fae mate. If he told her, she would then tell Kiril. And the more people at Dreagan who knew, the more chances that Henry would discover what was going on.

The only other Fae he could ask was Rhi, and since she was supposed to be off looking into the wooden dragon Faith and Dmitri had found on Fair Isle and the combination of Druid and Fae magic within it, he didn't want to bother her either.

Ryder worked fast, but right now, instantaneous wasn't quick enough for Nikolai. He dug into his bag for the mobile phone that had been supplied for him. The numbers for the Warriors and Druids at MacLeod Castle were in the contacts.

He scrolled through until he found Hayden. He hit the call button and brought the mobile to his ear as it began to ring.

"Ryder?" Hayden asked as he answered.

"It's Nikolai. This is just one of the many phones Dreagan has."

Hayden said, "Since the Kings doona call just to chat, I take it this is business."

"It is. The Ancients contacted Isla when Faith and Dmitri found the wooden dragon. Did they happen to say anything to her about a TruthSeeker?"

"Hang on," Hayden said.

Nikolai waited as he heard Hayden speaking in the background. He drummed his fingers and silently urged the Warrior to hurry up.

The voice that came on the line wasn't Hayden's, but his wife, Isla's. "Nikolai, tell me what's going on."

He quickly relayed the entire story about helping Esther find her lost memories, as well as what had happened while she slept.

Isla listened to it all quietly. Only when he finished did she say, "The Ancients told me nothing of a TruthSeeker."

"Damn." He squeezed his eyes closed. He'd held out hope that he might find some sort of answer.

"But I've heard of it."

His eyes snapped opened as he got to his feet. "And?"

"It's a term from an obsolete line of Druids. Each generation, there was a female born who was a TruthSeeker. There was also a male who was a JusticeBringer. Together, they regulated the Druids."

"Regulated?" He immediately thought of the Reapers.

"The family—the Clachers—was given that responsibility by the Ancients because they were driven to monitor the Druids."

Nikolai ran a hand over his mouth. "Should they no' have prevented Deirdre from taking control and unleashing the Warriors?"

"The last members of that family went to do exactly that. They intended to end Deirdre, but she knew they were coming, and she killed them, effectively ending their line."

"Are you sure? Could one have survived?"

Isla sighed. "That was before Deirdre held me captive, but she retold the story enough times. She didn't just kill the brother and sister, she wiped out the entire family. And just to be sure, she sent her wyrrans across all of Britain and Scotland to guarantee that none survived."

Nikolai was still asleep in his mountain during all of that, but Con had told him about the small, yellow creatures that Deirdre created, with their huge mouths full of sharp teeth.

"Esther can't be a Clacher," Isla said.

He didn't quite believe that, not when magic was involved. "Are you saying the Ancients couldna have given such power to another Druid family?"

"I can't speak for the Ancients. If they had the ability to do it, then I'd want to know why they waited so long," Isla said, bitterness tingeing her words.

"Aye."

Isla then said, "I know you and Esther want answers, and I wish I had them. But I keep coming back to the fact that neither she nor Henry have any magic."

"Could it have been bound?"

"Of course, but as soon as the Druid entered Esther's mind, she should've seen that."

"Maybe she did," Nikolai said.

"Has Esther displayed any magic at all?"

He looked at the floor. "None."

"I'm sorry. I wish I could be more help. It would've been nice if Henry and Esther were from the Clacher line so they could find and kill the Druid who has teamed up with Ulrik."

Nikolai didn't correct her. For all he knew, Ulrik was working with the Druid. Until they knew differently, it was easier to leave things as they were instead of mentioning Mikkel and how little they knew of him.

"Thank you for your help," Nikolai said and ended the call.

Just when he thought he'd learned something, he ended up with more questions than he had before the call. And if he felt like this, he could only imagine how Esther suffered. He put the mobile back into his bag. When he turned around, Esther was coming down the stairs. She smiled when she saw him.

"You can move your stuff up to my room," she said.

He nodded. "I will later."

She stopped at the table where the coasters were. "Shall we go to more pubs?"

"Certainly. What do you want to do?"

"Find the truth."

He grinned, because he'd known that would be her response. "The truth of what?"

"All of it." She licked her lips and moved the coasters around. "I feel like the more I look, the more hints I get, but the less I actually learn."

Nikolai walked to her. "I'm here to help. We'll find the answers. All of them."

"You've already spoken to Ryder, haven't you? He's looking into my past?"

"Aye." Nikolai worried that Esther might be upset that he'd taken the initiative without talking to her.

She gave a nod. "Good. Maybe he can sort out the facts."

"Do you want to call your parents?"

Her brown eyes lowered briefly to the table. "I'm thirty-two years old. In all of that time, I've never had a reason to doubt they were my biological parents. If Henry and I were adopted, they would've told us by now."

"We're talking magic. Perhaps they doona know because they were made to forget."

She laughed, the sound bordering on distraught. "See? More questions. If you're right, and it is logical that you are, who would do that? And why?"

"The only thing I can think of is that it was done to hide you and Henry."

"As well as to conceal the fact that I'm a TruthSeeker?"

Nikolai took her hand and brought her over to the sofa near the fire. Once she sat, he took one of the chairs across from her. "I made a call to MacLeod Castle."

"The Druids, yes," she said excitedly. "Did they know anything?"

He hesitated to tell her, not because he didn't want her to know, but because it might give her hope when there was none. "I spoke with Hayden and Isla."

Esther leaned back against the cushions. "I've only met a few of the Warriors and Druids, but I took an instant liking to Isla. She's the one the Ancients spoke to about the Druid who messed with my mind. What did she know?"

"There was a family—the Clachers. It seems the line had an affinity for monitoring and punishing the Druids. Each generation, there was a male and female born. The Ancients intervened and used the family's motivations to regulate the Druids."

"To keep Druids in check," Esther said. "Much like police agencies do with humans."

Nikolai leaned forward and put his forearms on his knees, clasping his hands together. He could see the excitement in Esther's eyes, and he hated to dash it. "The females were the TruthSeekers and the males the Justice-Bringers."

"Really?" she asked with a growing smile.

He took a deep breath and delivered the statement that would kill her expectations. "Deirdre, the *drough* the Warriors and Druids fought for centuries, had the entire family wiped from the earth."

CHAPTER TWENTY-FIVE

Hope was an emotion Esther didn't allow herself to feel very often. It often gave people courage, but it could also bring some to the pits of despair if lost.

She wasn't blind to the way Nikolai watched her as he spoke. The smile never waivered from her lips, even when he delivered the tragic news. "Magic, remember?"

His nostrils flared as he drew in a deep breath and straightened in the chair. "You said that E2 told you the Druid inadvertently released her."

"That's right."

"Have you felt differently?"

She wasn't fooled by his question. "You mean, have I done any magic? The answer is no."

"The members of the Clacher family were Druids."

"I understand that, and I'm also clear on the fact that Deirdre wiped them out." Esther crossed one leg over the other. "We're dealing with magic. The possibilities are endless."

He slowly leaned back and scratched his chin. "I'd caution you on pinning everything to that."

"How could E2 come up with TruthSeeker if it wasn't real? And Isla confirmed that it is."

"Hundreds of years ago."

Esther tried to keep an open mind, but she knew in her bones that she was the TruthSeeker. Yet there was no denying she had zero magic. Because if she had any, she would've used it on the Dark the previous day on instinct.

She let everything roll around in her mind for a moment. "There are some facts that haven't changed. I'm missing memories, and we're here to trace my movements before I encountered the Druid."

"Aye."

"I realize that there's a chance E2 isn't real, or that she was placed there by the Druid to lead me on a wild goose chase."

Nikolai quickly said, "We'll know about your parents soon enough. With Ryder's skills, it doesna matter how deep something is buried, he'll find it."

"I'm glad he's on our side."

That made Nikolai chuckle. "I agree."

"This is being kept from Henry for the time being, right?"

"It is, but I wouldna recommend leaving it that way for long."

She uncrossed her legs and pushed herself to her feet. "Agreed. Ready to start the day?"

"Go pick the coasters," he said while he extinguished the fire with magic.

At first, Esther had been frightened of the magic and the fact that those at Dreagan were really dragons, but she'd soon learned how beneficial magic was.

Within minutes, she was inside the SUV with the heated seats turned on as Nikolai drove them to the next pub—The Porterhouse in Covent Garden, which just happened to be the largest bar in London.

Just as before, they remained outside for about an hour as Nikolai sketched. Esther looked around, trying to remember the last time she'd been in the area to see if it matched up with whatever he drew.

Finally, they walked into the alehouse, ready to explore each of the twelve different levels. Nikolai opened the door for her, and she walked through. Not two steps in, he suddenly halted and grabbed her hand.

She looked back at him, concern filling her when she saw the same look he'd worn right before he fought the Dark on his face.

Then it hit her. Dark Fae. Ireland. The Porterhouse was owned by an Irishman. She let her gaze roam the area and saw that many of the guests were looking at them—and those patrons were Dark Fae.

"We can leave," she said.

A sound much like a growl rumbled from Nikolai's chest. "We came for a reason."

"But there are Dark everywhere," she whispered.

"Look at the mortals."

She wanted to roll her eyes at his statement, but she did as he asked. That's when she noticed that they all acted normally. The humans weren't yanking off their clothes or rubbing against any of the Fae.

"How?" she asked.

Nikolai kept his hold on her and turned to walk toward the back corner where a man sat reading the paper. She didn't have time to ask what Nikolai was doing before they were standing at the table.

The paper slowly lowered to reveal a man with short, thick, white hair and a neatly trimmed beard. His vibrant blue eyes looked from Nikolai to her. His lips curved slightly as he folded the paper and set it aside before he motioned for them to join him.

Esther wanted to walk away, but Nikolai held her hand tightly as if sensing her thoughts. He moved her toward the booth, so she slid in first. Nikolai tossed his sketchpad on the seat next to her and then sat. He braced his arms on the table as he and the man silently stared at one another.

"I don't believe a Dragon King has ever entered my establishment," the man said with a heavy Irish accent.

Nikolai lifted one shoulder. "We're no' here to eat."

"Ah, but Ms. North has visited us a few times before. She likes the steak, medium."

Just when Esther thought she was getting used to the world of magic, she felt as if she were tripping all over it again. She didn't know how the man knew her or Nikolai, or what Nikolai was, but she aimed to find out.

Nikolai didn't move so much as a muscle, but the atmosphere grew distinctly chillier.

The man laughed and moved the paper to the seat. "I'm not threatening her. There's no need for such a show."

"I disagree," Nikolai said.

"You came into my place, walked to my table. Who's threatening who?" the older man asked.

The tension lessened enough that Esther could take a deep breath. She wasn't at all keen on the knowledge that someone had been watching her movements in the bar to such a degree that he knew what she'd ordered.

Then she realized that she and Nikolai had a prime opportunity before them. She got the man's attention and asked, "Would you mind telling me the last time I was here?"

The man looked from her to Nikolai before returning his gaze to her. "You've lost your memory?"

"In a way," she said. "I'm missing some days, and I'm trying to piece it all together. And since you know who I am, might I have the pleasure?"

He smiled, his eyes crinkling in the corners. "I like you. I'm Donal Cleary."

She held out her hand despite Nikolai's frown. Donal took it, and they shook. She nodded. "It's nice to meet you, Mr. Cleary."

"Donal, please," he said. Then he looked at Nikolai. "And which Dragon King are you?"

When Nikolai didn't answer, she said, "He's Nikolai."

Donal's brows rose in his forehead. "Well, Nikolai and Esther, welcome to my bar. Now, about your query," he said as he turned his blue eyes to Esther. "You were in here about six weeks ago. You sat on the third floor, alone, and ate your steak."

"Six weeks," she repeated. That was during the time she was in London undercover.

"Was she followed?" Nikolai asked.

Donal was silent for a moment before he nodded. "She was."

"A man?" Nikolai sat back, keeping one arm on the table.

Donal waved away a server who came toward the table. "In a long, black coat."

Nikolai reached for his pad and opened it, his pencil moving quickly across the page. Esther knew he might be at it awhile, so she found herself looking into Donal's eyes.

"Are you Dark Fae?" she asked.

He smiled, chuckling softly. "Will you be disappointed when I say I'm not?"

"Relieved actually."

He glanced at Nikolai. "Then be at ease."

She noticed three Dark staring at them. "How is it that the Fae aren't affecting the humans?"

"An old family trick," Donal said. "When you grow up in Ireland, you learn the tales of the Fae early on. If you're really lucky, your ancestors acquire ways to keep them away. Mine did, and I carved the symbols all over my bar to make sure the Fae's appeal is blocked from the rest of us."

Esther was impressed. "Thank goodness for your ancestors."

"It does come in handy."

"How do you know so much about me?"

As soon as the question was out, Nikolai paused and lifted his gaze to Donal.

Donal didn't seem to mind the glare. "For one, I have cameras everywhere and recordings that I study daily."

"You wouldn't be able to review all the camera footage every day," she said.

He grinned, his blue eyes twinkling. "That's true. I'm an old man, and I'd rather fill my days with other things."

Esther raised a brow, waiting.

"I've one or two on my staff who are Druids. I also have a few Light and Dark Fae, though they use glamour to hide their beauty," he explained.

Nikolai said, "So they were watching Esther."

Donal's smile was gone as he nodded in agreement. "They take an interest in anyone with connections to magic, and Esther had a direct connection through her brother because of his affiliation with you."

"How do you know about Henry?" she demanded.

Donal released a long breath. "My dear, when you're in my world, you make it your business to know things. News travels fast about a mortal, an MI5 agent, no less, helping the Dragon Kings. Then he disappears? It's not a stretch to realize that Henry is at Dreagan."

"So you assumed Esther would have information?" Nikolai asked.

Donal's lips tilted down as he frowned. "Of course not. We were watching her to see if anyone approached her that might give me a clue as to movements in your war."

"You're a mortal, how do you even know about that?" Esther queried.

Donal gave her a wry look. "The video of the Kings shifting was a bloody good indication. Besides, I pay a good price for such information."

"How do you know about us?" Nikolai demanded.

"Like I said, I pay very well for any and all intel regarding all magical beings on this earth."

Esther pulled out her phone and found the picture of the Druid to show to Donal. "Have you seen this woman in here?"

As soon as Donal saw the picture, he jerked back as if struck. He yanked the phone from Esther and brought it closer. "Who is this?"

"We were hoping you might tell us," Nikolai said, his head tilting to the side as he watched Donal.

Donal was quiet for several minutes as he continued to gaze at the picture. Esther exchanged a look with Nikolai. There was something about the Druid that Donal knew, but would he share it with them?

"I need to find her," Esther said.

Donal slowly lowered the mobile to the table and watched as the screen dimmed, then went black. "She hasn't been here."

"But you know her," Nikolai said.

Donal ran a hand over his face, which suddenly looked haggard. "I take it you drew that picture," he said to Nikolai.

"I did," Nikolai agreed.

Donal scratched his beard. "Why are you looking for her?"

"She got into my brain and took over," Esther said. "It's why I have missing days. I want to know what I did during that time."

Nikolai leaned forward and caught Donal's gaze. "Who is she?"

"I don't know," Donal said. "But she looks very much like the woman I fell in love with and was suppose to marry."

"Where is that woman?" Esther asked.

Donal lowered his gaze to the table. "She disappeared."

CHAPTER TWENTY-SIX

The answers to just about anything could be seen in a person's eyes. Nikolai had learned that while still very young. It was how he knew he could trust Ulrik, and why he knew he couldn't return to the Ivories with Avgust.

As Nikolai stared into Donal's blue eyes, anything he wanted to know was laid out before him. The biggest truth was that the Irishman wasn't lying about anything. Nikolai wanted to hate Donal, as well as distrust him, but he couldn't. Donal's knowledge might be the very thing he and Esther needed.

"I looked everywhere for her," Donal continued. "She was the love of my life, and the only thing I ever wanted."

Nikolai knew people didn't just disappear. More often than not, the Fae were responsible in such situations.

"Everywhere?" Esther asked.

Donal lifted his hand to a passing waitress, who gave him a nod. "At first, I thought she might've run away."

"Why?" Nikolai asked.

Donal waited as the server arrived and set down a pint of ale and a shot of whisky. She looked to Nikolai, who waved her away, but Esther ordered a coffee.

The Irishman lifted the shot glass and drained the amber liquid as he squeezed his eyes shut and swallowed. He wiped the back of his hand over his lips, and Nikolai saw the way his hand trembled.

The waitress returned and set down Esther's mug of coffee and removed the empty shot glass before walking away.

Donal drew in a ragged breath and leaned both his forearms on the table. "Her family was very strict."

"So was mine," Esther said. "I might have contemplated running away, but I never did."

Donal gave her a sad smile. "I doubt your family was as strict as Eireen's. You see, she was a Druid."

Now things were beginning to make sense to Nikolai. "A Druid in Ireland isna so strange."

"Except that the line had been diluted so many times that most were born without magic. But not my Eireen. It was as if the magic had gathered and waited just for her."

Esther wrapped her hands around the mug of coffee. "So, she was powerful?"

"Extremely. I met her while she was attempting to locate other Druids. She came into my bar in Dublin. It was by happenstance. She had no idea there were other Druids and Fae about, but it didn't take her long to discover it. After that, she was at the pub nearly every day."

Nikolai said, "That's how you got to know her."

"She came to me," Donal said with a smile. "She wouldn't leave me alone until I told her what she wanted to know. Then she wanted me to introduce her to other Druids. She blossomed right before my eyes."

"How so?" Nikolai asked.

Donal shrugged, his lips twisting briefly. "She'd been hiding her magic from her family, who looked for any of their blood who had it. While within the walls of my pub,

Eireen could be the person she truly was. Other Druids taught her how to use her magic," Donal explained. "It was evident to all just how great her magic was by how quickly she learned."

Esther smiled at him. "So you fell in love with her because she was a Druid?"

"No," he said and looked down at the table. "I fell in love with her the first time she walked into my place, her black hair soaked from the rain. She was shivering and pale, and she looked at everything and everyone as if they were an enemy. Yet, despite the obvious fear within her, she squared her shoulders and held her head high as she walked through the pub."

Nikolai glanced at Esther. Donal's description matched Esther in many ways, so he understood completely how the Irishman felt.

Donal lifted his eyes to Esther. "I fell in love with her strength and determination. Her beautiful spirit and face were bonuses. But her magic? It destroyed everything we had. I wanted nothing more than for her not to be a Druid."

"I'm sorry," Esther said.

Donal waved away her words. "Don't be. It was a legitimate question."

"I take it her family discovered what she was about?" Nikolai asked.

"That they did, the slimy fekkers," he ground out, his face contorting in anger.

Intrigued, Nikolai pressed for more. "What happened?"

"We had six months of complete bliss. We were making plans to marry and leave Dublin and her family. Then, her sisters followed her."

Esther frowned. "Why leave? Once she was married, her family wouldn't be able to control her anymore."

Donal smiled. "Ah, if only it were that simple. When

I met Eireen, she was twenty-six. She had a place of her own, but that didn't stop her family from keeping watch over her. I still don't know how they found out about her magic. She used magic to conceal so much from her parents."

"Someone outed her," Nikolai said.

Donal shrugged one shoulder.. "That was my guess, as well. That meant it was most likely someone in my pub. I still remember the day her sisters came. Eireen and I were having dinner, talking about the wedding, and where we wanted to open a new pub. She chose London and this very location. I'd already begun the process of purchasing the building, but she didn't know that yet. It was to be a wedding gift."

"Obviously, she left with her sisters, but why?" Esther asked. "Why not tell them to go screw themselves?"

Donal gave a small shake of his head. "I don't know. I thought that myself. I don't know what the eldest said when she leaned down and whispered in Eireen's ear, but whatever it was worked. Eireen told them to wait outside, and then she tried to explain to me why she had to go. I wouldn't listen. I was so angry."

Nikolai leaned forward, his eyes narrowed. "Do you remember what she said?"

"I tried," Donal said with a look of frustration. "The only thing I recall was her saying that she had one last promise to honor with her family. My temper got the best of me. I was furious. I told her she was a grown woman and didn't need to keep bowing to the wishes of a family who didn't care about who she really was."

Esther lowered her cup of coffee to the table after taking a drink. "Do you know what that promise was?"

"It was the first I'd heard of it, which was odd since we shared everything with each other. But," Donal said as he ran a hand over his face, "I do recall how she looked sick at the idea of whatever it was. If only I had listened to what she had to say."

Nikolai grieved with Donal over the loss of his woman, but Eireen could be just the connection they needed to find the Druid who messed with Esther's mind. "Was that the last time you saw her?"

"It was. When she didn't come in the next day or return my calls, I went to her flat. I had a key, but it didn't look as if she'd been home. So I went to her parents'. They refused to tell me if she was with them. I went back every day for six months, but they never told me anything."

Esther asked, "And you don't have any idea what her family wanted?"

Donal pressed his lips together as annoyance crinkled his brow and narrowed his eyes. "I have my notions."

"And they are?" Nikolai pressed.

"It doesn't matter. I've looked into them," Donal said.

Esther reached over and put her hand atop Donal's. "You didn't have a Dragon King helping you."

Nikolai watched as Donal's gaze swung to him. Donal sat for a moment before lifting the pint of ale to his mouth and drinking half of it down.

Donal smacked his lips when he finished and set aside the glass. "Eireen despised her family. She rarely spoke of them. No matter how much I asked. I should've pushed harder. Maybe then, she would've told me what was really going on."

"Meaning?" Nikolai pushed.

"She tried to tell me that day, but I wouldn't listen. No private investigators or even the friends I've developed in the Druid and Fae world have been able to find her. I lost the love of my life that day. Not even her family would tell me what happened to her."

"But she loved you. I bet she was protecting you," Nikolai said.

Donal chuckled wryly. "Perhaps. I was ready to meet her family, but she told me it wasn't a good idea. She's the one who pushed for us to run away and get married. I only wanted to make her happy. I didn't care where the vows were spoken as long as she was mine."

"I'm so sorry," Esther said.

"I had six amazing months with her," Donal said as his gaze grew distant with his memories.

Nikolai knew that amount of time would never be enough with Esther. Six lifetimes wouldn't even come close. He wanted eternity with her.

Donal finished off his ale. "I even got the authorities involved in the search for Eireen, but whatever her family told them, they quickly ended their investigation."

"The police didn't give you any answers?" Esther asked.

Donal grunted. "They told me it was a family matter, and that I wasn't family."

Nikolai looked at Esther as she sat back, a frown furrowing her brow. "What are you thinking?"

"That I'd head into MI5 and see what I could find, but now, my first thought is Ryder."

"Ryder?" Donal asked.

Esther grinned. "Like I said. You've got a Dragon King helping now."

"You'd do that? You'd find her for me?" Donal asked.

The hope in Donal's eyes was enough to make Nikolai uneasy. "I've no doubt we'll get answers, but you might no' like what they are."

"I just want to know she's safe," Donal said. "If she wanted to be with me, she'd have come home. I reconciled myself to that fact many years ago. It's not knowing what became of her that haunts me."

Nikolai gave a nod. "I'll see what we can find out."

"And the woman?" Donal said, his chin jerking to Esther's mobile.

Nikolai and Esther exchanged a look. "We doona even know her name. The fact that she looks like Eireen could be what we need to discover who the woman in the drawing is."

"But she hurt you," Donal said to Esther.

Esther sighed and nodded. "This Druid might have nothing to do with Eireen."

"Or, she could," Donal insisted.

Nikolai wanted to get Donal off that topic. "What kind of magic was Eireen able to do?"

"Anything," he answered.

"But she was a *mie*?"

Donal grinned. "There was nothing evil about my Eireen. She was a *mie*. Though *droughs* did attempt to recruit her because of the strength of her magic. She turned them all away."

"Have you ever heard of a TruthSeeker?" Esther asked.

Donal frowned before shaking his head. "I can't say that I have."

Nikolai felt more than saw Esther's disappointment. He was just as frustrated as she at their lack of ability to resolve any of the questions that plagued her. But they were just getting started.

He would search every realm if he had to in order to give Esther the peace she so desperately sought.

"Thank you," Nikolai said to Donal as he gathered his pad and pencil. "We'll be back with any news."

He scooted from the booth and held out his hand for Esther. She took his pencil and jotted down her mobile number on a napkin before pushing it toward Donal.

"In case you want to contact us," Esther said.

She took Nikolai's hand and stood beside him. As they were turning to leave, Donal put his hand on Nikolai's arm.

"You've got a good one," the Irishman said.

Nikolai smiled because he knew more than anyone how special Esther was.

CHAPTER TWENTY-SEVEN

Somewhere in Canada...

With each breath that infused her body, her anger spread and intensified. And the darkness smiled eagerly.

If Rhi weren't so furious, she might actually be afraid of how the darkness responded, but she had other matters to deal with. Like the fekking betrayal of a so-called friend.

From the tree line, she stared at the movie set and all the people milling about as they finished one last take for the day. It was high time to tackle the issue that was Usaeil—or Ubitch as Rhi had begun to call her. The queen had done enough damage. She needed to be removed from power so she couldn't harm the Light anymore.

Phelan was the logical choice to take over since he had royal blood from both his human and Fae sides. Rhi had made sure Usaeil never knew of Phelan. Mainly because Rhi wasn't exactly sure what the queen would do. Call it intuition.

That hesitation had been valid. Thankfully, Rhi listened to her instincts. Otherwise, there was no telling what Usaeil would've done to Phelan.

After all the years the Warrior had suffered being locked away by Deirdre because his blood could heal anything, he'd finally found peace and love in the arms of Aisley, who was a Phoenix. Rhi would never forgive herself if Usaeil killed Phelan.

But the question remained. Would he want to take over as King of the Light? He had a life among the humans, and a family of his own at MacLeod Castle. Not to mention that Aisley was human, even if she were a Phoenix. It was doubtful the Fae would accept her.

Rhi felt more than heard a presence come up behind her. She didn't need to turn around. It was Con. His presence was . . . unique. He'd done a check of the perimeter because, well, that's what Con did.

"You're right," he said. "No other Fae."

She kept her gaze locked on Usaeil. "I once thought she was the most magnificent of us all. Kind and generous. She fooled me completely. I hate that."

"You can no' blame yourself."

She shot him a wry look. "Well, I do."

"The blame lies with Usaeil."

"Exactly. But what happened to her?"

"There are many possibilities. She might've just gotten lonely."

Rhi snorted. "She could've had any Fae she wanted. Everyone kept waiting for her to find a match and have children."

"I can no' imagine Usaeil with kids."

"Me either, if I'm honest." She looked over at Con, who had removed his suit jacket. His charcoal gray dress shirt was open at the collar, and the gold dragon head cufflinks flashed at his wrists. His black pants and shoes were untouched as if even the foliage and dirt knew to keep their distance.

Con turned his head toward her. His black eyes were

fathomless as usual. "What were you thinking about when I walked up?"

"That Phelan should be king."

Con raised a blond brow. "Phelan? You would take him and Aisley away from their world?"

"He's the heir."

"That may be, but he knows nothing of being Fae. He was raised as a human and only learned of his heritage when you sought him out. He's meant to be with the Warriors as host to his primeval god."

Rhi swallowed and looked away. "I realize that, but there's no one else."

"You really think Usaeil will just step aside?"

"Hell, no. She'll fight to the very last, and she'll make it bloody and long, taking anything and anyone near her down in the process."

There was movement as Con faced her. "You plan to battle her."

Rhi gave a slight shake of her head in irritation before looking at him. "You say that as if I have a choice."

"You do."

"I really don't." She turned to him fully and pointed toward the movie set. "She wants me dead. She went to the Dark Palace and asked Taraeth to kill me."

"And we both know Balladyn isna going to let that happen."

Rhi had told Con nothing of Balladyn's plans, but she should've known he would realize what her lover planned to do. "He's protecting me."

"By removing Taraeth and becoming King of the Dark?" Con's face was impassive as he stared at her. "Was it Balladyn's idea for you to go after Usaeil?"

"How dare you," she spat.

His tone was soft, calm. "How dare I what? Ask the obvious question?"

It was his lack of anger that outraged her. As if he'd been thinking about this for some time and had come to a decision, merely waiting until he could put it out there. It was so Con that she wanted to scream.

Instead, she crossed her arms over her chest and blew out a frustrated breath. "Balladyn wants me to rule with him."

"Together?"

She looked at him as if he were a dunce and leaned back against a tree. "That's usually what *together* means. He wants to unite our people."

"What do you want?"

What did she want? No one had asked her that. Everyone made decisions that affected her or pushed her into a corner, giving her few options. She looked to the side where Daire stood veiled. Even the Reapers were part of the problem.

"It's a good idea, but it won't ever happen," she said. "Nor will I give in and become Dark. I've told Balladyn as much. So, to answer your question, no, he didn't send me. He has no idea I'm here."

"With me," Con added.

She glanced at him and nodded. "I'm not keeping it a secret."

"If you didna tell him, you're keeping it from him."

He wasn't right. Or was he? She didn't have the energy or inclination to have this debate. She was too focused on Usaeil, and she wanted to remain that way.

Con let out a sigh. "The Usaeil we're about to confront willna be the queen you once knew."

"I'm prepared for that," Rhi said as she opened her eyes.

"I doona think either of us is ready for it."

That had her turning her head to him. They stared into each other's eyes for a long minute as she tried to discern what he was thinking. "I don't want to kill Usaeil. I want her to be the queen she once was."

"Perhaps that'll happen, but we should be primed for either eventuality."

A male voice yelling, "Cut!" had both of them shifting toward the set. Usaeil walked to her trailer where a note from Con awaited her.

"It's time," he said.

Rhi looked over her shoulder at Daire. The Reaper's earlier words, those warning her to be cautious, returned.

"What is it?" Con asked.

Rhi swung her head to him. "Usaeil will expect me."

"It's a possibility."

"I want the advantage, and right now, she has it."

A frown wrinkled Con's brow. "What do you propose, then?"

"You go. Keep the meeting."

"And you?"

"I'll be there."

"Veiled?"

"Yes."

His forehead furrowed deeper. "What are you no' telling me?"

"I have a . . . friend . . . who can help."

Con's gaze flashed dangerously. "If you tell me it's Balladyn—"

"It's not," she interrupted.

"Then who?"

"A Reaper," Rhi admitted after a brief hesitation.

Con's face went slack. "Cael?"

"No." Now it was her turn to frown. "How do you know Cael?"

"Is it Talin?"

"No," she repeated, getting more agitated. "How do you know them?"

Con shrugged. "They paid a visit to Dreagan recently."

"And you didn't think to tell me?"

He didn't reply, simply met her gaze.

Rhi blew out a breath. There was no use arguing since she hadn't told Con about Daire. "Fine."

"So, another Reaper," Con said. "Are you sure he will keep you veiled from Usaeil?"

"Yes," she replied.

"Then let's go," Con said as he turned on his heel and strode farther into the woods.

Rhi was surprised Con had given in so easily, but she didn't complain. She turned to Daire as he dropped his veil and gave her a harsh look. "Don't," she warned.

"This isn't a good idea. Usaeil is powerful," Daire stated.

"Maybe, but you're more formidable than she is."

Daire ran a hand down his face. "This is a bad idea."

"It's a good one, and you know it. Now, stop stalling."

The Reaper held out his hand. As soon as their palms were joined, they teleported to the meeting place Con had set up. Daire situated them about fifty feet away. No sooner had they arrived, than Usaeil appeared.

The Light Queen looked around, one hand raised, palm out as she used her magic to search the area for anyone veiled. Rhi tensed, waiting for Usaeil's magic to find them.

Beside her, Daire chuckled and leaned down to whisper in her ear, "I didn't think you were worried."

She glared at him, then turned her attention back to Usaeil. After two sweeps of magic, Usaeil dropped her hands and veiled herself.

Holding onto Daire while he was veiled gave Rhi the ability to see Usaeil shrouded with her magic. It wasn't something Rhi could do on her own, and it was an insight into just how powerful the Reapers were.

It wasn't long before Con strode into the small clearing. He stood in the center and merely waited. He didn't call out to Usaeil or look around.

Rhi heard Useail's laughter before she dropped the veil and allowed Con to see her.

"I knew you'd come to me sooner or later."

Con put his hands into his pant's pockets. "I warned you that I doona like ultimatums."

"I don't know what you're talking about."

Rhi wanted to gag as she saw how Usaeil blatantly put her hand on her hip and stuck it out. Con didn't seem to notice her leather-clad legs or the thin, gold sweater that dipped down to show ample cleavage.

"Enough," Con told her. "I've seen the picture."

Usaeil laughed and walked closer to him. She put her hands on his shoulders and smoothed her palms down his chest. "What are you so upset about, lover? Your face couldn't be seen."

"We agreed that our affair would remain secret."

Rhi heard the anger tingeing his words, but Usaeil seemed oblivious to it.

The queen lifted her face to Con and pressed her breasts against him. "You have what so many covet."

He merely stared at her.

She rolled her eyes. "What's wrong with letting the Dragon Kings know of our love?"

"And the Light? Who posted a copy of the picture all over the palace?"

"Oh, stop," she said, laughing. "You act angry, but I know you aren't. You didn't want to tell anyone for fear of the repercussions, so I did it for us."

Con grabbed her wrists and stepped back from her. "I warned you what would happen if you didna listen to my words. We're done."

Usaeil jerked from his grasp. Her smile vanished, replaced by a mask of rage that contorted her face into something hideous and evil. "I started this. I'll be the one to end it."

"Why? Because you're queen?" Con asked. "Well, guess what? I'm the fucking King."

Rhi wanted to clap her hands at Con's little speech, but it was Daire's tightening hold on her that prevented it. She glanced at the Reaper to see his brow puckered as he stared at Usaeil.

"What is it?" Rhi whispered.

Daire jerked his chin to Usaeil. "She's dressed like you."

Rhi blinked and looked from the queen down to herself. She had on her leather pants. Rhi had multiple pairs because she loved them so much. Today, she wore a sheer white shirt with a black tank beneath.

She tried to think back to the last time she'd seen Usaeil wearing leather pants. The queen preferred dresses because she thought them more revealing, and she liked to show off her legs.

"Whatever hold Rhi has over you won't last much longer," Usaeil stated to Con.

"This has nothing to do with Rhi."

"In fact, it does," she stated.

Con crossed his arms over his chest. "Why do you always believe everything is about Rhi?"

"Because it is. But I'm taking care of her. We'll talk again when you can admit our love and are more biddable. Don't worry, lover, I've already picked out my gown for the mating ceremony."

"I'll no' be taking you as my mate, Usaeil. No' now, no' ever," Con declared.

"We'll see about that," she said and vanished.

As soon as she was gone, Daire released Rhi. He remained veiled while she walked to Con. "Well, I think it's safe to say that Usaeil is off her rocker for sure. Now more than ever, I know she needs to be removed as ruler of the Light."

Con looked at her with a troubled gaze. "Her eyes began to change."

"To what?"

"Red."

CHAPTER TWENTY-EIGHT

As soon as Esther and Nikolai walked from The Porter-house, she turned to him and said, "We found a connection to the Druid."

"We doona know that for sure yet," Nikolai cautioned.

She smiled at him. "We found a connection."

They climbed into the SUV, but he didn't start the engine. Instead, he placed his hands on the steering wheel. "If what Donal told us is the truth, we have a thread we can pull and see where it takes us."

"It's going to unravel all around that Druid bitch." Not that Esther was bitter or anything. She just wanted to deliver her own kind of payback.

Nikolai swiveled his head to her. "I hope it does, but there's a chance it willna."

"I know you're trying to stop me from getting my hopes up, but this is the best lead we've had."

"And we've only been at this a few days."

She laughed and looked out her window. "A few days of searching, perhaps. But I've been locked in torment for weeks." Her gaze returned to him. "I need to cling to this thread, to grasp whatever hope I can."

"All right," he said.

Esther took a deep breath and fastened her seat belt. She felt good about the things Donal had told them. But it was the way the Irishman's eyes had widened and the recognition on his face after looking at the drawing of the Druid that sealed the deal for her.

Donal and the Druid were connected. Esther would bet her life on it.

"On to the next pub?" Nikolai asked.

She would rather return to the flat and talk to Ryder, but even if Ryder found out the woman's identity, Esther still didn't know when or how she'd come into contact with the Druid.

"Sure," she replied.

They drove to the next bar and repeated the same steps as the day before. While sitting in the Mercedes as Nikolai drew, Esther kept going over the images he had drawn of the man who'd been following her—the one Donal had confirmed was in The Porterhouse.

As a spy, she'd come to consider everyone a threat and would often check to see if she were being followed. She would use the screen on her mobile, or even the windows of shops to check. She would stop and talk to street performers, which gave her a chance to look around.

There were a thousand different ways she checked to see if she were being trailed, so there was no way she didn't know about the man in the coat.

She turned her mobile over in her hand as she debated whether to call Stuart. She'd already read over the reports that she filed, so she knew there was no mention of a man in a black coat.

Nikolai broke into her thoughts by saying her name. She looked his way, their eyes clashing. The desire that flared in his blue depths made her heart skip a beat. The longer she was with him, the more he filled her life—and the more she craved him.

The need was so intense that it almost seemed unreal. Because, surely, something so tangible and physical didn't exist. Not for her, a mortal who was as ordinary as one could get.

And yet . . . there was no denying it.

Nikolai reached over and took her hand, bringing it to his lips. Holding her gaze, he placed a kiss upon her knuckles. Something so innocent combined with the carnal look in his gaze had her wishing they were back at the flat so she could rip off his shirt again.

"Ready?" he asked.

Was he kidding? After that scorching look, she wasn't sure her legs would hold her. But she nodded anyway. They got out of the vehicle and walked into the pub. When she started toward a table, Nikolai maneuvered her to the back near the restrooms instead.

The lights were dimmed to such a degree that she could barely see, but he didn't allow her to run into anything. She turned to ask him what he was doing when he pushed her against a wall and silenced her with a kiss that curled her toes.

In an instant, her body was enflamed, need clawing through her that only he could quench. Even if she wanted to fight the temptation he offered, she couldn't.

Someone bumped into Nikolai. He tore his mouth from hers and snarled as he looked over his shoulder at the intruder. The growl rumbled through his body, the sound primal and threatening. The man mumbled an apology and stumbled away.

The entire event only fueled her desire. She put her hand on Nikolai's cheek and slowly turned his head back to her. With both hands cupping his handsome face, she looked into his eyes and knew one thing—she *yearned* for him.

"Esther," he mumbled before he seized her lips again.

The kiss was blazing hot as their desire sizzled and crackled between them. She couldn't get close enough to him. The need, the hunger that howled within her for Nikolai was only fanned by his seductive touch.

When he turned and backed her into a room, all she could think about was having him inside her. The door slammed behind them as she fell back against it. They tore at each other's clothes, yanking down pants to get free.

Then she was lifted in his arms, her legs instinctively wrapping around his waist. In the next heartbeat, he was inside her.

They didn't move. With her heart racing and their breaths loud, they looked into each other's eyes. The longer she was with him, the more she felt she'd found her place.

"I've looked for you my entire life," Nikolai whispered.

Her stomach fluttered at his confession.

"This," he said as he pulled out before thrusting deep inside her, causing her to shudder in need. "Has bound us."

There were no more words spoken as their bodies took over. The feel of his hard length filling her again and again soon brought her to the edge of oblivion.

It didn't matter that they were in a bathroom in a pub or that anyone could hear them. All Esther cared about was the man in her arms. Their passion flared, and all too soon, they climaxed.

The cocoon of their passion held them for long minutes after as they remained locked in their embrace. She held him tightly. He was quickly becoming the center of her universe, and that terrified her more than the Druid did.

Because she felt her heart reaching out to him.

He was everything she wanted and more, but she was a spy. And she had family. Could she give all that up for Nikolai?

To be with the man who brought her to unimaginable heights and gave her incredible joy? And children? She hadn't thought much about them, but as Nikolai's mate, she would be giving that up, as well.

She told herself to stop such thoughts because he hadn't spoken of love or asked her to be his mate. Yet, she couldn't cease thinking about being in love. And the reason for that was because she'd already fallen for him.

Hard.

Banging on the door behind her jerked them both out of their thoughts.

"Hold on!" Nikolai yelled through the door as he set her feet on the ground.

They hurried to dress, kissing and laughing between each item. A few minutes later, they walked out of the bathroom and past the glaring man to find a table.

"I'll be back," Nikolai said as he strode out the door.

Esther chided herself because had she been more aware of things, she would've realized that he hadn't brought his pad and pencil with him. But she'd been preoccupied with her thoughts. She walked to the bar and placed a drink order for herself and Nikolai. The bartender glanced at her as he began pouring a pint.

He set the glass before her and reached for the Scotch when he said, "I didn't think I'd ever see you back in here again."

Esther froze, her gaze jerking to him. "I'm sorry, what?"

"You don't remember?" he asked as he replaced the bottle and pushed the tumbler of whisky toward her.

She gave a shake of her head as she saw Nikolai return out of the corner of her eye. In moments, he was beside her. Esther kept her gaze on the bartender. "When was this?"

"I don't know," he said with a shrug.

She leaned forward and caught his gaze as he turned away. "Try."

"It was the end of December."

Six weeks earlier. Esther motioned the guy closer. "I don't remember the incident. Can you refresh my memory?"

The bartender glanced at Nikolai with narrowed eyes before he swallowed, his Adam's apple bobbing in his narrow throat. "Yeah. Sure. There was this man who kept staring at you. For a while, you ignored it, but then you walked up to him and started talking."

"What did he look like?" Nikolai asked.

The bartender scrunched up his angular face as he shrugged. "He didn't look as if he belonged here. He was dressed too fancy, and he wouldn't remove his coat."

"What color was it?" Esther asked.

"Black. Long."

She and Nikolai exchanged a look. Then she returned her gaze to the bartender. "Do you know what I said to him?"

"No," the bartender replied. "But he wasn't happy with whatever it was. He tried to get away, and I saw you pick his pocket."

Yes, that sounded exactly like something she'd do. "What did I take? His wallet? Or mobile?"

"Mobile."

"Then what happened?" Nikolai pressed.

The bartender pointed to a back corner. "There was a woman who had been here for a few hours. She kept to herself despite the men trying their luck with her. But as soon as you walked in," he said with a nod to Esther, "she watched everything you did."

Esther felt her heart jump with excitement. "What did she look like?"

"She was gorgeous," the man said. "Long, black hair and the most amazing skin."

Esther took out her mobile and showed the bartender the picture she'd shown Donal. "Like this?"

The bartender leaned down on his elbows and smiled as he looked at the drawing of the Druid. "Exactly like that. She has a face no man can forget."

"Anything else you remember about her?" Nikolai asked.

The bartender wouldn't stop looking at the picture until Esther put her mobile away. Then he blinked and cleared his throat as his gaze slid to Nikolai.

Nikolai raised an auburn brow and waited.

"She paid with cash, so I never got a name," he admitted. "She didn't speak except to ask for whisky. Irish whisky."

Esther was finding it difficult to keep her smile hidden. Donal was Irish, as was Eireen. It wasn't coincidence that the Druid had ordered Irish whisky.

"What happened after I stole the man's phone?" Esther asked.

The bartender straightened and grabbed a towel that he began rubbing along the bar, his gaze lowered as if he were suddenly nervous. "She approached you."

Esther wasn't in the mood to dig for answers, especially when he'd been so forthcoming with replies before. "And?"

The bartender flicked the towel on his shoulder. "She came up behind you and put her hands on your head."

Esther's skin began to tingle as the image filled her mind.

"Did you hear what she said?" Nikolai asked.

"She whispered." The bartender's gaze skated around

the bar as if looking for the Druid. "After she spoke, she took the mobile from your hand and walked out."

Esther licked her lips. "What did I do?"

"You returned to your table where you picked a fight with the waitress and broke two chairs."

She was only vaguely aware of Nikolai speaking to the bartender and money being exchanged before he took her arm and led her out of the pub. After he'd opened the SUV door and helped her inside, he pulled her against him and held her.

Esther closed her eyes, letting him comfort her.

"We found where you first met the Druid," he whispered. "It's another thread to pull."

She opened her eyes and looked up at him. "We're going to yank this one."

Nikolai smiled and nodded. "Aye. We are."

CHAPTER TWENTY-NINE

Despite his dragon magic and the fact that he was a King, Nikolai was powerless to help Esther. And it infuriated him.

After discovering exactly when and where she'd encountered the Druid, he returned them to the flat. She was busy mapping out her location based on his drawings and what memories those sketches jarred.

It wasn't much to go on, but she needed to occupy her mind. Which is just where Nikolai wanted her while he spoke with Ryder. Before he got the chance to open his mental link, he heard ringing coming from his duffel.

He glanced at Esther, but she was too absorbed in her work to hear anything. He walked to his bag and unzipped it to find his mobile and Ryder's name on the screen. Nikolai accepted the call and put the phone to his ear.

"Aye?" he answered.

"We need to talk," Ryder said.

Nikolai frowned, wondering why Ryder would use a human device to communicate. Not to mention the fact that he was on speaker. "About?"

"My sister," replied an angry male voice in a British accent.

Nikolai had known it would only be a matter of time before Henry discovered what was going on, but he'd hoped it would be later rather than sooner.

Ryder hurried to say, "Before you say anything, Nikolai, Henry came to me."

"What happened?" Nikolai asked.

There was a sigh, and then Henry said, "A dream."

"What kind of dream?" Nikolai pressed.

"I was searching through some of Esther's belongings, hoping I might find something to help her recall her lost memories. I didn't expect to discover anything."

Nikolai looked at Esther. "But you did."

"A small notebook. It was folded within a shirt."

"What was in the notebook?"

Henry hesitated, the silence lengthening before he replied, "One word, written over and over again."

Nikolai had a suspicion he knew what it was, but still he asked, "What was the word?"

"TruthSeeker."

"Not two separate words?" Nikolai queried.

It was Ryder who said, "Just one word. And that changed everything."

"How?" Nikolai hated having to pry the information out of them. Why couldn't they just tell him?

Henry's voice grew louder as if he'd moved closer to the mobile. "Reading that word triggered something. In my dream, Esther and I stood together. She looked at me and said, 'TruthSeeker.' And I replied, 'Justice-Bringer.' As odd as that was, it wasn't what woke me in a cold sweat."

"What did?" Nikolai was beginning to think that he should return to Dreagan immediately. Whatever was going on with Esther and Henry, being away from the safe haven of Dreagan wasn't a good idea with all the enemies the Dragon Kings had.

"We were chasing the Druid."

Henry's words were like a punch to the gut. Nikolai swallowed. "That brought you to Ryder."

"I told him everything," Ryder replied.

"Why doesn't Esther want me to know any of this?" Henry demanded.

Nikolai propped his back against the foyer wall as he watched Esther lean over the coffee table as her gaze moved from one paper to another. "She wanted to figure things out herself first."

"Well," Ryder said. "When Henry showed me the notebook, I revised my search. All this time, I had been putting TruthSeeker as two words. When I amended the search, I found something."

"A link to the Druids?" Nikolai asked hopefully.

There was a bang as if Ryder slammed his hand on one of the tables in the computer room. "Precisely. And Isla was right. That line of Druids was wiped from existence."

"Then why does my sister believe she's the Truth-Seeker, and why am I dreaming about being the Justice-Bringer?" Henry asked.

Ryder gave a loud sigh. "I'm working that out."

"Well, you two were no' the only ones to learn something," Nikolai said. "The coasters led us to The Porterhouse, where we encountered Donal Cleary, the owner."

As he spoke, Nikolai heard Ryder typing. A second later, Ryder said, "Donal Cleary from Dublin. He owns several pubs in Ireland as well as London. He's unmarried with no children."

No doubt there were more facts, but they could wait. Nikolai continued, "There were Druids as well as Fae in the pub. Donal, it seems, has knowledge of the supernatural beings in this realm, including us. He uses information from his ancestors in the way of carvings throughout the establishment to keep the humans from falling under the power of the Fae."

"That's a dose of information," Ryder said.

"I'm no' finished. We spoke with Donal at length. He remembered Esther. In my drawings, there is always a man following her. Donal confirmed it, but he said it appeared as if Esther knew about it when she was there."

Henry interrupted then. "If I'm on a mission and know I'm being trailed, I'll sometimes lead them on a merry chase to see if I can get information. Esther could've been doing the same thing."

"I believe she was," Nikolai said. "I'll get to that in a moment. Esther showed Donal a picture of the sketch I did of the Druid. Donal said she looked like a woman he'd been in love with."

There was a smile in Ryder's voice as he said, "Well, now. I like this. Give me something to search, Nikki."

Nikolai grimaced at the nickname but ignored it. "Donal said the woman's name was Eireen. She was a Druid but had been hiding it from her family. She and Donal intended to run away together, but her family had other ideas for her. One day, Eireen's sisters came for her, and Donal never saw her again. He searched himself, as well as contacted the authorities. He also hired a private investigator, but no trace of her was ever found."

"If the Druid looks like this Eireen, then they're most likely related," Henry said.

"I'm doing a search," Ryder mumbled.

Nikolai then moved on to the next story. He relayed the incident at the pub with the bartender and everything the mortal had imparted about the Druid and her encounter with Esther.

There was a long stretch of silence before Henry erupted with a barrage of curses. Nikolai understood his exasperation and anger because he felt the emotions, as well.

"How is Esther?" Ryder asked.

Nikolai hadn't taken his gaze from her. "She's strong. She'll get through this and find the answers."

"It feels like all we're getting is just enough to bring a deluge of additional questions," Henry said.

Nikolai pinched the bridge of his nose with his thumb and forefinger as he briefly closed his eyes. "Aye."

"You should bring her back," Henry declared.

Before Nikolai could reply, Ryder said, "Esther needs to be where the answers are. Her going from pub to pub is what has given her—and us—these clues. Bringing her back to Dreagan will get us nothing."

"You can find the answers right here, doing all the tricks you do on the computers," Henry argued.

Nikolai understood where Henry was coming from. Henry wanted to protect his sister, and right now, he felt helpless. And that was clouding his judgment.

"We need to find the Druid's name," Nikolai said. "Ryder—"

"Already looking for Eireen," he interrupted. "It would make things go quicker if I had her surname, but I'll find her. As soon as I know anything, I'll contact you."

Nikolai blew out a breath. "Henry, about your parents. Is there any way you and Esther are adopted?"

"None," he replied. "I'll get you papers to prove it."

A moment later, the sound of a door slamming echoed through the connection. Ryder blew out a loud breath. "I doona know what to think about all of this."

"You're no' the only one."

"How are Esther and Henry the TruthSeeker and JusticeBringer?"

If only Nikolai had the answer. "Henry intends to bring you birth certificates, but we both know those can be forged."

"Doona worry. Kinsey is looking into that. I've got her set up elsewhere. She's digging deep into the Norths, as well. If there's anything to find, Kinsey will uncover it."

"Ryder, I need your skills on this. I realize you're still looking for Ulrik as well as Mikkel, but I need to help Esther. She's . . . my mate."

"I'll be damned," Ryder said, a grin in his voice. "I'm happy for you, brother."

"I'll rejoice once she gets her memories returned, and we discover everything we can about this TruthSeeker."

"You know I willna let you down. I'll find what we seek," Ryder promised.

Nikolai ended the call and tossed the mobile into his bag. He kept coming back to Esther's and Henry's connection to the Druids. If they had magic, there was a chance that it had been bound. But with the dream Esther had about E2, something should've manifested by now.

He wished he could talk to the Ancients himself and question them to see if the titles Esther and Henry claimed were for Druids only. The designations had connections to magic, but when it came to that, things had a way of changing and evolving to fit the current atmosphere.

But it was all speculation on his part. He wouldn't share any of this with Esther until he had more information, and it wasn't as if the Ancients would talk to him. He wasn't a Druid. Hell, they didn't even talk to all the Druids, only a select few.

If only he could give Esther some kind of relief. And then he realized he could. It was a chance—a huge one. But he was willing to take it.

Nikolai opened his mental link and said, *"Ulrik. I know you can hear me. I need your help."*

He waited for Ulrik to reply. When minutes ticked by with no word, Nikolai tried again. *"The woman I've claimed as my mate is suffering, and I believe you have the means to aid her. I've no right to ask for your help, but I am."*

Once more, there was silence.

Nikolai had known what would probably happen, but he had to try. No matter how close he and Ulrik were, when it counted the most, he'd let his friend down. Now, when he needed Ulrik, he was learning just how deep the ripples of such a blow could go.

"Hungry?" Nikolai asked Esther.

She gave a nod but said nothing. He walked from the flat to find some food. Three blocks away was a pub with the amazing fish and chips he'd been craving. He was returning to Esther with the bag of food in hand and his mind circling the new facts he'd uncovered when his gaze locked on a figure leaning against the side of a building.

Nikolai halted, unsure if he was seeing what he wanted to see or what was actually there. He took a step forward as the man pushed away and came to stand in the light of the streetlamp.

Nikolai smiled. "Ulrik."

CHAPTER THIRTY

The bond that had once existed between him and Ulrik was strong and resilient. Nikolai still considered him a brother, but he couldn't even begin to understand what Ulrik felt.

Nikolai looked the King of Silvers over. They might've banished him from Dreagan, but he never doubted that Ulrik would make his way in the human world. By the handmade, designer, navy suit Ulrik wore, Nikolai had been right.

"It's good to see you."

Ulrik silently regarded him.

Nikolai wished he didn't see the wariness in his friend's gold eyes, but it was to be expected. "Whether you came to help me or no', I owe you an apology. I didna stand with you when you needed me. As your friend, I should have."

"I raised you to think for yourself," Ulrik stated in a soft voice. "I told you to make your own decisions and to follow your heart. You did that. You honored your vow to the mortals."

"I should've been with you."

"Why do you feel guilt?" Ulrik asked, a black brow raised.

For a brief instant, Nikolai felt as if he were a young dragon again, getting a life lesson from the King of Silvers. "You gave me a home, you taught me everything I know."

"You made your decision long ago. Do you regret standing with Con?"

"I regret no' standing with you."

"You can no' have it both ways."

It was a fact that Nikolai knew well. He'd made the right decision remaining with Con, but he still felt great remorse for abandoning Ulrik.

"Did you think an apology would grant you my forgiveness?" Ulrik asked.

Nikolai gave a shake of his head. "I've heard from the others how deeply your hatred runs for us. I doona assume, or expect, your absolution."

"What do you mean you've heard?"

"I've been asleep since you were banished. I woke briefly during the Fae Wars, but then returned to my mountain."

Ulrik took a step closer. His voice was pitched low as he asked, "Why?"

"Guilt, as you said. You were like a father and a brother to me. I let you walk away from Dreagan alone. I couldna change what had been done, or bear to see you no' among us where you belonged."

Ulrik put his hands into his pant's pockets and glanced up at the sky. "We must all live with the decisions we make."

When Ulrik turned on his heel and began to walk away, Nikolai said, "I know the Ulrik who saved a frightened young hatchling is still within you. The fact you've survived and come out on top all these centuries later proves how strong you are. How great we all knew you were."

Ulrik halted but didn't turn around.

Nikolai took a few steps toward him. "Sebastian believes you're blameless in the treachery that has befallen the Kings and our mates. Bast thinks the fault lies with Mikkel—your uncle."

Still, Ulrik didn't move, but he didn't walk away either. Nikolai used that to his advantage.

"I think Sebastian and his mate, Gianna, encountered Mikkel in Venice because they have memories missing. The same thing happened to Ryder's mate, Kinsey, and my mate, Esther. We know the party responsible is a Druid. A woman with immense power who no' only wiped Sebastian's memories but also got into Esther's mind and controlled her."

"And you believe I know this Druid?" Ulrik asked as he turned his head to the side.

Nikolai took another step closer. "I can no' say for certain whether you're working alongside Mikkel or no', but either way, I recall the tactician you were. The first rule you taught me was that I had to know my enemy better than I knew myself."

Ulrik slowly turned and faced him. "The way you speak, you make it sound as if Mikkel is my enemy."

"Even if you're working with him, you make sure to know everything." Nikolai didn't point out that Ulrik all but admitted that Mikkel was, in fact, real. "Do you know the Druid?"

"If I do, what makes you think I'll help you?"

"I doona expect you to deliver the Druid to me. I'll find her myself, but I was hoping you'd impart anything you can about her. She . . . unleashed . . . something within Esther. And the missing days are taking a toll on her because she doesna know what she did."

Ulrik's shoulders lifted as he inhaled deeply and then released the breath. "You freely share such information when you know I could use it against you."

"You willna."

At this, Ulrik smiled, though it lacked humor. "Doona be a fool."

"I'm no' talking to Ulrik, the dragon intent on killing us all. I'm talking to the Dragon King who was father, brother, and sometimes even mother to me."

Ulrik looked away. "Then, as the father and brother I once was, heed my next words." His gold eyes swung back to Nikolai. "Protect your Esther with everything you are. The Druid isna one to be messed with. She's no friend of mine, and in fact, she intends to kill me."

Nikolai was so shocked at the last part that he jerked as if kicked. "A Druid believes she can kill a Dragon King? Is she daft?"

"She's verra powerful. So much so, that I'm no' entirely sure she can no' do as she claims."

"Shite."

Ulrik's lips twitched as he gave a snort.

Nikolai's mind raced with different possibilities. Ulrik knew the Druid, but he wouldn't give up information easily. There had to be a trade of some kind. And if the Druid were after Ulrik, the likely reason was because she worked with Mikkel.

"What if you had something to tempt the Druid?" Nikolai asked.

Ulrik's gaze narrowed. "And you want me to use whatever it is you have. Why?"

"I need the Druid. She's the only one who can remove the last of her magic from Esther's mind so she can have her memories back. I'll give you the information so the Druid will take her attention off you. By helping her, you will no longer be a threat."

"And what do you want in return?"

"Tell me where I can find her."

Ulrik cocked his head to the side. "You would trust me when none of the others do?"

"I would."

"Then you're twice the fool."

Nikolai stepped in front of Ulrik before he could turn away. "Are you no' curious about what Bast discovered? Or do you already know?" When Ulrik just blinked at Nikolai, the truth of it was clear. "You know. Why have you no' gone to Con?"

"I've admitted nothing, nor will I."

"Help me help you. If you turn the Druid away from Mikkel to your side, we can regain everyone's memories. You willna have to tell Con anything. Sebastian will."

"Or perhaps he'll tell Con that there is no one named Mikkel," Ulrik said.

Nikolai gave a shake of his head. "Stop acting as if you doona care."

"It's no' acting. I can no' help you."

Still, Nikolai couldn't let him leave without gaining something, but there was still hope within him that Ulrik would do the right thing. So, he took a chance.

"There is a man in London who knew a woman who looked exactly like the Druid. We think it could be her mother. And I believe the man is the Druid's father. Since he only learned of her today, I doubt she knows of him."

Ulrik said nothing as he turned and walked away until the shadows took him and then vanished. Nikolai wasn't at all shocked at Ulrik's new trick. He always knew how to use things to his advantage. Somehow, Ulrik had learned how to teleport.

Which meant Ulrik could get into Dreagan at any time. Nikolai had to wonder why he hadn't gone there already to challenge Con.

There was no doubt in his mind that Ulrik had been to Dreagan, but it wasn't for Con. It was for the Silvers. No King would be able to stay away from their dragons no matter what barriers were put in place to stop him. Nikolai would do almost anything to see his Ivories again.

With the food growing cold, he returned to the flat. He found Esther still engrossed in the papers and the map. He laid out the food, and while doing so, opened his mental link and said Con's name.

A few moments later, Con said, "*Nikolai?*"

"*I spoke with Ulrik.*"

"*When? Where?*" Con demanded.

"*Just a few minutes ago, here in London.*"

"*Did he threaten you or Esther?*"

Nikolai sighed. He should've known Con would think such a thing. "*Nay, he didna. I called for him. I had a suspicion he knew the Druid, so I was hoping he'd tell me where to find her.*"

"*And did he?*"

"*Nay.*"

"*Nikolai,*" Con said, "*I know Ulrik was like a father to you, but—*"

"*Doona say it,*" Nikolai stated. "*Bast thought Mikkel was involved. After telling you he had information on Mikkel, Sebastian and Gianna lost their memories about him.*"

"*You can no' even recall if Ulrik had an uncle with such a name.*" A shred of anger could be heard in Con's words.

"*You can no' say for certain either, and you knew him longer than I.*"

"*I didna live with him.*"

"*Ulrik's family kept their distance,*" Nikolai argued. "*But talking to Ulrik, he didna deny anything about Mikkel.*"

Con blew out a breath. *"Did he confirm it?"*

"He didna, but you didna see his face or hear his voice."

"We can argue this for eternity. Bottom line—does he indeed know the Druid?"

"He does."

Con gave a snort. *"Just as I figured."*

"She intends to kill him."

There was a long stretch of silence before Con said, *"That isna possible."*

"Ulrik isna taking any chances. So, if she wants to kill him, it means she's no' working with him, but with Mikkel."

"It's useful information, but it doesna help you."

"Perhaps," Nikolai said. *"I told him about Donal. If the human didna know about the Druid until today, most likely she doesna know about him. Ulrik can use that to his advantage."*

Con said, *"You always did believe the verra best of him. I hope you're right, and this works. If no', then you just gave away something we could've used."*

"One more thing. Ulrik can teleport."

"Food," Esther said as she rose from the sofa and joined him at the table.

Nikolai severed the link and pulled out a chair for her. "Sit. I've something to tell you. I saw Ulrik."

CHAPTER THIRTY-ONE

Esther was in shock. No longer did she taste the delicious food. Her mind went blank as she listened to Nikolai speak of his encounter with Ulrik.

She didn't ask Nikolai why he'd contacted his old friend. The reason was clear, even if it did astonish her. Because with every word, every touch, every action, Nikolai was telling her of his feelings.

He hadn't spoken the actual words, but he didn't have to when his actions declared them for him.

"Why are you looking at me like that?" he asked.

She wiped her lips and set aside the napkin. "You're amazing. You didn't have to talk to Ulrik for me."

"Aye, I did. There was a way I could help, and I did."

Reaching across the table, she took his hand in hers. "That was the first time you spoke with Ulrik in thousands of years. Did it go as you planned?"

"I still see the man he used to be, but I also see what he's turned into."

"And that is?"

"It's like he's encased himself in armor and willna let

anyone in. He always wore a smile before, he didna grin once this time."

She shrugged one shoulder. "In his mind, he feels betrayed by those he thought would always stand with him. As you said, he was driven from his home and had no choice but to live among us mortals—who he deeply detests. Of course, he's changed. I live among my own kind, and even I put up armor."

"He willna help us."

"It's enough that you tried." She rose and moved to sit on his lap. She rested her cheek against his head. "So much could've gone wrong."

Nikolai's arms wrapped around her. "He wouldna harm me."

"You truly believe that after everything he's done to the other Kings?"

"I still believe Mikkel was responsible, but I know Ulrik well enough to know that he isna completely innocent. Despite all of that, aye, I knew he wouldna do anything to me. I was sure of it once I looked into his eyes."

She kissed his temple and ran her fingers through the cool strands of his auburn hair. "Regardless that he isn't going to help, I'm glad you got to talk to him. You needed that closure. He doesn't hold a grudge against you, does he?"

"He didna seem to."

"Then hold onto that," she said as she turned his head to look into his eyes.

One of his hands splayed along her back. "I'd rather hold onto you."

"You say that when you don't know what I've done. Those missing days—"

"Doona matter to me," he interjected. "It wasna you. It was the Druid controlling you."

"What if I killed someone?"

One side of his mouth lifted in a grin. "It wasna you."

"I've killed," she said.

His gaze lowered. Then he took her hand from his chest and brought it to his lips where he kissed her fingers as he looked at her. "So have I. Does that change how you see me?"

"No," she answered honestly.

He moved his hand so their palms were against each other, then he linked their fingers. "Nor does it change how I see you."

"You see deeper into my life than anyone ever has, or ever will, for that matter."

"Does that bother you?"

She looked at their bound hands. "At first, I was afraid you'd see the worst parts of me. Then I realized that, of course, you did, but you still looked at me the same."

"I always will."

Her gaze slid back to his baby blue eyes. "You said once that you don't feel as if you belong at Dreagan. That was because you carried guilt for not siding with Ulrik, and then because you didn't believe he was culpable of the crimes he was accused of."

"I never said the last part."

She smiled at his frown. "I'm an MI5 agent. I'm trained to read people. Even Dragon Kings. I'm right, aren't I?"

"Aye," he whispered.

"What I don't think you comprehend is that every Dragon King feels some of what you carry. They all mourn Ulrik's absence—Con most of all. If you shoulder such remorse for Ulrik, can you imagine what Con bears?"

Nikolai tightened his fingers on her hand as the lines smoothed away on his brow. "I was so wrapped up in myself, I didna think of the others. I wish you'd have mentioned this sooner."

"My point in all of this is that you do belong at Dreagan. You felt disconnected because of regret about Ulrik."

He pulled her toward him and pressed his mouth to hers. With one brush of their lips, a fire erupted between them. The kiss became uninhibited, hedonistic. She gasped when he lifted her and moved her so that she straddled him. She wantonly ground herself against his arousal.

When his hands cupped her breasts and massaged them, she dropped her head and arched her back. Skilled fingers played her body to perfection.

She didn't care when he grabbed the collar of her sweater and ripped it down the middle. Her bra soon followed. The moment the cool air brushed against her heated skin, her breasts swelled.

"I can no' get enough of you," Nikolai said before his lips closed over a hardened nipple.

Suddenly, his head jerked up.

Esther was instantly on alert. "What is it?"

"I'm no' sure." He gently set her on her feet and rose to walk to the window.

She wrapped her ripped sweater around her to cover her nakedness. In the heat of the moment, she hadn't thought about the blinds being open, allowing anyone to see inside.

"I feel magic," Nikolai said.

Esther wanted to recoil at the thought. "The Druid?"

"A Druid." He swiveled his head to her. "You might want to put on a new shirt. We're about to have company."

She raised her brows but didn't question him as she raced upstairs. Her feet hadn't hit the landing before there was a knock at the door. While she rummaged through her bag, she heard the voices below and stilled. That's when she recognized who had come. Esther yanked off her ruined sweater and bra and tugged on a sweatshirt, forgoing the bra this time.

She raced downstairs, a smile on her face when she saw Isla. But the grin faded when the Druid looked at her. The petite woman had her black hair pulled up in some intricate braid.

"Esther," Isla said.

Her gaze moved to Nikolai, who stood with Hayden and another pair. The man was tall with deep blue eyes and dark blond hair. He had his arm around a woman with curly, dark auburn hair and gray eyes. But it was the curious way the woman looked at Esther that brought her up short.

"I called her," Nikolai said. "While Ryder was doing his usual tricks, I thought we might learn more if I went to the source."

Esther glanced at Isla, realizing who the other woman was. "The Druids."

Nikolai nodded.

She swallowed, a pit of unease growing in her gut. "And?"

"I should've told you the rest," Nikolai said. "I'd hoped to have answers when I did."

"But we only seem to be gathering more questions," she replied. Esther might be a little miffed that Nikolai had kept something from her, but she knew he'd done it with good intentions. She turned to Isla. "Tell me, please."

Isla motioned to the sofa and chairs where they all took seats. Esther and Nikolai sat on the sofa with Isla, while Hayden stood beside his wife. The Druid and Warrior took the chairs.

Isla then indicated the other couple. "This is Reaghan and her husband, Galen. Reaghan has the ability to tell if someone is lying."

It didn't take a genius to figure out why Reaghan was there. Esther was trying really hard not to get pissed.

"Please don't take offense. It's not that I don't believe you," Isla said. "Once I explain the story, you might understand."

Esther gestured for her to continue. "Do tell."

After a glance at Hayden, Isla began. "When the Druids split into *mies* and *droughs*, it didn't take anyone long to conclude that if left unchecked, the *droughs* could do untold damage. Yet no one wanted to be the one to stand against them. The few *mies* who had the ability, wanted to protect their families."

"Understandable," Esther said.

Isla raised her brows and gave a brief nod. "It is. Luckily, there was a group of *mies* who had an affinity for monitoring other Druids. A brother and sister, together, began what no one else would do. They policed the *droughs*. They were so effective that the Ancients bestowed a great honor upon the Clacher family. Every generation, a brother and sister were born to continue the tradition of containing the *droughs*."

Esther heard every word, but as she did, she also saw it in her mind—as if she'd lived it. Which wasn't possible.

Chills raced along her skin. Esther tried to reach out to hold onto something, and then a strong hand grabbed hers. She didn't need to look to know it was Nikolai. Isla's voice grew quiet as if coming from a great distance.

"The brother and sister duo were soon labeled by the Ancients. The female was the TruthSeeker, and the male the JusticeBringer," Isla continued. "Unfortunately, the Clacher family soon caught the attention of one of the most evil *droughs* ever to walk this earth—Deirdre. I was her prisoner for years, so I know just how malicious she was. When she learned about the siblings, she wiped the entire family out in one afternoon. None escaped her wrath."

Esther drew in a shuddering breath at the foggy memory of a blade narrowly missing her throat. The brush of air as the weapon swooped made her jerk back. When she blinked, the images she saw vanished, replaced by the flat and those inside it. She turned her head to the side and looked at Nikolai, who gave her a nod of encouragement.

"They're all gone then?" Esther said as she returned her attention to Isla.

"Every last one," Isla replied.

Esther licked her dry lips. "Then I can't be the Truth-Seeker."

"That isn't true," Reaghan said as she leaned forward. "The Ancients and magic work in mysterious ways."

Nikolai's hand tightened on hers. Hadn't they just had this conversation? She looked from Reaghan to Isla. "I don't have a shred of magic. I'm not a Druid, nor do I claim to be one."

"We know," Isla said with a comforting smile. "But if the Ancients did appoint a new TruthSeeker, I'd like to know."

"Why wouldn't they use Druids again?" Esther asked.

It was Nikolai who said, "Because there are no' as many of them as before. Many doona even know they're Druids, while others refuse to practice."

"Shall we?" Isla asked.

Esther kept hold of Nikolai as she turned her head to Reaghan. "Yes, let's. I'd like to get an answer to something tonight."

She only hoped it was what she wanted to hear. The problem was, she wasn't sure what she wanted. If she were the TruthSeeker, it put her squarely in the magical world.

That in itself was alarming, but it was also comforting because she had Nikolai.

And if she weren't the TruthSeeker . . . she wasn't sure how she would feel.

CHAPTER THIRTY-TWO

Dark Palace

The time had come. No more planning, no more scheming.

Balladyn strode through the palace. He was focused and single-minded, which is probably why every Fae in his path quickly got out of his way.

As far as he knew, Taraeth hadn't sent anyone to kill Rhi, but it wouldn't surprise Balladyn to learn that Taraeth had done it behind his back.

There was no way the king knew of Balladyn's affair with Rhi, but Taraeth hadn't remained King of the Dark because of luck. He always thought the worst of everyone and ensured that no one ever double-crossed him.

Balladyn thought of Fintan. The infamous Dark Fae who had been Taraeth's personal assassin. Fintan had killed more Fae than any other in their history. He'd been completely loyal to the king, and despite all that, he had been betrayed.

The brief conversation Balladyn had had with Fintan was eye opening. Though Fintan didn't tell him much, the implications were there. Without a doubt, Balladyn knew the white-haired Dark was a Reaper.

And it was no coincidence that Rhi had asked him to do research on the Reapers. She knew about them. Balladyn was certain of that. Did she *know them*? That was the question.

His talk with Fintan had sent Balladyn back to his extensive library and the books that mentioned Fintan. Many speculated that Fintan had merely gone to another realm, but there was one book that cited a betrayal by Taraeth that put Fintan in the Light Queen's clutches.

Usaeil.

"Bitch," Balladyn mumbled.

He wasn't going to make Fintan's mistake. No, Balladyn would be the one to take down Taraeth. But first, he had to get the king out of the palace.

Balladyn reached the double doors to the throne room. The guards gave a nod as he approached. The doors opened of their own accord and shut behind him as he entered the throne room.

He spied Taraeth sitting on the throne with an empty glass in hand and his gaze on the floor. After a moment, he looked up and saw Balladyn.

"Just the Fae I wanted to see."

Balladyn walked to him. "Oh?"

"I know you have a history with Rhi."

Balladyn clasped his hand around his other wrist behind his back so he didn't attack the king right then. "I do."

Taraeth eyed him as he held up his glass. Balladyn ground his teeth together and pivoted to get the decanter of whisky to take to the king. Once Taraeth's glass was filled, the king took a long drink. Balladyn returned to the sideboard and softly set the crystal decanter down with the others.

"But I'm in a hurry to get to her," Taraeth said. "Take me to her. Now."

Balladyn bowed his head and turned on his heel. Taraeth was right behind him as they walked from the throne room to one of the Fae doorways Balladyn had made that would take them to Italy.

As they stepped through, Taraeth looked around the Italian countryside. "Where is she?"

Balladyn walked down the trail to the cottage Rhi had claimed. She'd left it months ago, preferring her island now. Since then, Ulrik had taken the cottage as his. But Ulrik wouldn't be there this time.

When they reached the cottage, Taraeth used his magic to prevent Rhi from escaping. If Rhi had been inside, Balladyn didn't think Taraeth's magic could hold her. That's how powerful she'd become.

Taraeth pointed to the cottage. "Get inside and bring me the Light."

"I thought Usaeil needed to be here."

"I want to see Rhi first for confirmation before I call to the queen."

Balladyn shrugged and made as if to take a step forward. He called to his sword as he did and pivoted at the last moment, thrusting his blade into Taraeth's heart.

The king's eyes widened. Blood dribbled from the corner of his mouth. "No," he muttered.

Balladyn smiled as he withdrew his sword. "How does it feel to be betrayed?"

Taraeth stumbled backward and swayed before dropping to his knees. He was dead before he hit the ground. Seconds later, he was only ash that floated away on the wind.

Balladyn took a deep breath and smiled. The grin turned into a frown when pain lanced through him. He touched his side, his fingers coming away bloody. It was

Rage boiled within him. It had been simn
stewing ever since Usaeil's visit. As difficult
Balladyn had to keep it hidden a while longer.
just his plans at stake, but Ulrik's, as well. And th
was Rhi.

"Your hatred ran deep," Taraeth said. "Howev
was when you thought she'd left you behind on th
tlefield."

Balladyn turned to the king. "That fact hasn't chang

"Usaeil didn't let Rhi return for you."

"Are you trying to dim my loathing of Rhi or Usaei

Taraeth chuckled. "I saw your anger at the discove
of how you ended up here."

"I was loyal to Usaeil, and she betrayed me. Of course,
I was furious," Balladyn stated.

"My thought was to find Rhi and turn her Dark as I
did you, but I don't think Usaeil will settle for that. After
you, she's demanded to be present when we kill Rhi."

Balladyn smiled, his blood pumping with excitement
as everything started to fall into place. "Then it's fortu-
itous that I know where Rhi is."

"And you're just telling me now?" Taraeth bellowed
as he sat up on the throne, the movement causing liquor
to splash over the side of his glass.

"I came to do just that."

"You shouldn't have let me go on like that. You
should've stopped me."

Balladyn bowed his head. "Next time, I will, sire."

Taraeth leaned his head back and drained the whisky.
He tossed Balladyn the glass as he stood. "Where is the
Light Fae? I'd like to get this taken care of so I don't have
another visit from Usaeil anytime soon."

"There's a small house on the Italian coast that I
tracked Rhi to. I gather she spends a lot of time there, so
I don't think she'll be in a rush to leave."

then that his gaze caught the dagger lying in the grass where Taraeth had fallen.

He'd been so intent on Taraeth's death that he hadn't realized the king had a weapon of his own—or that he'd used it to strike a mortal blow. Now that Balladyn knew about the wound, the agony of it consumed him. He pressed his hand against the injury and managed a step and then another.

No! He couldn't die, not after finally killing Taraeth. The throne was his. It was time for a new ruler. His rule. He had to make sure Rhi was safe from Usaeil. No one else could.

"Rhi," he said as his legs buckled.

He fell on his side and rolled onto his back, looking at the bright blue sky above him. How many times had he stared at the clouds with Rhi beside him? Before and after he'd turned Dark.

"Balladyn!"

At the sound of her voice, he felt something fall from his eye and roll down his temple into his hair. A tear. Because only Rhi could make him cry.

She fell to her knees beside him, her face a mask of shock and horror. Her gaze ran over him as she held out her hands, unsure what to do.

When her silver eyes met his, tears were streaming down her face. And, somehow, he found the courage to smile. "Taraeth is dead."

"You're . . . hurt," she said, sniffing.

"I'm dying."

"No," she said, shaking her head. "I refuse to let that happen."

It was out of her control, but he no longer had the strength to tell her that. He felt her hand slip from his, even as he said her name. He wanted her beside him as he breathed his last. Why wasn't she staying?

He fought to keep his eyes open as he searched for her, but soon, that became too much. His eyes closed while his heart bellowed for the only one he'd ever loved—Rhi.

Con heard his name being shouted throughout the manor as he entered the conservatory from the mountain. He recognized the voice and rushed toward Rhi. He found her running down the stairs. As she reached the bottom, she spotted him and came to a stop, breathing heavily.

Her hair was in disarray, and tear streaks ran down her face. It was the blood on her hands and shirt that gave him pause, however.

"Are you wounded?" he demanded.

She looked at him as if she didn't understand his words. Others gathered around them, but she didn't take her eyes from him.

"Con," she whispered.

This was Rhi unlike he'd ever seen her before, and frankly, he wasn't sure what to make of it.

A tear rolled down her face. "I need your help."

"Are you wounded?" he asked again, his tone deeper as he took a tentative step toward her, ready to heal her if necessary.

"It's not me."

At least there was that. Whatever brought her to him, it was important. The past and their animosity had been put on hold, though neither had spoken of it. And now wasn't the time. With enemies at every turn, Con wasn't going to push away an ally.

He gave a nod and held out his hand. She didn't hesitate to take it and teleport them away.

In the next instant, Con found himself on a mountain, looking down at a lake. It took him but a moment to realize he was in Italy. He saw Rhi rush to someone lying on the ground and watched her give the body a shake. Con spotted a dagger and the ash that remained nearby.

By the look of the small section of grass disturbed, there hadn't been a fight. Whatever happened, it had been quick. He lifted his gaze to the prone form and realized what had happened—Balladyn had killed Taraeth.

And the new King of the Dark now lay at Death's door.

Con turned toward Rhi as she looked at him over her shoulder.

"Please," she beseeched him.

He walked to her to see Balladyn clinging to life. The Dark wasn't a friend of the Dragon Kings, but he meant something to Rhi. There was no way Con could refuse her. Not now, especially not when it was Balladyn.

Rhi cried silent tears as her large silver eyes watched him. Con went down on his haunches and touched Balladyn's arm. Magic charged through Con and transferred into the Fae, healing the Dark's wound.

It took longer and more magic than Con had ever used on anyone—except for Rhi.

Con stood when he finished, staring down at Rhi, who clasped Balladyn's hand with her own. Had he been wrong to think that Rhi's affair with the Dark was fleeting? Because it was obvious she cared for the new King of the Dark.

It was even possible that she . . . loved . . . Balladyn.

Con began to turn away when Rhi was suddenly before him. She threw her arms around his neck and hugged him. He stood there for several seconds before slowly lifting his hands to place them on her back.

"Thank you," she whispered. She leaned back to look into his face. "I know you didn't want to do that."

"We doona always get the things we want most. I could give you this, however."

Her smile was sad as she teleported him back to his office at Dreagan. And then she was gone.

Con sighed. Then he walked to his desk and sat.

CHAPTER THIRTY-THREE

TruthSeeker. Was it ironic that while she claimed to be something, she was also hunting the truth within herself? Esther was fairly certain the answer was yes.

She looked into Reaghan's gray eyes and released her hold on Nikolai as the Druid held out both of her hands, palms up. Esther swallowed as she scooted to the edge of the cushion and placed her hands atop the Druid's.

Reaghan's lips lifted in a comforting smile. "Long, long ago, my magic was bound in order to keep the location of Deirdre's sister a secret. You see, she was the only one who could kill Deirdre."

"The same Deirdre who wiped out the Clacher Druids?" Esther asked.

Reaghan nodded. "The very one. Deirdre was ruthless in taking what she wanted, and there were times I wondered if we'd ever be free of her. Then Galen walked into my life. My magic was returned, and with it, my ability to see if someone is lying."

"Ask your questions. I would know the truth, as well."

Reaghan's gaze never wavered. "What is your name?"

"Esther Marie North."

"Truth," Reaghan said. "Do you have a brother?"

"Yes, Henry."

"Truth."

Esther didn't think she'd want to take Reaghan's place as a human lie detector. Sometimes, it was better not to know if someone were being dishonest.

"Do you have magic?" Reaghan asked.

"No."

"Truth. Do you want magic?"

"If it would allow me to help fight against the Dark Fae, yes."

Reaghan grinned. "Truth. Are you the TruthSeeker?"

"Yes." The answer was past Esther's lips before she even had time to consider it.

Suddenly, Reaghan released her hands and sat back. The Druid's brow was furrowed as she stared. Esther rose to her feet, as did Isla.

"Reaghan," Nikolai said.

She reached out a hand that shook slightly and touched Esther before repeating, "Are you the TruthSeeker?"

"Yes," Esther replied.

Reaghan's gaze slid to Isla. "Truth."

"How?" Galen asked.

Isla shrugged as she looked at Esther. "Perhaps the Ancients will tell us. Maybe Dani will glean some knowledge as our Seer."

"What does this mean for Esther?" Nikolai asked, concern in his voice.

Reaghan shrugged and dropped her hand. "I wish I had the answer."

Esther wasn't going to accept things quite so easily. She turned to Isla. "You said the last TruthSeeker and JusticeBringer were Druids. How can I be a part of that history and not be a Druid?"

"I don't know," Isla said with a shake of her head.

"Do you think the Druid put something in my mind to make me believe this? If I believe it, wouldn't it come out as truth?" she asked and swung her gaze to Reaghan.

Reaghan said, "It doesn't work that way. Whether you believe something or not, I can detect the lie. It goes beyond your words or your beliefs, to the very core of who you are."

"Exactly. And if the Druid made me believe, to the very core of my soul, that I'm the TruthSeeker, that could fool even you. Right?"

Reaghan frowned and glanced at Isla. "That's possible."

"Then that's your answer." Esther was disappointed, but she would keep that to herself until later. "Druids should be the TruthSeeker and JusticeBringer."

"Then why did Henry have a dream about him being the JusticeBringer?" Nikolai asked.

Isla's brows rose high on her forehead. "Did he?"

"Perhaps the Druid got to him, as well," Esther said.

Hayden crossed his arms over his chest as his black eyes locked on Esther. "Or it could be that you and your brother are the verra things you now want to deny."

"This comes back to something very vital. I don't have magic. Henry doesn't have magic. How can we police Druids when we have nothing to fight them with?" Esther demanded.

Nikolai nodded at the coffee table. "Look what you've been occupied with for the past few hours."

"My lost time," she said.

One side of his mouth lifted in a grin. "Seeking the truth. What did you do in MI5?"

"I hunted down threats to our country."

"And?"

She looked into his blue eyes for a long moment. "I dug into people's lives."

"Seeking?" he urged.

"The truth of their misdeeds."

"TruthSeeker," he said.

Esther ran her hands down her face as she sighed. "I'll admit, I still believe I'm the TruthSeeker. It seems so obvious to me."

"Then why are you fighting it?" Galen asked.

She glanced at the Warrior with his deep blue eyes that were locked on her. "Because the Druid fucked with my mind already. I don't know what's real anymore, but there is one thing I do know for certain, and that's that I don't have magic."

"What if you are the TruthSeeker?" Isla asked.

Esther shrugged and looked around the room. "I don't know."

"I do," Nikolai said.

She turned her head to him and reached for his hand. Their fingers curled around each other's. "I wanted answers."

"We need the Druid," Isla said.

Nikolai pulled Esther closer to him. "I believe the Druid has roots in Ireland."

"We've not looked there," Reaghan said to Isla.

Isla shrugged. "I think we'd better start."

"I'm sure we'll be back," Hayden said as he dropped his arms to his sides when Isla walked to him.

Esther stayed beside Nikolai as they followed the Warriors and Druids to the front door. With a wave, they were gone. Nikolai closed the door and then turned to wrap his arms around her. She rested her head against his chest and took comfort in the strength he gave her. The thought of going through all of this without him made her sick.

"Henry really had such a dream?"

Nikolai rubbed a hand over her back as he said, "Aye."

"That's too coincidental."

"No' if it's a fact."

"We don't have magic."

He took her hand and walked her to the sofa where they sat. Reclining, he rested one arm along the back of the couch. "If magic wasna involved, would you still fight the idea of being the TruthSeeker?"

"Probably not."

"Because?" he prompted.

She shrugged as she comprehended what he was doing. Esther faced him and said, "It's what I've always done."

"What has called to you from the verra beginning, aye?"

"Right."

"Both you and Henry."

She nodded slowly.

"If you believe that you could be the TruthSeeker, then you should also contemplate the rest."

Esther's stomach tightened painfully. "You're referring to the fact that the Norths might not be my parents."

"I am."

"That would mean that someone went to great lengths to keep such information from Henry and me."

Nikolai shook his head. "If it's the truth, then it means someone went to great trouble to *hide* you and Henry. Why?"

"I've been so wrapped up in the magic part that I've not thought about that angle." And it was even scarier than being without magic. "You're right. I need to think about it. Why would someone do that?"

An auburn brow rose on his forehead. "I'd like to know *who* did it."

"And where are our real parents?"

"Why could they no' keep you?"

She popped her knuckles as her mind filled with doubt. "Were Henry and I ever supposed to find out?"

"Is there a connection to the Clacher Druids?"

Esther shook her head. "More questions. I'm drowning in them."

"Then hold onto me."

She didn't need to be told twice. She scooted closer to him and sighed when he wrapped an arm around her, holding her firmly. "We could spend weeks here in London trying to piece together my missing time."

"I thought that's what you wanted to do."

"It was, but now I've another target in mind."

He looked down at her. "Ireland?"

"Ireland," she said.

Nikolai grinned and kissed the top of her head. "We'll leave first thing in the morning."

"Thank you."

They sat listening to the sound of the fire. Esther kept trying to focus on everything that had occurred that night, but she couldn't stop thinking about Nikolai—or more importantly, her growing feelings for him.

She'd had enough bad relationships to know that what she felt was something she'd only thought she knew before—love. And though she'd accepted that she'd fallen in love with Nikolai, she wasn't sure she could say the words.

Admitting them aloud might shatter the ease between them. If he didn't feel the same, she would then ruin everything she'd come to depend on. So she kept the secret locked tightly in her heart, all the while hoping that she didn't see more in Nikolai's gestures than what was really there.

That's what she dreaded the most. Because she'd definitely fallen for him. Was she now hearing his words and seeing his actions with a bias that hadn't been there before?

She might have briefly thought herself unworthy of Nikolai, but now she didn't care. Her love had grown to the point that she couldn't imagine life without him.

Her gaze dropped to his leg where their hands were clasped together. She lifted her arm and spread her fingers. He pressed his palm to hers. She raised her head and found her gaze snagged by his.

It became difficult to breathe as her chest constricted with the uncertainty of the future paired with the love she held inside.

"I see questions in your gaze," he murmured in that deep, sexy brogue that made her stomach quiver in anticipation.

She released his hand and slid her fingers through his thick, auburn locks. "I'm conflicted."

"About?"

"I want things solved, but once I find the answers, then this—what we've found together—will end."

His baby blue eyes searched hers. "Is that what you want?"

"No."

"Then it willna because I'm no' prepared to let you go."

CHAPTER THIRTY-FOUR

Dublin, Ireland

The farther from Dreagan he got, the more Nikolai felt the pull to return. And being in Ireland around so many Dark was making his skin crawl. Despite those issues, he would remain with Esther for however long it took.

He was the first to emerge from the private jet he'd chartered. After a quick look around the airstrip, he turned and nodded to Esther, who joined him. They walked down the stairs together before crossing the tarmac to the waiting, black Range Rover.

Nikolai put their bags in the back. He was walking to the driver's side when Esther smiled at him through the window, her hands on the steering wheel. With a wink, he made his way to the passenger side and got in.

"Well, you got us here," Esther said, her gaze staring ahead.

Nikolai buckled his seat belt and sat back. "It's a hunch. We could be wasting our time."

"Or, we could find her."

"Ireland isna huge, but there is still a lot of territory to cover."

Esther looked at him and shrugged. "We're in the process of yanking on a string. That will lead us somewhere. Until we hear back from Ryder, we go on your hunch."

"You're driving. You get to decide where we go."

She laughed as the sun came through the window and illuminated her face. Nikolai watched as the sunlight brought out the vibrant colors of her brunette locks and highlighted how her skin fairly glowed.

He'd almost told her last night of his feelings, but he hesitated at the last moment. It might have been the uncertainty that filled her beautiful, nutmeg eyes that stopped him.

Their gazes met as she started the engine and put the SUV into drive. Then she focused on the road as she drove them out of the airport. They had been driving for about fifteen minutes when Nikolai heard the buzz of his mobile phone in his bag.

"What is it?" Esther asked.

"Someone is calling." No sooner had the words left his mouth than the ringing ceased.

And then Esther's sounded.

She laughed and pulled the mobile out of her pocket and hit the speaker as she set it in the cup holder. "Hello?"

"I doona know why I expect recently woken Kings to keep their mobiles with them at all times," Ryder grumbled.

Nikolai flattened his lips. "We doona need those devices. We can speak with our minds."

"Aye," Ryder agreed. "Unless information also needs to be relayed to someone other than a Dragon King."

"Me," Esther said with a saucy grin.

Nikolai smiled at her. "Tell us you have news, Ryder."

"I do," he replied. "I've got a couple of things. First,

the I'm-no'-sure-how-to-classify-it news. Taraeth is dead."

Esther's gaze jerked to the mobile. "The Dark Fae king?"

"The verra one," Ryder said.

Nikolai asked, "Who did the honors to become the next king?"

"Balladyn."

Nikolai dropped his head back and sighed. "We should've seen that one coming."

"Con did."

"Why did he no' share that with us?"

Esther cut Nikolai a look. "Obvious reasons. Like he had no idea when or if it would happen, so why bother any of you with it when there were other things to deal with. Not to mention, it doesn't change anyone's stance in the war."

"That's pretty much exactly what Henry and Kellan said," Ryder stated. "Although, the thought of Rhi and Balladyn together still makes me queasy."

Nikolai rubbed his hand over his chin. "How did Con find out about Taraeth and Balladyn?"

"I missed it, as I usually miss everything, but apparently, Rhi was running through the manor, covered in blood, shouting Con's name. She asked Con to save Balladyn," Ryder announced.

Nikolai frowned and exchanged a glance with Esther. "And he did?"

"Aye, brother, he did. From what I could get out of Con, it looks as though Taraeth tried to get the upper hand, but Balladyn managed to kill him. However, Balladyn was gravely wounded in the process. I'm guessing either Rhi was there, or Balladyn called for her as he was dying."

Esther went around a slow car. "Do you think Balladyn used her because he knew she'd get Con to heal him?"

"It's no' a chance any Fae would take," Ryder said.

Nikolai nodded in agreement. "I'm surprised Con did it."

"Everyone is," Ryder muttered.

Esther tucked her hair behind one ear. "And the other news?"

"I uncovered some information on the Druid."

Nikolai watched as Esther's eyes widened in excitement as she gave him a quick glance.

"Do you have a name?" Esther asked.

Ryder made a noise. "No' exactly. I did find Eireen, however. There are still members of the Duffy family in Dublin. Only the two sisters and mother remain."

"Could one of them have raised the Druid?" Esther asked.

There were sounds of typing before Ryder said, "The eldest sister had a son two years before the Druid went missing. The middle sister had two bairns about three years after Eireen disappeared."

"That answers that," Esther said with a frown.

"And just as Donal told both of you, the youngest daughter fell off the face of the earth. There hasn't been anything on her credit report in over twenty years. Nothing is in her name. No' a mobile, no credit cards, no car."

"It's like she doesna exist," Nikolai said.

"But she's no' dead. There isna a death certificate."

Esther drove off the road into a field and put the vehicle in park. "She's using another name. Either her family made her, or she went off on her own."

"Aye, I thought the same," Ryder said. "It's why I've taken one of the last known pictures of Eireen and aged it. Then I'm going to start a facial recognition search."

Which would take days. Nikolai drew in a deep breath.

"If the Druid is her daughter, then there has to be birth records between seven and nine months after Donal saw Eireen."

"Unless she had the infant at home," Esther said.

Ryder grunted. "And that's a distinct possibility."

"But," Esther said eagerly, "there would still be some kind of paper trail, whether it be adoption records or even notice of her leaving the country."

"I'm looking as we speak," Ryder said, the sound of furious typing coming through the mobile.

Nikolai watched the cars pass them. "Just so you know, we're no longer in London."

There was a pause before Ryder said, "Let me guess. Ireland?"

"He's really very good," Esther said to Nikolai with a straight face. Then she ruined it by winking.

"Verra funny," Ryder stated dryly.

Nikolai said, "We're searching for the Druid. We'll begin in Dublin, but please send anything that might be helpful our way."

"Of course. I'll ring when I have something," Ryder said before ending the call.

Nikolai waited as Esther remained staring out the windshield. "What's wrong?"

"I've hunted people before. It's a long, arduous process. It can take years, especially if someone is good at hiding." She turned her head to him. "The fact that we know nothing of this Druid other than her face gives us very little to go on. She could be anywhere."

"She's no' far. Whether she's working with Ulrik or Mikkel, they would want her close to help them. That means she could be somewhere in the UK, Ireland, or possibly across the English Channel."

Esther held the steering wheel and straightened her arms so that she pushed back against her seat. After a moment, she relaxed her arms and let her hands drop to her lap. "That's a fair point. It helps to narrow down the area considerably, but that's if her power keeps to traditional Druid magic."

"Meaning what?" he asked. "That she can teleport?"

Esther shrugged. "Like I said, we don't know anything about her."

The thought of the Druid having the ability to move about like the Fae was distressing. That meant she could be anywhere in the world.

"She has a connection to Ireland," he said. "I still believe this is where she is."

Esther's gaze slid to him. "Then we look. I don't have any better ideas, and I trust your instincts more than I do mine at the moment."

"A Druid will naturally search out areas where there is magic and other Druids. That's what we need to look for," he said.

"I hope you can sense magic."

"I can."

Esther released her seat belt. "Then you'd better drive."

"Stay," he bade her. "I can concentrate more on the direction if I'm no' driving."

She buckled back up. "The Fae are here."

"Everywhere, in fact."

"That doesn't make me feel any better."

It dawned on Nikolai then. "Because you doona have magic."

"We're in the last place I want to be, searching for a Druid I'd love to pound into the ground. Yes, I definitely wish I had magic."

"You have me."

Her lips lifted in a smile. "That makes me lucky indeed. My very own Dragon King."

"Aye." He was hers. Only hers.

Their gazes tangled, and the passion between them sparked and filled the SUV.

He reached over and took her hand in his. "I'll kill any Fae who gets near you."

"I hope I'm not making a grave mistake."

"The one you should be worried about is Henry."

She winced at the mention of her brother. "I'm going to get an earful when we get back."

"It willna be half as bad if we return with the Druid."

"Right now, I'd settle for just finding and talking to her." Esther frowned then. "Perhaps you shouldn't be there when I do. If what Ulrik told you is true, she might hurt you."

Nikolai bit back a growl. "Let her try. I'll be with you when we approach her."

"All right, then. Which way?" Esther said as she put the vehicle into drive.

He pointed forward. "Keep heading this direction."

"Yes, sir," she replied with a grin.

Nikolai was well aware of the danger they were in, and he was ready and willing to do whatever it took to keep Esther alive.

He might not be the brawler Thorn was, but that didn't mean he didn't know how to fight. After all, he'd been taught by the best.

And when Nikolai fought, he always won.

CHAPTER THIRTY-FIVE

There was more magic around than Esther had first believed. Hearing the Dragon Kings talk, there wasn't much left. Yet she and Nikolai were headed to their fourth site in Ireland.

It made her want to visit every magical site in England and Scotland. If for nothing more than to record them and determine—through Nikolai—how much magic was there.

It would also be a good way to track Druids.

Her mind skittered to a halt at the thought. What did she care where the magic was?

No matter how many times she asked herself that question, there was never an answer. Just a driving need to know every place of magic around the world. And a surging necessity to seek . . . truth.

"You've gone pale."

She glanced over at Nikolai to find him watching her with soft blue eyes that saw everything. "I have this . . . urge . . . to locate every magical place on Earth."

"For?"

Her attention was briefly diverted as she slowed for an intersection. "So I'll know where the Druids go."

"And yet you keep saying you are no' the Truth-Seeker," he said in a soft voice.

"I don't know anymore."

He touched her hand, squeezing it before releasing her. "You will."

"You act as though you believe I'm this . . . thing." She couldn't even get the words out now.

Nikolai smiled as he looked out his window. "Because you are."

"What do you know that I don't?"

"Take a right up here," he said.

Their conversation halted as she followed his directions. As they continued driving, she saw a sign that indicated they were leaving the town of Ballina and were headed toward Dooncarton.

"There," Nikolai pointed to an obscure road.

Since he was the one who could sense magic, she took the road. Except it wasn't a road at all. It was more like a trail that was just wide enough for a vehicle. She cut her eyes to him briefly and found Nikolai sitting forward in his seat, a frown upon his brow with his eyes closed. Already, she caught a glimpse of blue from the ocean.

"Stop," Nikolai said as his eyes flew open. "We walk from here."

Esther put the SUV into park and shut off the engine. She looked out over the green grass as the rain started. "Where are we?"

"Outside of Dooncarton. There is a stone circle that lies on a slope facing Broad Haven, and the cliffs of Rinroe Point are across the water."

"Shall we go see them?"

He gave a shake of his head. "No' now."

Esther raised a brow in question. "I thought that's what we came to do."

"It is, but there are others there."

"Others as in . . . Druids?" As soon as she said the words, something inside her swelled and pulsed. It was all she could do to remain inside the vehicle and not rush out to see the Druids.

Nikolai turned his head to her. "No' Druids. Mortals."

"Oh." She puffed out her cheeks and drummed her fingers on the steering wheel. "Why do we care who's there anyway? It didn't matter at the other places."

"That's because the magic was faint at those. Here, it springs forth like a well."

Esther knew that meant the site would call to Druids. "She'll come then."

"I didna say that."

"You didn't have to."

He flattened his lips as he sighed. "It's a place that would certainly draw Druids to it. It's open, though. There's no way we could lie in wait for her."

Well, that just crushed her plans. "Do we go to the next site then?"

"Nay."

With no other explanation, Nikolai simply stared out the windshield. He might know where the stones were, but she didn't. As far as she could see, there was grass, more grass, and in the distance, the sea.

The rain pinged against the metal of the SUV as it fell. With the engine off, it didn't take long for the chill to penetrate the vehicle. Esther crossed her arms over her chest to help hold in her warmth while droplets covered the windshield, making it impossible to see out.

It wasn't long before her eyes grew heavy and she closed them to rest for just a moment.

"You don't believe me."

The voice—*her* voice—shocked her. She spun around and saw E2. Before, she'd been afraid, but now, she took the opportunity to learn more.

Esther noticed that this time, her mind was brightly lit, and the multitude of doors looked inviting instead of imposing. And, somehow, she knew that if she went to a door, it would open.

"I don't have magic," Esther said.

E2 rolled her eyes. "So?"

"The last TruthSeeker was a Druid. With a Druid brother. Do you see the issue?"

"You're making a problem where there is none."

Esther shot her a look of disbelief. "How can I fight Druids without magic?"

E2's smile was slow as it filled her face. "You have something more powerful than magic."

"What could that possibly be?"

"Not only do you hold the title of TruthSeeker and Henry that of JusticeBringer, but there is also something else that awaits both of you. Yours will come first."

Esther was past the point of frustration and fully into the pissed column. "Stop with the cryptic words. Just tell me."

"There are some things you need to figure out on your own."

"Well, that's certainly helpful."

E2 shrugged and walked closer. "If you want to end the questions haunting you, then embrace who you are. Accept that you are the TruthSeeker, believe that you are exactly where you need to be in life—and with exactly who you need to be with."

"Nikolai."

E2 tilted her head to the side as she regarded Esther. "He's accepted everything about you."

"I know, but why?"

"Because it's who he is. Also, he's seen it."

Esther took a step forward. "Seen it, as in he's drawn it?"

"You would've seen that sketch if he had. It's his gift to see what others overlook. His mind memorizes things so he can make them into art later, but that is only the tip of what he can do."

"How do you know this?"

E2 laughed as she gave a shake of her head. "I'm a part of your mind, Esther. I know this because you know it. He's told you, but you've also witnessed it yourself."

"So he has."

"Ask him to show you the woman he sees when he looks at you."

Esther wrinkled her nose. "I'm not so sure I want to know."

"Yes, you do. Just like you want to be with him."

She didn't want to talk about Nikolai, not when she was still coming to terms with her love for him. "What does it mean that I'm the TruthSeeker?"

"You'll know when the time comes," E2 said.

"That's not helpful at all."

E2 merely smiled as she began to fade away.

Esther's eyes snapped open as she woke. She turned her head to find the seat next to her empty. Sitting up and dropping her arms, she used the windshield wipers to clear the window so she could see out. Yet there was no sign of Nikolai.

She twisted in her seat to look behind her, but it wasn't until she turned back around that she saw him standing alongside the SUV.

Crawling into his seat, she rolled down the window and stuck her head out. "Fancied getting wet, did you?"

He smiled at her. "I hoped to get a better sense of where I feel the magic."

"Straight ahead," she said. "Where the stones are."

"There's another source. And it's powerful."

That made her smile. "Let's go see what it is. We can always return here."

He thought about it for a moment before he gave a nod of agreement. "I'll drive this time."

She rolled up the window and got buckled in by the time he was in the driver's seat. Within moments, they had backed up and were leaving the stones behind.

"I need to make a map," she said.

"Of all the places with magic?"

Esther looked at his profile. "Yes."

"Then you must make it."

"Do you believe in destiny?"

His lips softened into a smile as he gave her a quick glance. "I suppose so. I should've died with my parents, but I lived. I should've been given over to Avgust since he was King of the Ivories. In both instances, Ulrik intervened. I've always believed I was meant to be trained by him."

"To become King of Ivories."

"I saw firsthand the weight of responsibility Ulrik bore as King of Silvers since I was with him nearly every day. I didna want to be King, but I knew that I couldna always remain with the Silvers."

"Why?"

"Though no one forbade it, dragons usually didna look outside of their clans to find mates. It happened, and the dragons were accepted into the different families, but it didna occur often."

She rubbed her hands together. "And you wanted a mate?"

"Someday, but there was a drive within me to return to my clan. Yet I couldna do it with Avgust as King. We have a sense that we're meant for more, which is why a

King is challenged. I could feel my magic and power growing each day, and I knew what I was supposed to do."

"Do all those who challenge a King become the next Dragon King?"

Nikolai slowly shook his head. "Some crave the mantle so badly that they make themselves believe they have what it takes. And they die because of it."

"How did you know the difference?"

He shrugged and briefly met her gaze. "I can no' explain it other than to say that it began as a thought in the back of my mind and grew until it became a bellow. The day I accepted that I must challenge Avgust, was the day I knew I'd be the next King of Ivories."

Acceptance. Isn't that what E2 told her? Esther wasn't craving something she hadn't known about until E2 told her. But now that she knew it, she was ready to become the TruthSeeker.

"I imagine my face looked just like that," Nikolai said.

She jerked her gaze to him.

His smile widened. "You've acknowledged who you are. That's the first step."

Esther took a deep breath and looked forward. The first step of many, but it had been a doozy to be sure.

CHAPTER THIRTY-SIX

Locating magic was as easy for a Dragon King as breathing, but sometimes, it was discovering the kind of magic that led to battle.

Nikolai found a spot along the wet street to park the SUV once they reached the small village. He shut off the engine and sat back. The rain ceased a short time ago, leaving everything wet.

"What do you see?" Esther asked as she watched the people walking along the street.

He propped his elbow on the side of the door. "On the surface, all is normal."

"Because that's what people like me, who don't have magic, are supposed to sense," Esther said.

They shared a look, and he nodded. "And no' be any wiser."

"So what am I not seeing?"

"The Fae walking among the humans."

Her head jerked to look out her window. "Even if the Fae use glamour, shouldn't the mortals be falling all over themselves to get to them?"

"They should be, aye."

"Something else I'm not seeing." She looked at him once more. "Donal used carvings to control the Fae in his pub. I'd say the entire village has done the same, but these people don't look as if they know what's beside them."

Nikolai shrugged. "Because they doona. When the Fae chose Ireland, they had to walk among the people here. Most times, they want to blend in and no' be noticed."

Esther's eyes widened as she figured it out. "That's right. They can mute their appeal."

"Exactly. The Fae choose when to turn it on or off."

"Which is why Henry isn't yanking off his clothes anytime Rhi is near."

Nikolai grinned. "The last time I looked at Henry's mapping of the Dark, I noticed that while the Fae were returning to Ireland, they didna all go to one place. They were scattered."

"That may change if Balladyn becomes king."

"He is king," Nikolai said. "But I'm curious to know if the Dark's movements shift, because I suspect they will."

Esther motioned to the town. "Tell me what you see beneath the surface, besides the Fae."

He looked out the window. The cars and buildings melted away, leaving only the land and the people. "There is a peace here I've no' felt in any other place."

"Peace?" Esther questioned.

"There is no strife, no friction. The village is protected."

"By what?"

He traced the magic that ran along each of the streets and around homes and businesses until he finally came to the source. "No' a what, but a who."

"Who is it?"

Nikolai blinked and slid his gaze to Esther. "Someone verra powerful."

"The Druid?" she asked hopefully.

"I'm no' sure."

Esther grabbed for the handle of the door. "I want to find out."

He reached across her and placed his hand over her. "Wait," he cautioned.

Her brown eyes met his. "We could've found her, and you want me to wait?"

"Aye, I do. We doona know what we're walking into, and I'll no' take you somewhere you could be killed. I swore to protect you, and I plan to do just that."

"I'm not used to waiting behind in the car," she said. There was no anger in her eyes when she met his gaze. "But I don't want to die. Since I'm without magic, I'll heed your words."

He smiled before he leaned in for a quick kiss. "I'll no' be long."

"You'd better not be, or I might leave you here," she teased.

He grinned and exited the vehicle then made his way down the street. Just as he recognized the Fae, they knew he was a Dragon King. Word would spread quickly. If the Druid were here, he wanted to find her before she discovered that he was in town.

Nikolai followed the magic and found himself staring at an ordinary brick building that was several hundred years old. What was extraordinary about it was that Fae, Druids, and mortals were coming and going from it freely.

This wasn't the first time the Kings had encountered a bar for the paranormal. *An Doras* was a pub Kiril had watched for a long time.

How many more of these establishments were around

that the Kings weren't aware of? Perhaps it was something they needed to look into.

Nikolai watched the place for several minutes before he began to turn away. Something caught his attention out of the corner of his eye. When he looked, his gaze snagged on Ulrik right before he walked around a corner.

Nikolai quickly followed after Ulrik, but in a blink, his old friend was gone. It wasn't coincidence that Ulrik was in the village where such strong magic was. That meant that this was where the Druid hid. Nikolai hoped Ulrik hadn't lied about working with her. Then again, it didn't matter.

One way or another, the Druid would answer for her crimes.

The sound of a car door opening got Nikolai's attention. He looked toward the pub and saw a man exit a vehicle. He had his back to Nikolai as he buttoned his suit. Nikolai frowned since the man's long, black hair resembled Ulrik's. The angle Nikolai was in prevented him from getting a look at the man's face before he walked into the building.

He debated going into the bar himself, but Nikolai hesitated. If the Druid were in there, he might have to fight every occupant inside just to get to her. If she weren't there, then she'd be alerted almost immediately to his presence.

Nikolai turned on his heel and retraced his steps back to the Range Rover. As he neared, he noticed that Esther wasn't in the car. Halting, he turned his head one way and then the other, searching for her. He caught sight of her hair in a group of people and hurried toward her.

When he reached her, she was standing still, her hands in the pockets of her jacket as she stared at a young child on the playground with others.

"What is it?" he whispered.

She didn't take her eyes off the boy. "He's a Druid."

Nikolai was surprised at her statement, because she was right. He felt the child's magic. "How do you know?"

"He looks different than the others."

"Different how?"

"Fuzzy around the edges." She looked up at him. "I'm right, aren't I? He has magic."

He wrapped an arm around her. "Aye."

"I can't see it in the others. I still don't know who is Fae and who isn't."

He turned her toward the vehicle and began walking her back. "A day ago, you didna know who was a Druid either."

"I saw one child."

"It's one more than before."

She changed the subject then. "What did you find?"

"A pub. One that caters to the paranormal."

"Really?" she asked excitedly. "When do we get to visit?"

He got her inside the Range Rover and waited until he'd climbed into the driver's side before he said, "We have one shot to corner the Druid. No doubt she'll learn of my appearance shortly, which takes away any advantage we might have."

"Then we need to draw her out."

"Easier said than done. She'll be on the defensive."

Esther scratched the side of her nose. "Maybe we should have more Dragon Kings here."

"And risk a battle? This village hasna been ravaged by the damage the Fae can do."

Her eyes widened in outrage. "You think the Druid is responsible for that?"

"It's a verra good possibility. We risk that by having more Kings arrive. The Fae will see that as an act of war and retaliate. I doona want innocent lives lost."

Esther's anger deflated quickly. "I don't either. It just seems damn impossible to get near this woman."

"We found her, though."

"You saw her?"

He gave a shake of his head. "I saw something better. Ulrik."

"Did he lie to you about working with her?"

"Ulrik always warned me that I should know my enemy better than my friends. If Ulrik's here, it's because he's trying to learn more about the Druid."

Esther lifted one shoulder half-heartedly. "Or he's working with her. All the Kings are searching for Ulrik. Shouldn't you tell them you've found him?"

"I followed him, and he disappeared."

She sighed loudly. "We should get off the streets. The fewer people that see us, the better."

"I know just the place."

Nikolai started the Range Rover and drove down one of the back streets. He'd spotted the empty building when he walked to the pub. Pulling alongside the curb, Esther was out of the vehicle before it came to a full stop.

By the time he joined her at the back of the building, she'd already picked the lock. They walked inside and quickly shut the door behind them. He watched Esther as she walked through the lower floor. Little by little, she had changed since leaving Dreagan.

It wasn't just that she had come out of the shell she'd been in since her mind was infiltrated. It was that she was gaining back control of her life. But there was something else, as well, something that teased him every now and again as it did now.

A part of her that hinted at magic.

The more confident she became, the more she believed she was the TruthSeeker, the more he saw the magic.

She didn't possess power to use, but it was still within

her. He thought about telling her since it was something that worried her. Yet he held back. Soon enough, she would figure it out for herself.

Esther looked his way and smiled as she crooked a finger at him. "Who knows how long we'll be waiting before we can draw the Druid out."

"Do you have a suggestion on how we might pass the time?" he asked as he slowly walked to her.

She shrugged, giving him a sexy look. "I've got an idea or two."

"Hmm. So do I."

"Is that right?" she said with wide eyes. "Care to share them with me?"

He reached her then and lifted her so that her legs wrapped around his waist. Turning, he pinned her against the wall and looked deeply into her eyes. "I'd rather show you."

"Yes, please," she murmured.

He ground his aching cock into her as he claimed her lips.

CHAPTER THIRTY-SEVEN

Italy

"What did you do?"

The accusation in Balladyn's voice pierced Rhi like the dullest of blades. She looked at him and forced a smile. "You're alive."

He glanced down at his black shirt soaked in blood as he paced angrily before her. His forehead was creased in a frown and his lips were compressed tightly as his chest heaved. Ever since she'd brought Con back to Dreagan and returned to Balladyn, his rage had been barely leashed.

"What did you want me to do?" she demanded, letting him hear her growing ire. "Let you die?"

His steps halted as he whipped his head to her. "I called to you because I wanted you by my side. I thought you knew that."

"No," she said with the shake of her head. "You knew I had the means to save you."

His lips pulled back as he sneered. "Con."

"Yes, Con. He healed you."

If she hadn't been so distraught, she might've tried to heal him herself since she had somehow been able to mend Cael, the Reaper leader. That wasn't something she'd shared with anyone else yet, though, especially since she wasn't at all sure how she'd done it.

Balladyn sliced his hand through the air furiously. "I never wanted Con's help!"

"I wasn't going to let you die!"

He stomped to her until they were nose-to-nose. "Now I owe the bastard."

Was that what this was all about? Rhi wanted to roll her eyes at men's egos. "That's not how Con works."

"You would know, wouldn't you?"

She jerked back as if his words had physically assaulted her. "You're King of the Dark now. You've removed Taraeth and taken the throne. No one needs to know what occurred here."

"But *I* will!" he shouted as he thrust his finger into his chest. He drew in a deep breath and dropped his arm to his side. Then he bit out, "And so will Con."

Rhi hadn't thought about Balladyn's reaction when she asked for Con's help. All that had mattered was saving Balladyn's life. Not once did she imagine that he would be so angry to be alive.

The only way for him to get past this was to make sure whatever debt he felt he owed Con was paid immediately.

"There's a way you can easily wipe the slate clean," she said.

Balladyn's red eyes narrowed in suspicion. "How?"

"Stop the attacks on the Dragon Kings."

For a moment, he stared at her before he gave a bark of laughter. "You expect my first decree upon taking the throne to be that? The Dark will revolt. Scores will attack me to take control."

"Then stop them. You're the king now. Act like it."

"I'll act like a king. I'll do the things Taraeth never dared."

Rhi swallowed as unease churned in her gut. His words and tone hinted at actions she wouldn't like.

This was a side of Balladyn she hadn't seen before—the Dark side. And it frightened her, because she knew if matters continued on this course, she'd be fighting him once more.

They had come so far, and yet she felt as if he was going to do something that would back her into a corner and force her hand. She needed Balladyn. Didn't he know that? Couldn't he see past his ego to that simple fact?

With what was going on with Usaeil, Balladyn was someone she leaned on, someone who wanted nothing more from her other than her love. He was her friend, her lover. And now . . . now he was altering his course to a place she couldn't—and wouldn't—follow.

"What things?" she inquired.

He shrugged and took a step back. "Nothing you need worry about."

She stared at the spot he'd been in before he teleported away. Their conversation wasn't finished, but she didn't follow him. Balladyn would go to the Dark Palace and take the throne.

This . . . discussion had the potential to go nuclear. They both needed some time to cool down. Actually, he was the one who needed to get his undies untwisted. She'd done him a favor, and he hadn't bothered to even thank her.

"Damn you, Balladyn," she muttered.

The small amount of peace Rhi had found was gone. Balladyn was now furious because he felt he owed Con. Con wasn't happy because she'd put him in a position he didn't want. Yet Con had saved Balladyn, knowing he'd be fighting him later.

For once, her anger wasn't directed at Con. Something was very wrong in the world if she could actually think those words and have them be true.

Rhi drew in a shaky breath. It was then that she remembered she wasn't alone. Daire had witnessed everything as he stood silently—veiled—behind her. But she
didn't want to talk to him. Not now, not when her agony
over Balladyn's words was still fresh.

She thought of her island and teleported there where
she could lick her wounds and try not to think how everything around her was falling apart.

Ireland

The passage of time seemed like milliseconds to some—
eons to others. For Ulrik, he'd been counting down the
hours until he could get his revenge.

It had taken him years to set the board, and even longer to move everyone into place. Every situation and re-
sulting development had been meticulously thought out
as well as maneuvers planned in defense and offense.

But the one thing he'd never accounted for was
Mikkel.

His uncle had made him wipe the playing board clean
and start all over when he made himself known to
Ulrik. Centuries of plans had to be rethought and re-
mapped in days.

And yet, Ulrik was still going to come out ahead despite Mikkel's advantage.

That gain tipped toward Ulrik because he knew his
uncle. He was aware of how Mikkel fought without
honor, how he would trick, bribe, and betray his way to
the top.

Which was why Ulrik had suspected Mikkel would
find a Druid to help him. Only Ulrick hadn't been prepared for Eilish's power or beauty.

Ulrik's alliance with Balladyn would pay off. He knew

without a doubt that Balladyn had defeated Taraeth. There was no need for him to check in at the Dark Palace to see who was king, he was that confident in Balladyn.

Staring out into the night from an alley in the small village, Ulrik contemplated Nikolai's arrival. A part of him wanted to help his old friend. Nikolai had been the closest thing he'd ever have to a son, and it had stung when Nikolai hadn't stood with him against Con.

It was Nikolai's innate sense of right and wrong, his morality that never wavered, which reminded Ulrik of the dragon he'd helped raise. Perhaps that's why he harbored no ill will toward Nikolai.

He strode out of his hiding spot to the building where Nikolai and Esther had taken refuge. As he reached the back door, he paused when his hearing picked up their voices within.

"Shift," a woman asked in a soft British accent, a smile in her voice.

Nikolai laughed softly. "There isna enough room. I'd bring the entire building down upon us."

"Then when can I see you? The real you?"

"Soon," Nikolai promised.

Esther made a sound at the back of her throat. "We could drive out in the middle of nowhere. It's night now, and I know Con lifted the ban. You could fly. I'd love to see that."

A curious pain tugged in Ulrik's chest on his left side. All the times he and Nikolai had spoken of Nikolai finding a mate. Nikolai had been patient, often telling Ulrik that he didn't mind waiting until he found the perfect one.

It appeared his perseverance had given him the prize every Dragon King—whether they admitted it or not—wanted.

Love.

"I'd feel better if we waited until we returned to Dreagan," Nikolai said.

Why should he or any Dragon King have to be on Dreagan land in order to be their true selves? Why did they have to continue to hide?

His anger at the humans began all over again. Ulrik clenched his fists and brought the rage back under control. He didn't bother to knock. Instead he said, "Nikolai."

Ulrik moved away from the entrance as he heard Nikolai approach. The door opened, and Nikolai stepped outside, the edge of light from the streetlamp just reaching his feet.

Ulrik remained in the shadows. It had become a comforting place where he felt disengaged from the mortals, a place where he could pretend that they weren't standing all around him.

"I saw you earlier," Nikolai said.

Ulrik nodded. Neither of them needed light since their eyesight was better than any other animal on the planet. "I wasna trying to hide from you."

"She's here, is she no'?"

"Aye."

"At the pub."

Ulrik nodded once more. "It's called Graves, but I wouldna suggest going inside."

"I didna intend to. Mostly because I know Esther would attempt to follow me. Why have you come?"

The words got stuck in his throat. Not because Ulrik feared them, but because he knew that helping Nikolai would change things.

It would change *him*.

This was one step in all of his planning throughout the countless millennia that he'd never even considered. Because he'd believed all the Dragon Kings were against him.

But then he'd discovered Sebastian in Venice looking for Mikkel. Bast going to the shop and leaving the ring Ulrik had made for him was another piece he'd never counted on. Sebastian and Nikolai were making Ulrik re-evaluate things. And damn Nikolai for saying the right things so he wanted to help.

Nikolai took a step closer, seemingly uncaring of his bare feet on the cold, damp pavement. "You've come to help."

"It may no' work," Ulrik cautioned.

"I doona care. The fact is that you've come to me. To us."

Ulrik looked to the side for a moment, giving himself one last second to consider his next move. But it was already too late. He wouldn't walk away from Nikolai now, just as he hadn't left the hatchling he found.

"Her name is Eilish. She was raised in America and only returned to Ireland a few years ago."

"She was born here?"

"It's in her voice if you listen carefully."

"Was she was raised by someone from Ireland?"

Ulrik glanced behind Nikolai to the building and the window where Esther watched them. "I believe so."

"I wonder what brought her back."

"You mentioned the man you found in London."

Nikolai crossed his arms over his chest. "I believe he's her father, aye. You should've seen his face when he saw the picture I drew of Eilish."

"You saw her?" Ulrik asked, shock settling in his gut.

"No' as you think," Nikolai said with a slight shake of his head. "I only saw her through Esther's eyes."

That's when it dawned on Ulrik. "Your powers. They've grown."

"It appears so."

"The only way this will work is if I can get Eilish out of the pub."

Nikolai dropped his arms. "I've given you a reason. Tell her you know of her father."

"That could do it."

"And if it doesna?"

Ulrik grinned as he thought of the Druid. "Then we'll see if she really has enough power to kill me."

The door suddenly opened again, and a woman stood there. Her brown hair was mussed, and her clothes wrinkled. "My memories aren't worth your life."

Her words came as a surprise to Ulrik. Then again, he should've known Nikolai would've told her of their past. Yet Ulrik was still astonished that she wouldn't readily sacrifice his life for her own.

All the mortals he'd come across in his years being banished from Dreagan had shown him that there were very, very few who wouldn't do almost anything to keep from dying.

"Esther," Nikolai said as he turned and walked to her.

But she ignored him. Ulrik found her gaze locked on him, and he was intrigued. He didn't want to be because she was a human—and because of what he'd been through with his own mortal.

"Ulrik, this is Esther," Nikolai said. "Esther, Ulrik."

To his surprise, she held out her palm, her gaze daring him to take it. Damn if Ulrik didn't find himself liking her boldness.

He took her offered hand and shook it. "You doona seem afraid of me."

"I'm not," she replied as she released him. "Not after having a Druid in my head, controlling me and wiping my memories."

He gave a bow of his head, acknowledging her words.

It didn't go unnoticed that Nikolai hadn't introduced her as his mate. That must be because Nikolai had yet to broach the subject with her. Understandable since so much was in flux with the Druid and the war.

And yet, Ulrik knew how quickly happiness could be snatched away.

"Are you really going to help?" Esther asked.

Ulrik glanced at Nikolai. "I am."

"I've heard many things about you, and they weren't good. That was until Nikolai told me how you saved him and brought him into your clan."

Ulrik's past with Nikolai had been bombarding him since he'd heard Nikolai's voice in his head a few days ago. Before that, he hadn't thought about the day he saved Nikolai. It felt like a hundred lifetimes ago. A single decision had altered not only his life but also Nikolai's.

Esther continued, unaware that his thoughts had wandered. "Nikolai trusts you, so I'll trust you. But if you betray him, I'll hunt you down. I don't care that I'm human and can't kill you. I'll make your life hell."

"I believe you would," he said. Then he looked at Nikolai. "You chose well."

Nikolai smiled as he looked down at Esther.

Ulrik turned on his heel and began walking away before they invited him inside. "Meet me behind Graves in an hour."

CHAPTER THIRTY-EIGHT

It was going to work. It was going to work. It was going to work.

Esther kept repeating the mantra in hopes that Ulrik kept his word. Nikolai didn't seem the least bit worried. That was because she had enough anxiety for both of them.

"Ulrik doesna lie," Nikolai said as they walked from the building toward the pub.

They'd already had this conversation multiple times in the past hour, so she decided to change the subject. "Who names their pub Graves? I mean, really. *Graves*? It's so morbid."

Nikolai glanced up at the dark sky as thunder rumbled. "Ask her."

"Right," Esther said, rolling her eyes. "I'll do that between demanding she return my memories and kicking her ass."

"I'm looking forward to seeing you kick some ass."

She smiled despite herself. A glance in Nikolai's direction showed he was looking at her, a crooked grin upon his lips. "Are you now?"

"I am."

"I'll only do it if you shift so I can see you."

He reached for her hand, their fingers knotting together. "That might have to wait since I could be doing some ass-kicking of my own."

"Hmm. I might have to hold off on mine then since I do love watching you fight."

He quirked a brow. "Are you teasing?"

"Not at all. I've seen more fights than I like to admit, but no one compares to you. It's the way you move."

And the confidence that billowed off him in waves. It made her so hot.

He halted and looked at her. The way his eyes locked with hers made warmth spread through her. His blue gaze blazed with something deep and profound.

Her heart skipped a beat as she stared up at him. The smile was gone, his face now tight with uncertainty and indecision.

"I wasna going to do this now. I planned to wait until a better time, but I'm no' sure there is one."

"You're freaking me out." Her blood drummed in her ears, and she couldn't catch her breath. All because she feared what might fall from his lips.

He faced her and caressed her cheek with his free hand. "I love you."

It felt as if a rug had been yanked from beneath her feet. Her lips parted, but her mind froze as she searched for words.

"I'm no' good with words," Nikolai said. "I spend my time sketching or drawing, always behind one canvas or another. I watch the world, but rarely am I involved in it. You make me want to take part. You're all fire and bravado. The storm to my calm. It shouldna work, but it does."

She shook her head, wanting him to stop talking. "Why are you telling me this now?"

"Because you're mortal. I could lose you, and I want you to know that you hold my heart. You have from the beginning. When you walked into my rooms and saw the pictures I'd drawn of you, I feared you'd see my feelings."

"You can't say these things now." Esther tried to pull away, but he held her tightly.

"I can, and I will. They need to be said."

She shook her head. He had to stop. If he continued, all she'd be able to think about when they met up with Eilish was that Nikolai loved her. And she needed her mind focused on the Druid.

"You're my mate," Nikolai said. "The one I've searched thousands of years for."

Esther put a finger to his lips, needing him to stop but longing to hear the words. "Don't do this now," she beseeched.

He kissed her finger and gently moved it away. "I know you love me. I've seen it in your eyes, felt it in your touch. We belong together. I'd take you for my mate right now to keep you safe, but that isna possible. We walk into the unknown in a few moments. Do it knowing that I'll move Heaven and Earth for you."

"Damn you," she said as a tear fell. She wasn't the romantic type. Life as a spy had wiped that from her quickly enough, yet Nikolai was giving her everything she hadn't known she needed.

A smile tugged at his lips. "I love you."

"And I love you."

"Say you'll be mine," he demanded, his voice low, and his gaze boring into hers.

It was her turn to grin. "Only if you'll be mine."

His head bent, and they shared a soft kiss that felt as if it reached into her soul and healed whatever parts had been scarred and lost.

"It's settled," he replied. "Let's go find the Druid."

They started walking again. Esther wiped away a tear track. She was so happy, she thought she might be able to dance upon the air, which would be some feat since she couldn't dance at all.

By the time they reached Graves, Ulrik was already there. He didn't speak to them, only gave a slight nod and entered the pub.

"Now, we wait," Nikolai said.

This was the part Esther hated the most. They had no idea what was going on inside. No eyes or ears to get a clue of what was happening.

After Nikolai hid them in the shadows, she counted the minutes. When she hit seven and a half, the back door swung open, and Ulrik walked out. Behind him was a tall woman clad in an all black outfit that skimmed every curve.

Her long, midnight hair was slicked back in a high ponytail. It was the glint of light off something shiny that had Esther lowering her gaze to see the silver finger rings that came up to the second knuckle of each of the Druid's fingers on her left hand.

"I can't believe you're dumb enough to return here," Eilish said to Ulrik.

Esther heard the American accent with just a hint of Irish. It was hard to look at the Druid, knowing she was to blame for so much that was wrong in Esther's mind.

Ulrik faced the Druid and put his left hand in the pocket of his trousers. "I told you, I have information you're going to want."

"And you couldn't tell me inside?"

"It's because I doona have the information. A friend does," Ulrik said.

Esther followed Nikolai as he walked from the shadows. The Druid's gaze landed on her, and she paused for just a moment. There was no spark of recognition. Did they have the wrong woman?

"I'm not in the mood for games," Eilish said and turned to leave.

Nikolai said, "I spoke with your father the other day."

She halted and looked at him over her shoulder. "I highly doubt that."

"He didna know of your existence," Nikolai said.

Esther watched as frown lines formed on the Druid's forehead. Eilish faced Nikolai and walked right up to him. "You're lying."

There was only a smidgen of heat in her words. The rest was filled with dread and unease. Eilish had been so sure a moment before that Nikolai hadn't spoken to her father, but there must be something they didn't know about her family. Otherwise, she would've dismissed them instead of pursuing things further.

"He's not," Esther said. "I was with him."

The Druid's gaze, indiscernible in the shadows, landed on Esther. "My father raised me, so he knows who I am."

"Perhaps he isna your real sire," Ulrik said.

Eilish's gaze jerked to Ulrik. "You thought you could come here and tell me this insane story and I'd believe it. All so that you might tell me this man's name in exchange for me not killing you?"

"I doona fear you, Druid," Ulrik stated in a clipped voice.

She shifted to face him, one hand on her hip. "You should."

Esther then stepped forward. "We tell you this and offer the man's name in exchange for you returning my memories."

The Druid swung her head toward her. "I don't know what you mean."

"Aye, you do," Nikolai said. "I heard the subtle uptick of your heartbeat when you first saw Esther."

Eilish drew in a breath and released it. "Why should I believe anything you say?"

"When I showed your father a picture of you, he said you looked just like the woman he'd loved and wanted to marry," Esther said.

She watched as Eilish's gaze lowered to the ground as she struggled to make a decision.

"Why are you in Ireland?" Ulrik asked. "Something brought you here."

"My father is from Ireland," Eilish replied.

"That he is," Esther said. "So must the man who took you to America."

Nikolai said, "I think it's because you're looking for something. Or someone. You said your father raised you. Where was your mother?"

Eilish ignored the question as she faced Esther. "You believe this man you speak of is my father. Why?"

"He and your mother were going to marry," Esther said. "Her family, however, was against it. Her two elder sisters came to get her from the pub one day, and it was the last he ever saw of them."

"Where was this?" Eilish asked tightly.

Esther glanced at Nikolai and said, "Dublin. Your mother's name was Eireen."

Eilish walked to her and put her hands on either side of Esther's head without hesitation. "This isn't going to be pleasant."

That was all the warning Esther had before pain exploded in her mind. Her stomach rolled as white lights flashed behind her closed eyelids. She was locked in agony, unable to move or make a sound. It felt as if eternity passed before the Druid finally removed her hands. Instantly, strong and familiar arms came around her.

"I've got you," Nikolai whispered in her ear.

Esther clung to him as the missing days were suddenly there, as well as everyone she'd spoken with and saw. Including Eilish. She opened her eyes and looked at the Druid.

"I held up my end of the bargain," Eilish said.

Nikolai steadied Esther before he said, "Donal Cleary. He owns pubs all over, but you'll find him at The Porterhouse in London. It was the place your mother wanted him to buy, so he's been waiting there for her all these years."

"Who are you working for?" Esther asked as the pounding in her head began to diminish.

Eilish gave her a wry look. "You don't want to know."

"It's Mikkel, isn't it?" Esther felt Nikolai's arms tighten in warning, but she was done being nice.

The Dragon Kings needed to know this information, and so far, they'd only gotten hints that it might be him. Esther was going to deliver on it.

TruthSeeker.

"If you knew, why did you ask?" Eilish stared at her, unblinking.

Esther looked at Nikolai and smiled. "Because until just now, we weren't sure."

"Leave," Ulrik told them.

Nikolai looked at his friend for a long, silent moment. "Come back with us."

"I can no'."

"You can. Stand with me as I tell Con everything."

Esther watched as Eilish locked her gaze on Ulrik, taking in every move he made. The longer Esther watched the Druid, the more she felt as if she needed to do . . .

something. "You took away Sebastian's memories of Mikkel."

Everyone turned their gazes to Esther.

She smiled at Eilish. "It was obvious from the beginning. Sebastian went to Venice to find evidence of Mikkel in order to prove that Ulrik was wrongly accused, and then he returned without any knowledge of Mikkel at all. After he'd already spoken to Con about having information about Mikkel."

Out of the corner of her eye, Esther saw Ulrik pull his hand from his pocket and look at something in his palm. She glanced at his hand and saw a ring.

"Why are you working with Mikkel?" Esther demanded of the Druid.

Eilish held up her left hand with the finger rings and wiggled her fingers. "I can take away those memories again."

"Touch her, and I kill you," Nikolai stated in a voice that was pitched low and dangerous.

Eilish slid her gaze to Nikolai. "You've outstayed your welcome. Leave before I make you."

With one last glance at Ulrik, she turned on her heel and strode back inside the pub. There was a beat of silence as they took in everything that happened.

Nikolai looked at Ulrik, who disappeared without a word. Then Nikolai's head swung to her. "We did it."

"You were right about Ulrik."

"Aye," he said, but there was sadness in his gaze.

CHAPTER THIRTY-NINE

Dark Palace

Balladyn stood at the entrance to the Dark Palace. One by one, the Fae around him grew silent as they noticed him. There was just a handful of Dark, but that's all it would take.

The guards on either side of the double doors were who he looked at first. "You have a new king. Me."

At once, the guards knelt, showing their fealty. Balladyn slowly turned his gaze to the group watching. Their expressions were a mixture of surprise, delight, and fear. He looked at each of them, memorizing their faces. A heartbeat later, they each fell to their knees.

More guards were suddenly before him. They knelt and then rose to move on either side of him. Balladyn turned to face the group.

"Spread the word throughout the palace and across the world to every Fae," he ordered.

"But we're supposed to follow you," one of the guards said.

Balladyn walked around the group. "You're my King's Guard. There may be times I need you, but if I can't defend myself in my own palace, then I shouldn't be king."

The six men smiled.

He gave a nod, and the guards disbursed to carry out his command. Balladyn then turned and made his way to the king's quarters. They sat at the very top of the palace, overlooking a particularly beautiful spot in Ireland.

Balladyn walked to one of the windows and looked out across the land. He almost felt bad that none of the mortals could enjoy the scenery because once they ventured too close to the palace, they became property of the Dark.

His mind drifted to Rhi, but he couldn't think about her. Not now. Not when he was still so angry. A part of him wondered if she'd saved him so he would be indebted to the Dragon Kings.

Because in the back of his mind, he knew she still loved her King. If only he could kill the bastard, Balladyn would get rid of him once and for all. But would that end her love? Balladyn didn't think so.

He turned away from the window and looked about the chambers. With a wave of his hand, everything that had been Taraeth's vanished, wiped away in a blink.

Balladyn then snapped his fingers, bringing all of his belongings—including his library. He walked through the spacious rooms one at a time, making sure everything was in its place.

The room on the left end was where he decided to house his library. The books were still protected with magic, so the sunlight coming through the many windows didn't harm them. He stopped at the long table where books were scattered.

His gaze landed on the passage about the Reapers. Immediately, he thought of Rhi again. She was keeping secrets from him, secrets about the Reapers. If he asked, would she tell him? Should he question her?

He halted his thoughts about her because, in any form, the mere thought of her infuriated him. He turned away and strode from his new rooms down to the main part of the palace where the Dark gathered.

The ferocity of his fury in regards to Rhi left him needing to lash out and show his dominance. He needed to prove to her that she didn't control him. That whatever she'd intended with Con saving him, it wasn't going to work.

That he wouldn't bow down to the Dragon Kings.

More importantly, Balladyn needed to prove to his people that he was the right king for them.

"Hear me," he bellowed as he reached the main floor.

All around him, conversations ceased, music quieted, and eyes turned his way.

"The Dark was called to Ireland recently in preparation for war. Taraeth was going to send us into battle for Mikkel, a dragon who has been trapped on this realm in mortal form. Mikkel covets being a Dragon King, and he struck a deal with Taraeth. I'm revoking that deal," he stated. "We're Dark Fae. We don't make any sort of bargains with dragons. Return to wherever you were."

A Fae toward the back asked, "And the humans?"

"It's open season," Balladyn said.

There were smiles all around as Fae began to teleport, spreading the word.

Balladyn ignored the twinge as he imagined Rhi's face when she learned of his decree. He still wanted her to rule beside him, but he was coming to realize that was a farfetched dream that might never come to pass.

The one thing he could say for certain was that he would love her until the end of time. His feelings would never dim or die.

As Dark continued to teleport from the palace, Balladyn thought of his accord with Ulrik. None of the Fae would learn of it, and despite his words, he would keep his promise to the King of Silvers only because he and Ulrik had the same goal.

Balladyn turned on his heel and walked to the throne room. The first thing he did was remove the red velvet sofas Taraeth had loved so much. Then he focused his attention on the doorway Usaeil had made to get inside.

She would never set foot inside the palace again.

Unless she was in chains.

After so much disaster, was it possible that something had gone right? Nikolai turned his head to Esther. They silently walked away from Graves. But instead of heading back to the building they'd been hiding out in, she turned the other way.

Perhaps it was because Esther's steps seemed lighter than before, but he didn't question her as the village fell behind them. With every stride away from the Druid, her smile grew.

When they were a mile out, she suddenly released his hand, jumped the stone fence, and ran into a field of sheep, her laughter filling the air. The animals scattered, baaing their annoyance, but she paid them no heed.

He watched in awe as Esther paused in the middle of the field and flashed him a bright smile. Then she held out her arms and began to twirl around and around. With one hand on the rock wall, Nikolai leapt over it. Her exhilaration was all the answer he needed.

"I'm me again!" Esther shouted, her laughter following the statement.

She stopped twirling and swayed as she looked his way. Everything that had weighed her down over the last few weeks was gone. It showed in her eyes, through her smile, and in the way she stood.

He made his way to her, his arms aching to wrap around her. When he was just a few steps away, he felt the air move around him. To his horror, Dark appeared. He turned and counted seven of them. They were outside of the village, which meant the Fae were free to attack.

"Well," said a Dark with his black and silver hair shaved into a mohawk. "It looks as if you're a long way from home, Dragon King."

Another let out a whistle, while yet another said, "No kidding? A Dragon King?"

"And a human," said another.

A fifth said, "This is going to be fun."

It was the lone woman of the bunch who winked at Nikolai. She stuck out her impressive breasts and said, "I hear sex with a Dragon King is something all Fae should try at least once."

"Not with my King," Esther stated.

Nikolai bit back a smile at Esther's words. He turned away from the female without commenting and moved to stand beside Esther. "Stay near me," he whispered.

"Why are you in Ireland?" the female asked as she circled around until she stood before him once more.

Nikolai shrugged. "Why are any of you in Scotland?"

"It's really a bad time for anyone to be human," the female said, puckering her lips. "Our king has called open season."

"I thought that was Taraeth's common practice," Nikolai said, wanting to see what the Dark would tell him about Balladyn.

The female laughed, and the males joined in. Nikolai's power allowed him to see that the leader of this band was the female. She hid it from others to appear the weakest of them. Yet she was the strongest—and the one he needed to kill first.

Two of the males were in competition for her, which meant the men were divided. That could be useful, or it could backfire when he killed her.

"Taraeth?" the female said with a sly smile. "It looks

like you're a little behind the times, dragon. We have a new king. Balladyn."

Nikolai took a deep breath and sent a quick message to all Dragon Kings about Balladyn's new command. Perhaps they would be able to save mortals so they didn't have another night like Halloween.

He saw the subtle shift in one of the Fae, seconds before the first orb of magic was thrown his way. Nikolai grabbed Esther and dove, rolling as balls of Dark magic pelted the ground. The sound of the globes hissing was loud as they dissolved into the earth.

Nikolai jumped to his feet as the Fae closed in. He looked for the female, but she was too far away. Instead, he reached for the one closest to him, yanking the Dark against him just as the other six pelted Nikolai with magic.

He clenched his teeth through the agony as several of the orbs hit him in the back and sides. The Dark he used for protection screamed in pain. Nikolai thrust his hand into the Fae's chest and yanked out his heart, ending his shrieks.

Nikolai tossed the heart at the female as he flung the dead Fae aside. Then he shifted.

He heard Esther's quick intake of breath. He glanced down at her as she ducked beneath him. The female let loose a bellow as she directed her magic toward Esther.

Nikolai drew in a breath and opened his mouth as he blew out fire. It engulfed the female, killing her instantly. All the while, the others were pelting him with magic.

That's when he heard a roar, one he recognized.

Nikolai looked up to see Ulrik flying overhead. One Dark tried to use the spell that would prevent Ulrik or Nikolai from being in dragon form, but Nikolai cut the Fae in half with his tail.

Ulrik dove, swiping up one Dark in his jaws while Nikolai breathed fire at the remaining three. Two got out of the way in time.

The ground shook as Ulrik landed beside him. Side by side, they battled the last two Dark, who kept teleporting here and there, keeping just out of the way while they continued to throw balls of magic.

Nikolai anticipated one of the Dark's movements and opened his wing, catching the Fae as he materialized and killing him.

The last one, Nikolai and Ulrik both blasted with dragon fire.

When Nikolai turned his head to Ulrik, his friend wasn't looking at him but over his shoulder. Nikolai swiveled his head to see the silhouette of a woman watching from the road.

Eilish.

Nikolai turned back to Ulrik. *"Thank you."*

"You didna need my help."

"Then why did you come?"

"Your woman likes the look of you," Ulrik said, changing the subject.

Nikolai then felt Esther's hands on his scales. Her touch sent chills racing through him, followed by heat as he hungered to claim her right then, to bury himself deep inside her.

"Take her and leave," Ulrik said. *"Fly her to Dreagan before more Dark arrive."*

"Come with me," Nikolai urged.

Ulrik nudged him with his wing before he leapt into the air and flew away. Nikolai watched him until Ulrik was a speck in the sky. Then he looked down at Esther.

"What now?" she asked.

He held out his paw, which she climbed onto without question. Then he brought her to his back where she hurriedly settled. At the feel of her tight grip on his scales, Nikolai spread his wings and jumped.

CHAPTER FORTY

True bliss wasn't something Esther had ever experienced until she met Nikolai. Being loved by a Dragon King was amazing.

But riding atop one was truly epic.

She closed her eyes as the cold air blasted her face. She didn't even care about the frigid temperatures. Because she was riding a dragon!

A smile pulled at her lips when she felt a rumble run through him. They couldn't talk to each other, but she recognized that he was checking on her.

Opening her eyes, she patted his neck. "I'm doing great. No, scratch that. I'm doing amazing!"

There was another rumble that sounded like laughter, and she soon joined in. It seemed weird to be so joyous after being terrified just a short time earlier. When the seven Dark Fae had surrounded them, Esther wondered if they would survive it. Rather, she wondered if *she* would.

She'd wanted to fight. In fact, she'd had to hold herself back, which she readily did when the first orbs of magic appeared. It was Nikolai that left her speechless. He was as nimble and agile as a feline, but much deadlier. And that was before he shifted.

She looked down at the ivory scales beneath her. The moonlight cast them in a soft glow. They were warm and hard beneath her palms. The beat of his large wings was loud and comforting as they soared across the sky.

When he shifted, she had been in turns amazed and shocked at the size of him. She might've seen the Silvers a few times, but they had been curled up with each other, sleeping. Nikolai had been standing, his head held high, and his tail flicking in agitation.

While his enormous size had been mind-boggling, she thought him gorgeous. From the five splayed digits on each foot to the bony spikes that sprouted from the back of his head to the thin ridges that separated his nostrils to the two short horns that curled backwards from his forehead. And his eyes!

They were a bright, vibrant orange. When she met his gaze, she saw the Dragon King that he kept hidden while in human form.

The same qualities she'd glimpsed in Ulrik—cunning, ingenuity, absolute devastation, and certain peril—blazed in Nikolai's dragon eyes. Even the Fae had hesitated upon seeing him.

Esther had forgotten her own safety as she watched Nikolai and Ulrik battle the Dark. It all felt so surreal and yet tangible at the same time. She'd observed two dragons fighting a group of Fae. Magic had flown all around her, as had dragon fire. It was a fantasy geek's dream come true.

And she was actually living it.

No one had to tell her how lucky she was. She was well aware, but nothing could compare to being blessed by love.

Esther glanced below her and glimpsed lights through

the clouds. She felt sorry for everyone who didn't know the grandeur and beauty that were the Dragon Kings. Her life was in peril because of her association with them, yes, but she didn't care. Because she'd been changed by them. Her thinking had altered.

She shivered and watched as land gave way to water. The wind whipped at her face, stinging her eyes, but all of it was worth being taken on such a ride.

Her thoughts turned to Henry. Would her brother approve? She knew he would. He understood the worth of the Dragon Kings, which was why he'd befriended them and was working with them. If only Henry would let go of his love for Rhi.

Esther wanted her brother to find the kind of love she had. He deserved it. Though it would be difficult with her parents.

Her thoughts halted. Questions rose about her family. E2 suggested that the Norths weren't her parents. Esther needed the truth, not because it would solve a question, but because she was the TruthSeeker.

While she contemplated her new role and what it might mean for her future, her mind drifted to Eilish. Esther jerked when she realized that while the Druid had been returning her memories, she'd spoken to Esther in her head.

With her heart pounding, she closed her eyes and concentrated. Eilish's words were but a faint whisper that she couldn't quite make out at first, but the longer Esther focused on them, the louder they became.

"I didn't know I was unlocking something buried when I entered your mind. Never did I imagine I'd be facing the TruthSeeker. You question your function without magic, but you have something better. You have innate knowledge inside you to seek out what you need. Follow that.

"I'm sorry for what I did to you. I'd say I didn't have a choice, but I did. I won't ask for your forgiveness, but I can tell you that you're right about Sebastian. I have been working with Mikkel."

Esther's eyes flew open. Sebastian and Nikolai had been right from the beginning. Mikkel was involved, and that's who Eilish was working with, not Ulrik.

This would change everything for the Dragon Kings. Especially since Ulrik had helped her and Nikolai. Now, she felt ashamed for believing all those horrible things about Ulrik. She couldn't wait to get to Dreagan to tell Nikolai.

She looked down and saw land once more. It was closer than before, which meant that Nikolai had begun his descent while she had been in her mind. Soon, they were flying between snow-covered mountains. She glimpsed a river and several partially frozen waterfalls.

It wasn't long before she caught sight of Dreagan Manor. Nikolai dipped his wing and turned them. He flew in the back of the mountain and landed softly. She ran her hands through her hair to tame it after such a ride. Her gaze then turned on Henry, who came toward them along with the other Dragon Kings and mates.

When Nikolai lay down, she swung her leg over his neck and slid to the ground. Her brother was suddenly there, his arms around her. It was the way he held her that caught her attention. The last time his arms had wrapped around her so tightly was when her cat died.

"What is it?" she asked. She pulled back to look into Henry's hazel eyes.

Con walked up as Nikolai shifted and put on the jeans someone handed him. "You two have had quite an adventure."

Esther looked at the King of Kings and then Nikolai.

That's when she realized everyone knew whatever it was Henry didn't want to tell her—including Nikolai.

Her gaze returned to her brother to see the hint of sadness that was being drowned out by anger. Eilish had told her to seek the truth. It wasn't just the questions that kept prodding Esther forward, but the fact that she knew the answers she was being given were lies.

TruthSeeker.

She stepped out of Henry's arms. The one question that everything kept circling back to was her parentage. The truth was staring her in the face.

"The people who raised us aren't our parents," she said.

With the words spoken aloud, she'd thought she might feel some sorrow or even resentment at having been lied to her entire life. But there was nothing but the calming existence of honesty.

Nikolai came up behind her and rested his hands on her shoulders. For long minutes, Henry wouldn't meet her gaze. She saw him struggling with what she'd already accepted.

Was that the difference between the TruthSeeker and the JusticeBringer? She was driven to pursue truth, but Henry was compelled to beget righteousness.

Two sides to a coin. They each needed the other to carry out the roles destiny had bestowed upon them.

"I'm going to find who did this to us," Henry said as he looked at her.

She took his hand in hers. "Yes, you will. I know there's more, but it needs to wait." Esther then turned to the side so she could see Nikolai and the others. "There is much that needs to be said."

Nikolai frowned at her. "I already told Con about how Ulrik aided us."

"And I told everyone else," Con said.

Esther held Nikolai's gaze. "There's even more. When Eilish returned my memories, she spoke to me inside my head."

"Why did you no' say anything sooner?" Nikolai asked.

"Her words didn't become clear until we were on our way here."

Henry crossed his arms over his chest. "What did the Druid say?"

Esther hesitated, and Nikolai took her hand. She grinned at him and told the group, "Eilish said she never meant to unlock what had been hidden, but that I was the TruthSeeker, and I should do what I'm destined to do. She also admitted that she was working with Mikkel."

"I knew it," Nikolai said with a smile.

Warrick shook his head. "But Ulrik was the one who tried to kill Darcy."

"Eilish said something else," Esther interrupted before an argument could ensue. "She said she wouldn't ask for my forgiveness because she had a choice."

Thorn shrugged, his forehead furrowed in a deep frown. "So?"

Esther looked around the cavern. "While I've been here, I've heard how Ulrik manipulates and uses people."

"You think that's what Mikkel is doing to her?" Henry asked.

Nikolai squeezed her hand to get her attention. "You're the TruthSeeker. What did you see in her words?"

Esther opened her mouth to answer and then stopped. She thought back to Eilish's statement and felt something . . . powerful . . . move through her. Suddenly, she saw the truth of each word. It was as clear as day.

"She feels as if she doesn't have an option. She's look-

ing for something, which is why the information about
Donal surprised her."

Esther blinked, and whatever she'd seen in her mind
vanished as the world came into focus again. Nikolai was
smiling at her, pride showing in his eyes.

"No magic, aye?" he whispered.

"That wasn't magic."

"Was it no'?"

Maybe he was right. Perhaps it was magic. How else
would she know the truth in each word? Her head swung
to Henry to find him glaring at the floor. She knew what
it was to have something foreign and strange pushing at
her to follow a path she wasn't sure about. Would his path
be as complicated?

"It appears as if we need to search for Mikkel," Ryder
suddenly said. "Guess it's a good thing I've been doing
that since Bast left for Venice."

There were a few chuckles, but the mood in the cavern was grim. Because everyone was wondering the same
thing—was Ulrik working with Mikkel?

After all, Ulrik had told Con he was going to challenge him. Ulrik had spoken with several Dragon Kings
and made his hatred for them clear. Not to mention him
wanting the Kings to rule the world.

Just how did Mikkel fit into all of that? And what
exactly was Ulrik's role? Was he the main player, or a
pawn?

When others began to disperse, Nikolai stopped
Henry. "I'd like to speak with you."

Henry flashed a smile at them. "There's no need. I see
the way the two of you look at each other. I'm happy for
you."

"I need your blessing," Nikolai said as he glanced Esther's way.

Esther thought her heart might burst from her chest. She slid her gaze to her brother to find him watching her.

Henry looked between them and took one of their hands in each of his. "You have my blessing." He then leaned over and kissed her cheek.

"Thank you," Nikolai said.

Henry dropped their hands and took a step back. "I'll tell you as I've told every man she's dated. Hurt her, and I'll fuck you up."

There was a moment as the two stared silently. Esther rolled her eyes and shoved at Henry's shoulder, causing him to smile as they all laughed. Henry gave them a wink before he walked away. But if Esther thought they would get to leave, she was wrong. Con waited for them.

She swallowed nervously as the King of Kings approached. Nikolai's fingers tightened around hers, but that didn't stop her from shaking.

Con gave a nod to Nikolai before he looked at her. She stared into the King's black eyes and tried to determine what he was thinking, but she could grasp nothing.

"It seems something good came out of Eilish controlling your mind," Con said. "You discovered you're the TruthSeeker. And Nikolai found his mate."

No matter how she tried, she couldn't use her new power. It was as if it didn't work with Con. "Do we have your blessing?"

"Of course. Welcome to the family, TruthSeeker," Con said.

When others became to walk up, Nikolai pushed past them. "Enough," he growled testily. "I'd like some time alone with my woman."

Esther looked back at everyone and smiled. Could life get any better than this?

CHAPTER FORTY-ONE

One simple decision could change the course, the ripples affecting dozens if not thousands. Rhi saw Rhys's lips moving as he spoke, but she'd stopped hearing him after he told her that Balladyn had declared open season on the mortals.

"Say something," Kellan urged her.

She turned her head to him. When had Kellan walked up? Or had he always been there? Confused, her gaze moved around the Dragonwood. She spotted Con standing off to the side as if he were there to observe but not take part in the conversation.

Now, she knew why Rhys had called for her so far away from the manor. They wanted time to contain her if she let her anger consume her and she began glowing.

Except it wasn't rage that filled her.

It was sadness. A great sorrow.

"Rhi?"

Her gaze swung back to Rhys. "I heard you."

"We expected . . . well, another reaction," Kellan said.

She looked down at her studded black boots that were

sunk into the snow. The sun reflected off the white surface, causing her to squint against the glare.

Was it a sign from the higher powers? It was a beautiful day, with bright blue skies and the sunlight making the ice and snow sparkle all around her. All while she received devastating news. Again.

The Kings were quiet, waiting for her to reply. But how could she? One blow after another. How much more could she take before she said "Enough!"?

She lifted her head and caught sight of a red stag. He was peeking around a tree at them. She met the animal's gaze and suddenly had a longing to return to the Fae Realm—though there was nothing to go back to. Not really.

The stag turned away, continuing his forage for food. She didn't want to talk to anyone. She didn't want to even contemplate . . . well, anything. She tried to think of somewhere she could go, but she could teleport to the end of the universe, and her troubles would still hound her.

Balladyn's decree was a blow she hadn't expected. Perhaps that was her problem. She'd thought she knew him, when in fact, he was proving once again that he was Dark. The Fae she'd grown up with, looked up to, and trained with wasn't the same man.

She blinked and found Rhys standing before her. When had he moved? When had he grabbed hold of her hand? He was speaking again, but she couldn't hear his words.

". . . help you. Do you understand?"

She preferred it when she couldn't hear him. Now, he wanted her to reply, and she didn't know what she was answering. There was no sassy retort, no saucy comment.

The Kings thought that by having Rhys deliver the news about Balladyn that it would be easier for her to hear. That might be the case in other situations, but it didn't matter how close of a friend Rhys was, nothing softened this.

Kellan stepped toward her, and she immediately moved away, pulling her hands from Rhys's.

"Leave her," Con demanded.

She felt Kellan's gaze and looked into his celadon eyes that were full of pity. For her. It was too much. The entire scene reminded her of when Kellan and the other Kings had given her that same kind of look when the affair with . . . *him* . . . ended.

"Don't you dare," she said through clenched teeth.

Kellan bowed his head. "You helped me once. Let me do the same for you."

Her typical response was to snort and ask him what he thought he could do. But she couldn't even manage that.

Her eyes grew unfocused. She couldn't scream, she couldn't cry. She couldn't feel . . . anything. Maybe that was a gift. Because she wasn't sure she could handle such pain—or the anger that would surely follow.

She wasn't sure how long she stood there before she focused her gaze once more, but Rhys and Kellan were gone. Con remained some distance away. She looked at him, their gazes clashing.

"There's nothing I can say that will make this better," he said.

That was a fact, and yet, somehow, his words did just that. He didn't use the opportunity to tell her what a mistake it had been for her to get mixed up with Balladyn. He didn't berate her for taking a Dark for a lover.

Nor did he give the it'll-be-all-right speech.

She felt a presence beside her. Daire. She'd forgotten about the Reaper. His hand briefly touched hers before he dropped his veil. Con and Daire exchanged a nod.

"What do you want to do?" Daire asked.

Do? They expected her to do something? For once, couldn't she just sit by and let others handle it?

"We'll take care of Balladyn," Con stated.

She wasn't sure who was more surprised by his declaration, her or Daire.

Con inhaled as he looked her way. "No one should ask you to do this."

"I'd like to help you," Daire said to Con. "But I'm not sure if I can."

The King of Kings shrugged. "If you or any of the Reapers want to join us, we welcome it."

She looked from one male to the other. Her mind couldn't quite grasp what they were discussing, and in truth, she didn't care.

How silly she'd been to actually think she'd found some happiness. Was it madness that had allowed her to believe she might turn Balladyn back to Light? Was it folly that she could take a Dark lover and not suffer the consequences?

It was so stupid that all of this started simply because she wanted to save Balladyn. If only she'd thought about how she'd somehow healed Cael—maybe she would've been able to do the same with Balladyn instead of going to Con.

Perhaps then Balladyn wouldn't have reacted so harshly. But even she knew that regardless of how Balladyn was saved, his next steps would have been the same. She would still be standing in the Dragonwood, her boots covered in snow, wondering how all of this had come to pass.

Her thoughts immediately shifted to Usaeil. How long would it be before she visited Balladyn? Would he still defend her, or would he join Usaeil as Taraeth had done?

Rhi was no longer sure of anything.

Every time she helped someone, she wondered if she

were really causing more harm than good. An argument could be made that her friendship with the Dragon Kings made things worse.

She inwardly winced as she thought of Phelan. He was like a brother to her, and if anything happened to him, she wouldn't be able to take it. He wasn't responsible for his heritage, and he shouldn't be harmed because of it.

"Phelan," she said. Daire and Con jerked their heads to her. "Nothing can happen to him."

Con frowned. "He's a Warrior and," he paused, looking at Daire, "capable."

"He's a Halfling," Daire said.

She should've known the Reapers would know about Phelan. "If Usaeil discovers him—"

"She won't," Daire spoke over her.

Con held her gaze. "And if she does, we'll intervene. She'll have to face the Dragon Kings, Warriors, and Druids."

"And the Reapers," Daire added.

Rhi knew Daire couldn't make such a statement since Death gave the orders to the Reapers, but it meant a lot to her that he did. "Precautions need to be made with Phelan."

"I'll bring it up with Death."

"Invite Death here," Con said.

Rhi was suddenly weary to her very core. She wanted to curl up and sleep, to forget about everything.

"You can no' disappear," Con stated.

She looked at him and frowned.

"Doona pretend you doona know what I'm talking about. I can see it on your face."

Daire nodded in agreement. "So can I."

"Go do something that is just for you," Con said. "Forget Usaeil, Balladyn, and all of it for a little while."

"I know just the place," Daire said.

Before Rhi could react, Daire took her arm and teleported her away. The next thing she knew, she was standing outside of Jesse's nail place. There were so many other places she should be, but this was a place where she could forget the outside world for a short while.

She looked around, but Daire was gone. That's when she saw the bag in her hand. She peered inside to find several bottles of her favorite brand of nail polish—OPI. She walked into the salon and handed the bag to Jesse.

The nail tech took out each bottle, reading the color in her Texas accent as she did. "Oh, a pretty light blue called I Believe in Manicures. A gorgeous maroon named Can't Read Without My Lipstick. Here's a glittery pink called Sunrise . . . Bedtime. Last but not least, a lustrous silver titled Girls Love Pearls. What shall we use?"

"Whatever you want," Rhi said as she removed her shoes and set her feet in the hot water of the pedicure chair.

"I'm going to use them all. I've got a new design I want to try out on you."

Rhi forced a smile and nodded as she closed her eyes. She was supposed to forget about everything. So that's what she would try to do.

Somewhere in Canada

The excitement that filled Usaeil could barely be contained. She knew it wouldn't take Taraeth long to corner Rhi.

She couldn't wait to see the look in Rhi's eyes when it was Balladyn who killed her. Oh, the irony! It was almost too much.

As she walked past a mirror on her way to the movie set, she paused and looked at herself. Perfection. There was no way Con would refuse her. He was making a show of it, but she knew he'd cave.

It didn't matter how long it took, the King of Kings would be hers.

That was something else she'd tell Rhi right before the pesky meddler breathed her last. The need to have Rhi wiped from existence consumed her.

Usaeil wouldn't be able to concentrate on anything else until Rhi was gone. Forever. No one would stand between the Queen of the Light and what she wanted. Especially not someone like Rhi.

She'd taken the Light in and treated her like a sister. And what had Rhi done? Ruined everything.

Well, no longer. Soon, Rhi would be nothing but a memory, and then not even that. Usaeil would make sure there was no mention of her in any record of the Fae. It would be as if she never existed.

But she still hadn't forgiven Taraeth for keeping Balladyn alive. Perhaps it was time she showed Taraeth what happened when someone displeased her. It would have to wait until Rhi was taken care of, though. Then she'd turn her wrath on Taraeth. Perhaps she might even kill the King of the Dark.

"Now that's a thought," she murmured.

Maybe she would take control of the Light *and* the Dark. The Dark would learn what it meant to have a real leader.

She smiled at her reflection, her decision already made.

CHAPTER FORTY-TWO

If this were ecstasy, Nikolai prayed it never ended. Not only did he have his mate in his arms but he'd also cleared the air with Ulrik and once more felt as if he were a part of Dreagan and his brethren.

That wasn't to say that everything was fine. Far from it, actually. Soon enough, the outside world would intrude. But for the time being, he and Esther were cocooned within his chamber where they had made love for hours.

She'd been sleeping peacefully, so he was loath to wake her. Dawn had streaked the sky two hours prior, and he knew it wouldn't be long before Ryder and Henry would want to talk to them.

Esther might have halted anything more Henry would've said about the couple who raised them, but it couldn't be put off any longer. Nor should it be.

"You're frowning," Esther said groggily.

He looked down to see her gazing up at him with one eye barely open a slit. He smiled and kissed her forehead. "Did you sleep well?"

"You know I did," she said after a long yawn.

She then arched her back as she stretched her arms

over her head and rolled on top of him. After blinking several times, both eyes opened completely and met his. "Tell me what you're thinking?"

"That the others are expecting us."

"You should've woken me then."

He smoothed her hair back from her face and held her hand between his. "They can wait. You needed rest."

"It sounds suspiciously like you don't want to see them."

"I don't."

She nodded slowly. "Because you think it'll upset me."

"Aye."

She turned her head and kissed the inside of his palm. "I have you, Henry, and the others here at Dreagan. Whatever happens, whatever we find out, I'll be okay. Promise," she said as he gave him a quick kiss.

Then she was up and running into the bathroom to shower. Nikolai put one arm behind his head and looked up at the ceiling. Esther was being pragmatic, but either she hadn't let the news that the people who raised her weren't her parents bother her, or she was pushing it aside.

For the next ten minutes as she showered, Nikolai tried to figure out the best way to help Esther. It wasn't until he was under the spray of the shower that he realized the only thing he could do for her was be there for support.

Because no matter what she said, it did upset her. She kept it concealed from others, but she wasn't able to do the same with him. He didn't bother to call her on it because he knew she was handling things the only way she knew how—one day at a time.

Thirty minutes later, after Esther had finished her cup of coffee, they made their way to Ryder's office. Halfway there, Henry stopped them in the hallway.

"Everyone is waiting in Con's office," Henry said.

Esther shrugged. "Doesn't matter where we have this discussion."

"Why aren't you angry?" Henry demanded.

"What difference will it make?" she asked. "Will it make it go away? No. So why get upset?"

Nikolai wrapped an arm around Esther. "Doona let your sister's words fool you. She's hurting just as much as you."

Henry's hazel eyes moved from Nikolai to Esther. He stared at her a long time before he said, "Why hide it?"

"Why show everyone?" she retorted.

Henry glared at her. "I've hidden everything for years. I'm bloody tired of it."

"Let him go," Nikolai said when Henry stormed off.

Esther sighed and leaned against him. "Am I wrong to hold it all in?"

"No' as long as you share with me."

"Always."

They remained there for another few minutes. "Ready?" he asked.

She nodded and straightened. They walked hand-in-hand to Con's office where Henry stood against one wall, his face flushed with anger. Ryder and Con were talking together off to the side, but both looked up when Nikolai walked inside with Esther.

Ryder flashed them a smile. "I was wondering if we'd see you two today."

"Sorry," Esther said with a grin.

Con motioned for her to take one of the chairs. Since Henry didn't intend to sit with his sister, Nikolai took the other seat.

"Your trip to London has uncovered much," Con said as he made his way to his desk and sat. "I was uncertain if you would find anything, and I was glad to be proven wrong."

"We had help," Nikolai said. "Ulrik and the Warriors and Druids."

Esther was quick to nod. "That's right. We wouldn't have gotten close to Eilish if it hadn't been for Ulrik."

"But she still intends to kill him?" Ryder asked.

Nikolai shrugged. "I wouldna say they were on friendly terms. She wasna interested in anything he had to say."

"It was only our information on Donal Cleary that caught her attention," Esther added. "If we hadn't visited The Porterhouse and spoken with Donal, she wouldn't have returned my memories."

Con leaned forward and rested his arms on the desk. "As interested as I am in all the specifics, I think it's time we discuss what Ryder found."

Nikolai glanced at Henry, who was staring at the floor, his arms crossed.

"I agree," Esther said. "Tell me."

Ryder opened his mouth to speak when there was a knock on the door. Con bade the person enter, and Kinsey stuck in her head.

"Sorry I'm late," she said and hurried inside to stand beside Ryder, a file in her hand. She flashed Esther a quick grin.

But Nikolai saw the forced expression that hid Kinsey's nervousness.

"Is that for us?" Esther asked, nodding at the file.

"Uh, it is," Ryder said. "But first, I'd like to explain."

Henry said, "Get on with it."

"Ryder didn't tell you all of it, Henry," Kinsey said.

Nikolai exchanged a look with Con before he focused once more on Ryder. "Go on," he urged.

Ryder took a deep breath. "It took some digging, but I was able to determine that Jack and Lucy North never had children. The records were falsified, as were the documents signed by a midwife."

"Midwife?" Esther repeated. "We were born at a hospital."

Kinsey said, "That's what your birth certificates state, but they aren't real. We didn't learn that until we tried to locate the doctor who delivered both of you. He doesn't exist."

"Well, he did, but he'd been dead fifty years before Henry was born," Ryder added.

"Would that no' be easy to discover?" Nikolai asked.

Kinsey snorted loudly. "You'd think, but for some reason, no one found it."

"That seems a big risk to take," Con said.

Esther nodded. "Too big."

Ryder shrugged, his lips twisting. "No' when there are thousands of those certificates coming in every day. As long as there are signatures and the right stamps on them, the information gets recorded and filed."

"Someone had to have done this before to know it would work," Henry pointed out.

Kinsey said, "That was my first reaction, as well."

"How does the midwife fit in?" Esther asked.

Ryder's eyes flashed with excitement. "I looked at hundreds of forms from both of your births, and it was only by chance that I found the one with the midwife's signature. I did a search on her and discovered that she died five years back, but she was verra skilled at her profession. She delivered hundreds of bairns."

"Is this how you uncovered that Mum and Da—the Norths weren't our parents?" Esther asked.

Ryder glanced at the ground. "Actually, I found that first. It was in Lucy's medical file. She had endometriosis, which caused so much damage that doctors confirmed that she would never have children."

Nikolai reached over and took Esther's hand. Her fingers were cold, speaking to how hard all of this was for her to hear.

"That led to the forged birth certificates," Ryder continued. "It was obvious that Lucy couldn't have birthed either of you, so it was then a matter of determining how deep the conspiracy went."

"Mum, I mean Lucy, once told me about how different her labor was for me compared to Henry," Esther said. "I was even named after a North ancestor."

"And this is where things get complicated," Kinsey said softly, regret lining her face.

Nikolai nodded to Ryder to continue. For things like this, it was better to get it all out at once instead of a little at a time.

Ryder ran a hand down his face. "The more we looked into the midwife, the more things got weird."

Henry barked with laughter. "A Dragon King calling things weird."

Esther flashed him a glare before turning back to Ryder. "Proceed."

"I was able to . . . procure . . . the midwife's notebook," Ryder said.

Kinsey interjected, "He means he located it through an algorithm he developed on a hunch that the woman kept one. Then he bought it."

By the way Henry sat up, suddenly interested, Nikolai realized he didn't know this part of the story. "What did you find?" he asked Ryder.

"She didna deliver any babies on the days listed as Henry's and Esther's birthdays," Ryder said. "But I did find a listing for a baby girl born on the Isle of Eigg three weeks before Henry's listed date."

Esther's grip tightened on Nikolai's hand. "And me?"

"The midwife made another trip to the Isle of Eigg where she delivered a boy four weeks before your birth-date."

"That's no coincidence," Nikolai said.

Kinsey shook her head. "I don't believe so either."

"But we can't know for certain," Henry said. "Everyone who would know the truth is dead."

Ryder pressed his lips together and made a sound. "That's no' necessarily true."

"You know the woman's name who birthed the children?" Con asked.

"I didna say that," Ryder said. Then he smiled. "But I will say that I'm good enough that I figured it out."

Silence filled the office as everyone let that sink in.

Nikolai blew out a breath. "Surely I'm no' the only one who recognizes the significance of Eigg."

"What about it?" Esther asked.

"It used to be where a set of powerful Druids ruled," Con said. "Gwynn from MacLeod Castle discovered her Druid roots there."

Henry pushed away from the wall. "Druids?"

"I want to talk to this woman," Esther said.

"What's her name?" Henry asked at the same time.

Ryder hesitated a moment. Then he said, "Rebecca Hendry."

CHAPTER FORTY-THREE

Sometimes, whether something was right or not, it had to be done. Esther knew that was the case with speaking to Rebecca Hendry.

Whether the woman was her and Henry's birthmother or not, she might know something. The midwife switching the gender and dates of her and Henry's births was too coincidental to be ignored.

And if Rebecca were their mother . . .

Esther wasn't sure she could think about that yet. She would have to face it eventually, but she needed just a little more time.

"I want to talk to her," she announced to the room.

Nikolai squeezed her hand, his silent way of telling her that he would be by her side for whatever she chose.

"No," Henry stated.

Everyone turned their gazes to him. He gave a shake of his head, his gaze directed at her.

"Henry," she began.

"No!" he shouted. "I've no interest in finding a woman who gave us up."

It was Con who said, "You assume she willingly let you be taken."

"One child, maybe," Henry said. "I could make concessions for that. But both of us?"

Ryder said, "You're making judgments without knowing facts."

"I know facts," Henry said. "I know that some woman on an isle that used to be inhabited by Druids gave us up. I know that some midwife helped her do it. I know that documents were forged. I know that the person I believed I was, is nothing but a lie."

Without giving anyone a chance to reply, Henry stormed out.

Esther didn't try to stop him or go after her brother. Henry needed to calm down, and the only way he'd do that was with some time alone.

She looked at the others in the room. "I'm going to talk to Rebecca Hendry. I need to know if she gave us up and why."

"And if she didn't willingly hand you and Henry over?" Kinsey asked.

Esther looked to Nikolai. "Then I'm going to track down the people who took us from her. Now, tell me more about Eigg."

Con sat back in his chair. "There used to be more Druids in Scotland and England. The *mies* and *droughs* didna fight as the Fae do, but that doesna mean the two sects didna clash. The *mies* learned to gather at spots where magic amassed. Eigg was one such place."

"But that didna keep them out of Deirdre's reach," Ryder said.

Esther nodded, remembering how Isla and the others from MacLeod Castle spoke of the powerful *drough* they had fought for years. "Go on."

Ryder threw up his hands helplessly. "The Druids of

Eigg slowly died out. Those who can trace their history back to the isle will likely have Druid blood running through them, but it's doubtful they can do any magic. Rebecca is such a woman."

"Your ancestry isna important," Con told her. "I know you want answers, and I think you should get them. There is magic that remains on Eigg. Gwynn and Logan found it when they were searching for a clue to something that could help them defeat Deirdre. It's how Gwynn learned she was a Druid and discovered her heritage."

"So the same could happen to me," Esther said.

Nikolai shook his head. "Doona focus on that. If you do, it's a bonus, but I think we'll find out more by talking with Rebecca."

"If she'll talk to you," Kinsey said. She handed the file she'd been holding to Esther. "I thought you might want to visit her."

"Why don't you think she'll talk to me?" Esther asked.

Kinsey wrinkled her face for a moment. "She's become a hermit. She lives alone and doesn't speak to anyone. The villagers only get an occasional glimpse of her when she walks the beach near her house."

"We willna know until we try," Nikolai said.

Esther slowly nodded. "He's right. I have to try."

"When do you leave?" Con asked.

She fully expected Con to want Nikolai to remain at the manor for a few days since they'd been gone, but she couldn't and wouldn't hold off on the trip. "As soon as possible."

"I alerted Denae that she might be making another trip," Ryder said. "She's waiting on you."

Nikolai got to his feet and pulled her up beside him. "Then I guess we'd better pack."

"I suppose the mating ceremony will be put on hold then?" Con asked.

Esther had totally forgotten about the ceremony with everything else. She and Nikolai had spoken of love, but not about the ceremony.

He raised a brow as she turned to him. "You know I want you as mine."

"Do you?" she asked with a grin.

He flashed her a wicked smile. "Shall I show you?"

"Ugh," Ryder said as he strode past them. "Please don't."

Kinsey laughed as she followed Ryder out.

Esther watched the couple leave before turning her gaze back to Nikolai. "I'm yours. I always have been. If you really want to do the ceremony first, then I can wait before going to Eigg."

"I'm the one who will wait," he said. "Let's go talk to Rebecca. When we return, we'll have a grand ceremony."

"I'm lucky to have you."

His crooked grin made her heart skip a beat. "Damn right you are."

She widened her eyes and laughed, playfully pinching him. "Oh, really?"

His smile fell away as he grew serious and smoothed a strand of hair away from her cheek. "I've waited an eternity for you. As long as we're together, we can do anything."

"Together," she said and linked her hand with his.

"You're still in my office," Con warned.

Esther started laughing, because she had forgotten they weren't alone, and apparently, Con had realized that.

"I can remedy that," Nikolai stated.

The next thing she knew, she was cradled in his arms as they walked from the office. When Esther looked back, she thought she spied Con's lips relaxing just a bit. She wouldn't call it a smile, but it was close.

"Are you sure about this?" Nikolai asked as he walked them to his room.

She looked into his baby blue eyes before running her fingers through his cinnamon locks. "I'm the Truth-Seeker, remember?"

"I'll never forget." He stopped walking. "I doona have a good feeling about what we're going to find."

"Neither do I," she confessed.

He gave her a quick kiss. "Onward then?"

"Yep." As he started walking, she smiled at him. "I could really get used to this. You know, I think you should carry me everywhere we go."

He acted as if he were going to drop her, their laughter filling the corridor.

She had been through hell, and there was likely more to come, but she could face it all with a smile and conviction for the truth with Nikolai by her side. Because she was a Dragon King's mate. Nothing else mattered—not even her being the TruthSeeker. Nikolai was her heart, her soul, her very reason for putting one foot in front of the other.

When they reached his—their—chamber, he gently set her down and gave her a heated kiss. When he pulled back, he gave her a wink. "Together?"

"Together," she replied, eager for the next leg of their adventure.

EPILOGUE

Ireland . . .

Harriet breathed easier now that she was in Ireland. There was little chance that a Dragon King would be on an isle infested with Fae.

She grabbed the small bag as she exited the plane. There was still work to be done, and she was more than ready to do it. The Dragon Kings would pay for taking Stanley, and she knew just the person who could help her.

"Mikkel," she said when she caught sight of him waiting for her.

He smiled as she walked up. "Welcome, my dear. We've much to do."

"Then let's get started."

"Yes," he said as he led her to his car. "Let's."

London . . .

For long moments, Eilish stared at the entrance to The Porterhouse. Did she dare go inside? What if Nikolai and Esther had lied about Conal being her father?

Well, she knew exactly what she'd do to the mortal if that were the case.

But . . . what if they were telling the truth? That's what kept tripping Eilish up. If she discovered that Donal Cleary was her true father, then she would be demanding answers from the man she'd called Dad all these years.

That brought her back to her mother. Donal had been looking for Eireen for decades with no luck. The only one who knew anything about Eireen was Mikkel. Which meant that Eilish had to continue working with him.

She turned and walked away before touching her finger rings together and teleporting back to the top floor of Graves.

Con watched the helicopter containing Esther and Nikolai take off as V walked up.

"Another one found his mate, aye?" V asked.

Con nodded, not taking his gaze from the chopper. When the helicopter was out of sight, Con turned to V and saw the King's blue eyes filled with concern. "What is it?"

"There's a lot of flux around here, Con. I'm no' just talking the dragon skeleton on Fair Isle or Eilish. I'm talking about Faith's connection to Fair Isle and her father possibly being a Druid, Devon's association with the Skye Druids, and now to learn that Esther and Henry are the TruthSeeker and JusticeBringer as well as from Eigg."

Con put his hands into his pockets. "Despite our powerful magic, none of us can see into the future, but I know something is at work here."

"Meaning?" V pressed.

He sighed, not wanting to give anything more away than he had to. Not because he didn't trust V, but because Con wasn't ready to alert the others to his fear that the Kings were about to be betrayed on a scale so grand that it could very well be the ruin of them.

"Con," V urged, a frown marring his brow.

"Ryder is doing all he can. Nikolai is going with Esther to get more answers. Faith, along with Ryder and Kinsey, are still searching for Faith's father. It's going to take time."

Even if it was time they didn't have.

V's lips flattened. "Do you believe Faith's father is a Druid?"

"It's a possibility."

V clasped his hands behind his back. "And Mikkel?"

Just the mention of the name was enough to make Con seethe. "I doona know if Ulrik is working with him or no'. Did they conspire to make us believe Ulrik was in charge of everything?"

"Or was Mikkel using him?" V asked.

Con gave V a flat look. "Ulrik isna the type to be used. Ever."

"Unless he was doing it to get information. You know his motto."

"Know your enemies better than your friends," Con said.

V shrugged. "We willna know anything until Ulrik wants us to."

"And that doesna work for me. His challenge is coming, and regardless of his connection to Mikkel, only one of us can win."

"I should have told you what I knew of Mikkel when I returned."

Con stared at him. Anger rose swiftly upon learning that V kept information that could have helped them, but it quickly evaporated once he realized it was V. The King was known for taking time making choices and keeping his thoughts to himself before he reached a decision.

"I knew you spoke with Ulrik," Con said after a moment. "I understood that Ulrik told you things. I assumed if it was important you would've told me."

"You should be angry. The information on Mikkel was vital."

Con thought of all the balls he was juggling. "I doona have time to be angry at you."

Inhaling deeply, V glanced away. "I went to see Dorian."

Con briefly closed his eyes. "He woke as I asked him to. It's enough for now. Dorian will be there for us when the war begins."

"We could use him and his magic now."

"That time may come, but I'm going to give him the space he needs. For now. Dorian has never let us down before. He willna when the time comes."

V gave a nod before turning on his heel and striding away.

Con shook the snow from his hair and made his way into the mountain connected to the manor. Though he would never admit it, all the things he was juggling were becoming more difficult with each day. If he dropped or mishandled anything, the implications could be catastrophic.

He walked until he stood in the cavern where the Silvers were kept. He wasn't sure what brought him there, only that he had to see the dragons. Once in the cavern, he stilled, listening, his gaze searching the shadows as his gut warned him that he wasn't alone. That's when he spotted the shape half hidden behind a stalagmite.

Several minutes passed in silence before the form moved and Con's gaze landed on Ulrik.

Coming soon. . .

From *New York Times* bestselling author

DONNA GRANT

TORCHED

Ulrik's Novel

Available in June 2018 from
St. Martin's Paperbacks

Stay updated at
www.donnagrant.com